EVELYN EVOLVING

A NOVEL OF REAL LIFE

MARYANN MILLER

To my sister, Juanita. Thank you for all the years of love and dedication you gave to our mother. And thank you for being the best sister ever.

ACKNOWLEDGMENTS

This novel would not have been completed without the help of Kathryn Craft, a wonderful developmental editor and friend. When I was hopelessly lost in the middle of the first draft of this story, Kathryn took the manuscript, and me, in hand and helped me figure out how to write a novel so different from the mysteries that I had previously written. After I finished the first draft, Kathryn again offered the best guidance for the rewrites.

I must also acknowledge my muse, or the spirit of my mother, that started speaking to me one day in the shower and compelled me to go to my computer to start this project.

EVELYN – JUNE 1923

E velyn Gundrum sat in the shade of the leaves adorning the branches of the sweeping elm, digging in the sandy dirt with a tarnished silver spoon Miz Beatrice had given her to play with. She also had a blue plastic bowl. It was cracked but still held dirt if she balanced it carefully. When she was allowed to go outside, Evelyn liked to play in the sand near the front porch, methodically filling the bowl, dumping it out, then filling it again. Her sister, two years older, thought that was silly. Viola preferred to stay on the porch with her dolls, closer to Miz Beatrice, who sat on the porch swing slowly pushing it back and forth with one toe on the faded wood planking.

Only four years old, Evelyn didn't remember why they were living with Miz Beatrice or why they didn't call her Mother. Evelyn couldn't remember for sure how long they had been here, either. She had vague recollections of living some-where else before, but she got confused easily, and Viola had to explain why they were supposed to call this lady Miz Beatrice. Wasn't she their mother? "No," Viola had said. "Our mother brought us here months ago. Beatrice is a friend."

"Why did Mother give us to Miz Beatrice?"

"I already told you."

"Tell me again."

Viola sighed. "Okay. But this is the last time. Promise you won't ask again."

"What if I forget?"

"Then you forget. I'm tired of telling you. After Daddy left, Mother went to Detroit with a man named John."

"Why did Daddy leave?"

"I don't know. Now hush so I can tell you the rest. Mother said she was going to come and take us to Detroit too, but something happened, and she couldn't. So she took us here and wants us to live with Miz Beatrice."

Evelyn wasn't even sure where "here" was, but she did remember that Viola told her before that Detroit was far, far away. Now and then, her mind worried over the reason that their mother had not taken them to that place called Detroit. Mothers didn't leave babies. That's what Miz Beatrice had said when showing them the kittens under the porch last summer. That day, Miz Beatrice had been putting some food under there for the mama cat.

They weren't supposed to feed that cat, even though Evelyn would sneak her a piece of bacon when Miz Beatrice wasn't looking. The cat was supposed to feed herself, and her kittens, by catching the mice that often got into the bags of flour in the pantry.

"Why are you feeding the cat? You said not to," Evelyn had asked.

Miz Beatrice patted Evelyn on the shoulder. "This is just for a little while. The mama cat needs food to keep her close to her babies until they're older."

"Why?"

"To keep close to take care of the kittens."

"But she didn't," Viola said. "Yesterday, she pushed that little one away. It died."

"It was the runt." Miz Beatrice sighed and rose slowly to her feet. "It probably wasn't going to live anyway."

The kittens were gone now. And so was the mother cat. She'd disappeared sometime in the winter. Evelyn checked every day, hoping the cat was back, but she wasn't. Looking at the empty space, she thought about what Miz Beatrice had said about mothers and babies. Evelyn didn't understand about the runt and why the mama cat pushed it away. Had it been a bad kitten? Is that what being a runt meant? Was it the same for real mothers? Their mother?

When the questions threatened to clog Evelyn's brain, she took them to Viola, even though her sister hated the deluge of questions that Evelyn sometimes couldn't hold back. Viola had just laughed. "Don't be silly. We aren't kittens. And there's nothing wrong with us."

Evelyn tried to believe that. She tried really hard. And sometimes, she could forget about those fears and just be happy.

Sometimes.

Today was going to be a special day. That's what Miz Beatrice had said at breakfast this morning. A surprise guest was coming, and now Evelyn's tummy was full of eggs and toast, and she was wearing her favorite sundress, yellow sprinkled with white daisies. When they came outside, Miz Beatrice told her to be careful not to get the dress dirty, so Evelyn pushed the skirt between her knees as she squatted to dig in the dirt. The sun streamed through the branches of the tree, making light and dark dance on the sand with every wisp of a breeze. Birds sat on high branches, adding their song to the dance, and every now and then, a bit of conversation between Miz Beatrice and Viola floated her way.

"Please tell me who's coming?"

"No, child. You must be surprised like your sister."

The questions Viola asked stirred more excitement, and Evelyn's stomach fluttered with anticipation. Then the voices faded, and Evelyn heard only the song of the birds as she played.

Moments later, a cloud passed over the sun, and Evelyn shivered in the sudden chill. Miz Beatrice had been right about it being too early in the summer for a sundress. Maybe she should go change.

Evelyn stood and started toward the house, noticing that Miz Beatrice was slumped on the porch swing asleep. Lately, she'd taken to sleeping frequently during the day, which Evelyn thought was very odd. Only babies took naps. Right?

Miz Beatrice didn't eat much at dinner or supper anymore either, and Viola had said the other day that maybe they were running out of food. For some reason, Viola always worried that one day there would be no more to eat. But Evelyn had a feeling something wasn't right inside Miz Beatrice. Once, she had walked past the open bathroom door and saw Miz Beatrice hunched over the sink. She was coughing hard, holding a rumpled handkerchief over her mouth, and Evelyn had seen bold splatters of red on the white fabric before Miz Beatrice noticed her and pushed the door closed with her hip. While Evelyn knew that the splatters were probably from blood— she'd cut herself often enough to recognize the spots—she didn't know what the blood might mean. Yet, she did know that it was probably not right that it was on the handkerchief. The fact that it was had shot a bolt of fear so deep that Evelyn couldn't say a word about it, not even to her sister.

But if Miz Beatrice was sick, Viola should know so she could help figure out what to do if the lady died and left them all alone.

Evelyn glanced at her sister, who was next to Miz Beatrice on the swing. Maybe she could tell her now. It looked like Miz Beatrice was good and asleep. She started to walk toward the porch steps but turned when she heard the sound of a motor. A big, gray car rumbled to a stop in front of the house, and a tall woman wearing a navy-blue dress with white ruffles at the top, white gloves, and a hat with a wide, curved brim got out. When the woman walked toward the house, the dress flared around her legs, lifted at the hem by a slight breeze. It was not any of the ladies who visited Miz Beatrice before, and curiosity distracted Evelyn from her worries.

Suddenly, Viola jumped up, raced down the four steps to the front walk, and launched herself at the woman. "Mother!"

The lady disengaged herself from Viola's wild embrace and just stood for a moment, looking first at Viola then up the walk toward Evelyn.

Mother?

Another chill washed over Evelyn. This lady was their mother? She didn't know if she should run to hug her too, but then Miz Beatrice roused and called out. "Regina. It's good that you could come so quickly."

Miz Beatrice slowly rose from the swing and walked to meet the lady at the steps to the porch. The two women hugged, and Viola ran over and tugged at Evelyn. "Come on. Say hello to Mother."

Evelyn planted her feet in the sand, and Viola tugged again. "Come on!"

Cautiously, Evelyn took a few steps closer. "Hello." The word was barely a whisper.

The woman who was Mother leaned down and touched Evelyn lightly on the cheek. "You're a pretty little thing."

"Both of your girls are quite lovely," Miz Beatrice said.

"Please come inside. We need to talk about what we're going to do."

The two women entered the house, leaving the girls in the yard.

Once more, Viola tugged at Evelyn. "Let's go listen."

More willing to eavesdrop than talk to a stranger, Evelyn crept quietly into the house, following Viola to the doorway to the kitchen, careful to stay out of sight. After a few moments, Evelyn dared to peek around the doorjamb and saw Miz Beatrice pouring glasses of lemonade. Miz Beatrice made the best lemonade, and Evelyn wished she could have a glass. She started to step into the kitchen to ask for one, but Viola held her back.

"I'm thirsty," Evelyn said.

"Shhhh." Viola held her fingers to her lips.

"Girls? What are you doing out there?" Not much escaped Miz Beatrice's sharp hearing or watchful eyes.

"Now look what you've done," Viola said in a quiet whisper. Then she called out. "Nothing, Miz Beatrice."

"Then go do nothing somewhere else."

Evelyn followed Viola back out to the porch and scrambled up on the swing. "Push me."

If Viola sat on the edge of the swing and stretched her leg as far as she could, she could toe the swing into action like Miz Beatrice. So that's what she did. "Maybe mother came to take us home," Viola said after a moment, raising her foot and letting the swing slowly sway back and forth.

"I don't understand."

Viola put her foot down and gave the swing another push. "You were too little to remember."

"Remember what?"

"Anything. You keep forgetting everything. I have to keep telling you things over and over again."

Evelyn thought about Miz Beatrice maybe being sick. Was that what brought their mother here? Was everything going to change? "Are we going to have to move?"

"I don't know." Viola jumped off the swing. "Stop asking so many questions."

Evelyn fought back tears. She always made her sister mad. She didn't mean to, but she always did. "I'm sorry," she whispered, but Viola was already off the porch and running around the side of the house to the backyard.

Evelyn kept waiting for something to make sense, but nothing that was happening did. That night at supper, silence was served up with the ham and potatoes. Miz Beatrice always said that suppertime should be pleasant, and she often had stories to tell as they ate a meal. Sometimes she even told jokes, but tonight, she was more reserved. Because of the company?

Appetites were not as usual either. Evelyn's stomach was so tight with nerves she had to force each morsel of food down her throat. The visitor took the smallest portions of mashed potatoes and green beans and hardly took more than a nibble of each. She just pushed her beans into her potatoes and stirred them around. Evelyn couldn't quite believe this woman was really their mother, no matter what Viola said. So maybe Evelyn should just call her Regina like Miz Beatrice did.

No, she should say Miz Regina. That was the polite way to address an adult.

Knowing she didn't dare leave food on her plate, Evelyn forced down her few remaining bites of potatoes, and then looked over to Miz Beatrice. "Finished. Excuse please?"

"Not yet. Your mother has something to say."

"No, no. You tell them," Miz Regina said. "They're more comfortable with you."

Miz Beatrice sighed and held her breath so long Evelyn

wondered if she was ever going to speak. Then she stuttered over her words. "Well, uh ... I—"

"Oh, for heaven's sake. There is no need for such dramatics." Miz Regina looked intently at each girl for a moment. "This is what you need to know. You can no longer stay here. Beatrice has The Cancer, so she can't keep you anymore. I can't take you back with me, so I've made arrangements for you to go to another home here."

The words spun around in Evelyn's head, and all she caught was "Cancer" and "I can't take you back."

If Miz Regina was their mother, why couldn't she?

Viola voiced the other question, "What kind of home?"

———

The next day, Viola helped Evelyn pack her few panties and two other dresses in the small suitcase they shared. At breakfast that morning, Miz Regina had made it clear what they could bring with them, some clothes and one small toy, but that was all. She told them that the institution where they were going had firm rules. Evelyn didn't understand about an institution. She had never heard that word before, but the cold sweat of apprehension had kept her from asking what it meant.

Now, Evelyn was overcome with uncertainty. She stood for several minutes, looking at the small shelf that held her toys: a rag doll that Miz Beatrice had made, an empty wooden spool, three wooden blocks with numbers and letters, and a small metal horse. What should she take? It was so hard to decide. She loved them all and each was so special.

"Hurry up," Viola said. "We have to leave soon. Here, take the doll."

"No." Evelyn whirled away from the shelf and ran outside

where she grabbed the silver spoon from the sand pile. When she came back in, Viola said, "That's what you're taking?"

Evelyn nodded.

"Why?"

Evelyn shrugged and started to put the spoon in the suitcase. Viola reached over and snatched it away. "Don't. It's dirty. Go wash it."

A few minutes later, Miz Regina came and told the girls to hurry. She hustled them out of the door and into the back seat of the car, barely giving them time to hug Miz Beatrice. Evelyn tried not to cry when she said goodbye, but a few warm tears escaped and trickled down her cheeks. She clambered into the car next to Viola and waited until Miz Regina said her goodbyes and got behind the wheel. Evelyn had never been in a car before, at least not that she could remember, and when the engine started, the noise it made drowned out the music of the birds, and Evelyn could barely hear Miz Beatrice calling out one last farewell.

A short time later, the girls sat in an office at St. Aemilian's Orphan Asylum while their mother talked to a lady dressed all in black. The woman in black wore a funny white thing on her head that hid her hair and was so tight on her face there were ridges where it met her cheeks. A black veil was draped over the white thing. Evelyn knew it was not polite to stare. Miz Beatrice had told her that once at the market when they had seen a woman with a large wart on her chin, so Evelyn glanced down at the suitcase that stood on the floor between the chairs.

Words that were exchanged between the two women drifted in and out of Evelyn's awareness, and she rested one hand on the suitcase, trying to stay connected to the things that belonged to the time with Miz Beatrice; to the time when they were all happy. Listening to her mother and the other woman talk, Evelyn had a sense that this might be the end of happy.

Apparently, this is where she going to stay, Viola, too. Miz Regina told the lady that she had no room for her girls in Detroit. She also had no money. That seemed odd, as she certainly wore a nice dress and she drove a car. Miz Beatrice had old, faded dresses and no car. She walked to the market. But she had been able to keep Evelyn and Viola.

Evelyn glanced at her sister, who had formed her face into an expressionless mask. Questions bubbled up inside Evelyn that she wanted to ask her sister. Primarily, why did their mother keep calling them "her girls" instead of using their names? But the hard set of her sister's jaw made her force the questions down.

Maybe later she could free the questions. When Viola might be smiling again.

Miz Regina twisted the handkerchief she was holding as she listened to the woman in black. When papers were pushed across the desk for Miz Regina to sign, she put the handkerchief in her lap before picking up the offered pen. Evelyn looked at the handkerchief lying there in a crumpled mass, then reached over and pulled it quickly to her. Then she stuffed it into the pocket of her dress. She wasn't sure why. She just did it.

Once the papers were in order, Miz Regina stood and grabbed up her purse, not saying a word. She turned and quickly hugged each of the girls, barely a touch, and then walked out of the room.

When they had first driven up to this place, Evelyn thought the tall, gray building, shaded by large trees, was pretty. Some of the trees were covered in white blossoms, and they looked just like the tree in Miz Beatrice's backyard. Late in the summer, it gave them pears. Children played on an expanse of lawn, and Evelyn had wondered if this was some kind of school. Wouldn't it be nice to stay at a school and learn things?

Now she didn't think it was going to be so nice.

Tears burned in her eyes.

Evelyn leaned close to Viola and whispered, "Where are we?"

"It's an orphanage," Viola hissed back.

"A what?"

"A place for orphans."

"What are orphans?"

Viola sighed and whispered, "Children who have no parents."

"But—"

The lady in black cut off the question, taking each girl by the arm and leading them out of the office and down a long hall that opened into a large room. "This is the girls' ward," the woman said. "This is where you will sleep."

The room was lined with bunk beds along all four walls, and the woman stopped at one set. "There is a wooden bin under the bed," she said, pointing. "Put your things there. Stay here until the bell rings for lunch. You may call me Sister Honora. Do you understand?"

Evelyn glanced at Viola, who nodded, so Evelyn did too.

"Is she our sister?" Evelyn asked after the woman left.

"No."

"Then why—"

"I don't know."

Evelyn looked around, trying to count all the empty beds. She kept losing track of the numbers, but there were a lot. Definitely more than twenty. A chill made her shudder, and she pulled her sweater tight. "I'm scared."

Viola squatted down and hauled the bin from under the bed. She took things out of the suitcase and put them inside the bin, dividing the space with her rolled up sweater. "This is your half," she said pointing to the side that was empty.

"Is our mother going to come back and get us?"

Viola didn't answer. Her lips became a tight, straight line.

"Will we see Miz Beatrice again?"

Viola stood so quickly Evelyn had to take a step back.

"Stop! Stop! Stop your stupid questions!"

Sobs burst out of Evelyn. She tried to stop them, but they defied her. Viola opened her mouth as if she wanted to say something, then closed it. After a long moment, her expression softened, and she drew Evelyn to her chest, whispering, "I don't know. I don't know."

That scared Evelyn even more. Viola always knew everything. If she stopped knowing, who could Evelyn rely on?

2

REGINA – JUNE 1923

Regina didn't look back as she walked away from the large gray building, her back stiff and her head held high. She cursed the tears that threatened to spill down her cheeks. She had kept them and her emotions at bay so she could get through what she had to do. It wasn't her fault that she wasn't able to take care of the girls. If only she hadn't been stuck in that tiny apartment in Detroit. If only it had worked out with John, who had whisked her away from Milwaukee with promises of a grand life on Grand Boulevard in Detroit. And it had been grand until the accident, and she became a widow before she was a bride again. John's mother had kicked her out of the house, allowing her to only take her clothes and nothing else. So here she was two years later and worse off than when she was married to Fred.

It seemed like Regina never had any luck. Or maybe she just brought the bad luck on herself.

First, there had been Fred. He was so dashing, tall with dark hair that tumbled across his forehead, so beguiling with that wicked smile. And he did like to party. They both liked to party, even after they were married, and when her monthly was late, she prayed so hard not to be pregnant, but God had stayed silent.

In the blush of new love and Fred's initial eagerness to have a family, she had gone along with the first pregnancy.

Actually, she'd gone along more because she was afraid to sneak away and have an abortion. Her friend Millie had almost bled to death in a dark, dank apartment where a woman "took care of things."

The second pregnancy had been an "oops" when the rubber broke and one little sperm survived the cleansing Regina had done after the fun. Still more afraid of a back-alley abortionist than having another child, Regina resigned herself to being a mother of two. Fred was no longer so eager to be a father, so when her time came, he took Regina to the hospital and left her alone in the labor ward. It had been one of the worst days of Regina's life.

She didn't want another baby. She'd never wanted to be a mother at all.

It wasn't something she'd ever allowed herself to say, even to herself, but it was the truth. She wasn't like other women who couldn't wait to have children. Those women who fussed and cooed over the babies in the hospital. The hard work of raising children in difficult circumstances dimmed the glow of maternal love.

At the time, she told people she was doing the best she could under the circumstances. Folks who knew Fred understood that and would nod in empathy, but in her heart, Regina knew she was not doing the best she could. The best would mean no more smoking or drinking. That could pay for one more dinner a week. And she would be sober enough to cook one more dinner.

The marriage had started to unravel shortly after Viola had

been born. That's when the reality of having a baby had sunk in. During the first few days in the hospital, Regina had thought the tiny thing was just the loveliest thing she had ever seen and named her for the flower that was her favorite. The child deserved a pretty name. But three weeks later, that lovely baby face started contorting in the most awful red-faced screams. Day in and day out the baby wailed, until Fred started spending more and more time out of the house, and Regina wondered how much longer she could listen to the noise without doing something awful. That's when her mother pointed out that the baby was probably just hungry. It didn't appear that Regina had enough milk. "But if you drink a beer just fifteen minutes before you want to feed the baby, your milk will flow like a river."

Turned out, Mother was right. The milk flowed and the crying stopped. Well, not entirely, but enough that Regina no longer had the urge to stuff a sock, instead of her breast, into her baby's mouth.

When the second girl was born and Fred showed little interest, Regina gave the child the first name that came to her—Evelyn Louise, using her middle name. Maybe that would spur some emotional bond. Since Fred wasn't there to object, Regina could choose whatever goddam name she wanted.

Fred wasn't much for visiting hospitals.

To his credit, Fred did come to take her home from the hospital after her two weeks of laying up, but once they were home, he wasn't much help with the children. Babies both of them really. Viola was just barely two, and if the baby wasn't screaming, she was. "She's probably jealous," Regina's mother had said. "First children can be horrid about others. I was thankful to only have one."

Five months later, Fred said he was going out for some smokes and didn't come back. If she hadn't been angry enough to kill him if he showed his face again, Regina would have laughed at the whole cliché. How many men had used that same line, and how many women had believed the husbands would return? Waiting for hours, then days, then weeks, only to end up being stuck at home with kids. No job. No money. And no hope?

A week after Fred left, a man came to the door asking about him. Regina didn't like the looks of this well-dressed man— neatly-pressed suit, colorful tie, and hat like any other salesman who tried to separate her from a dollar or two. But his eyes were different. They didn't have that friendly sparkle framed by laugh lines. They were hard and empty, and the man didn't lead with some pleasant banter. Instead asking, "Do you know where your husband is?"

Regina hated saying the words out loud, but his eyes compelled her. "No. Haven't heard from him since he left days ago."

"He say where he was going?"

"Out. Just out." Regina couldn't bring herself to repeat the tired reason that Fred had used. This man would see right through that.

"Do you expect him back?"

Indignation stiffened her spine and gave weight to her voice. "If he intended to come back, he'd be here by now."

The man took a half step closer. "Do not use that tone with me, little lady. You understand?"

He spoke softly, almost conversationally, but the menace was like ice in his deep blue eyes. Regina nodded, swallowing her pride and her fear.

"Good." The man eased back, but the hard look in his eyes didn't change. "Fred owes my boss money. A lot of money."

Momentarily, Regina flashed on the large satchel Fred had slung over his shoulder when he'd walked out that Friday night.

Was that...? She masked any outward reaction as best she could.

"It's my job to get that money back."

"Don't know anything about your money," Regina said, hating the way her voice broke over the words. "He left me with nothing. Just the kids and a pile of bills."

The man didn't respond and didn't move. As they stood there, silent, a trickle of sweat ran hot down Regina's back. What if he didn't believe her? What if he forced his way in? Searched the place? She was trying to figure out if she could close and lock the door before he made a move when he took a half step back. Regina fought to keep relief from showing as she maintained eye contact.

"When that husband of yours comes back, tell him Bernie wants his money." He paused, as if wanting to give time for that to sink in, then added. "Understand? Bernie don't like hurting women and kids. But he does what he's got to do."

The man stood for another few seconds on the front stoop, then turned and left. Regina quickly closed and locked the door. Then she leaned her forehead against the wood. Oh, Fred, what have you gotten yourself into?

The answer to that question would have to wait. Evelyn was screaming to be fed again, and Regina felt the warm rush of milk filling her breasts. The beer trick still worked.

Fred stayed gone for six months, and then one day, he came back. When he walked through the front door, as casually as if he'd only been gone a few hours, he didn't say where he'd been. He had a noticeable limp, but he wouldn't explain that either. He did very little explaining, just resumed his routine of talking to people on the telephone and answering the door when the bell rang. Since he was home day and night most of the time, he didn't seem to care if Regina went out by herself, as long as she fixed meals and tended to the kids first. The marriage was all but over, but he never asked for a divorce. Neither did she, because he was now supporting them again. There was something to be said for security.

Regina didn't ask where Fred got the money he gave her to buy groceries and pay the bills. She was just thankful that he was able to do that. He wasn't much of a father, keeping a rather aloof distance between him and his offspring, but he did serve them the dinners Regina left. When she was home, it did hurt just a bit to see him brush any attempts at affection aside, but she rationalized that it would make the girls strong. They'd learn how to handle disappointment and frustration. Just in case their lives weren't going to be any better than hers had been.

Two months later, Fred left again.

That time, he never came back.

Regina didn't like to think about what it had been like in those months after Fred and before John. She wasn't proud of some of the things she'd done, and she'd certainly been a terrible mother to the girls. Leaving them for hours when she went out to hustle for some money. But she was still convinced that the hardships strengthened the girls for what might come in the future.

And now, a few years later, it appeared that she was right. Life was not going to be wonderful for the girls. Regina had no delusions about how they would be treated at the orphanage. It wasn't like a home, a real home, and they would be lucky to just have food and clothes.

Was it better than what she could offer?

Her steps faltered as she considered turning around and grabbing them out of there. But then what would she do? Take them to that dumpy little apartment in Detroit? Feed them hot dogs every night from the Coney Island where she worked? Have them sleep on a pallet in the corner of the living room?

The girls might come to hate her for what she did today, and that was a painful realization. Still, she kept on walking away. It was the best thing for them all. Regina might not be the best mother in the world, but a part of her did care about her daughters and fervently hoped for a happier future for them. She didn't pray for one, however. She was long past the days of prayers, figuring God had given up on her years ago.

3

EVELYN - SEPTEMBER 1925

Sister Honora made Evelyn tremble. She always made Evelyn tremble. Sometimes, when looking into the stern face pinched tight by the wimple, Evelyn was afraid her bladder would let go and she would be punished twice. Once for not scrubbing the floor fast enough and again for soiling herself. That's what the sisters said about pee and poop. "Soiling oneself." As if she had rolled in the dirt outside. If she was not locked in such terror of the nun before her, Evelyn would find that thought amusing.

Two years had passed here at St. Aemilian's Orphan Asylum, and Evelyn still didn't understand why they had to stay. Couldn't Miz Regina or Miz Beatrice not come and take them away from this horrible place? Everything was all so confusing, and Evelyn kept hoping that someday, someone would love them enough to come back and get them. Sometimes in her dreams, she lived with both women. Miz Beatrice not sick anymore and Miz Regina happy to have her girls back. Viola said it was silly to wish. Pointless to dream. Nothing was going to change.

"Child. Are you listening?"

The harsh words tugged at Evelyn. She nodded, unable to push words past the lump in her throat.

"Why have you not finished this floor?" The nun gestured down the hall with her walking stick. "You are as slow as molasses in winter. What good are you?"

"I don't know, Sister." A soft whisper.

That was met with a sharp crack along Evelyn's backside. "Don't talk out of turn."

"But, I—"

Another smack. "I said no talking."

"But, you—"

This time, when the walking stick landed, Evelyn's bladder did let go.

"Now look what you have done. You dirty, nasty little child. Take those panties off. Right now."

Evelyn did as she was told, holding the wet garment gingerly between thumb and forefinger. Sister Honora took the panties on the end of her walking stick, then draped them over the child's head. "You will wear these to supper."

"No! Please, Sister. No!"

"Enough. Go!"

Standing in the middle of the dining hall, the rotten stench of old urine swirling around her while the other children pointed and laughed, was the most humiliating experience of Evelyn's young life. She swallowed hard and held back the bile that rose in her throat. She couldn't vomit. She wouldn't vomit. If she didn't want more humiliation, she didn't dare vomit.

She looked past the rows of tables and the laughing children, focusing on the picture of the Virgin Mary at the back of the large room. Mary, Mother of God, was supposed to be their mother too. Their friend, but she didn't feel like a friend or a mother to Evelyn. She was just this lady in blue in a picture.

21

As the serving carts were brought out and the children lined up with their metal bowls to get their supper, the aroma of meat and gravy momentarily blocked the acrid smell of dried urine. Evelyn's mouth watered. She glanced at the carts. Dinner that evening was roast with potatoes and carrots and onions. A favorite of Evelyn's that she would not be allowed to eat. Children who broke the rules had no dinner, but not everyone was forced to stand in such embarrassment. This was reserved for the worst transgressions.

Viola walked past with her bowl to take a seat at a nearby table. She stared straight ahead, not even glancing at Evelyn. Maria, a girl of eight who had been friendly to Evelyn, gave her a quick look, then averted her eyes, taking a seat next to Viola.

That disregard, as if Evelyn was a stranger they had never seen before, cut deeper than the sneers from the others. Why couldn't Viola even look at her?

For the rest of the dinner hour, Evelyn's legs trembled from standing in one position for so long, and hunger rumbled in her stomach. And still nobody looked at her, except for Sister Honora, who seemed fixed on watching, as if wanting to catch Evelyn in some other transgression. She didn't know if Sister Honora would make her wear the dirty panties during evening prayer. She fervently hoped not. But she tried to steel herself for the possibility. She didn't want to cry. Not for hunger or for humiliation. She wanted to be strong like her sister. Viola never cried when the sisters hit her or insulted her or made her do horrible things. Viola would just set her jaw and look them in the eye and hold the tears back.

Somehow, Evelyn needed to find the strength to do that too. Otherwise, the other kids would learn how weak she really was and take advantage.

Evelyn stood for another painful hour as evening prayer followed dinner, and her only plea to a God she wasn't even sure was listening was that the session would end before her legs gave out and she fell. Once, when Maria toppled over in a heap during a punishment, she had received ten hard smacks with Sister's cane on the back of her legs. The same fate would have Evelyn hobbling for days.

Finally, when Evelyn thought she could stand there no longer, it was over. Sister Honora closed the book of evening prayers and walked down the aisle to Evelyn. "Take that filthy rag off your head and get washed."

"Yes, sister." Evelyn turned quickly and headed to the washroom. She took off her clothes and stepped into the large washtub that was used for bathing. The water was cold, but she didn't care. She took the bar of lye soap and scrubbed her hair, and then went under the water, holding her breath for a long time. She wished she could stay under forever. Never have to face Sister again. Or be hungry. Or be teased by the other children.

Sputtering, Evelyn burst out of the water, gasping for breath. Two older girls were in the washroom. "Hurry up," one of them shouted. "Get your stinky self out of here."

Evelyn quickly got out of the tub and dried herself with a rough towel. Then she pulled on the clean clothes she had grabbed from the sleep room and dressed. She took the wet underwear to one of the sinks and washed them, soaping and rinsing and soaping and rinsing again to get the odor out.

After lights were out for a little while and all was quiet in the sleeping area, Evelyn heard a rustle of sheets and then felt a tap on her shoulder. She looked up at her sister. "Here," Viola said, holding out a hunk of bread wrapped in a napkin.

Evelyn grabbed the bread and took a large bite, sending a cascade of crumbs down the front of her nightgown.

"It's making a mess."

"Oh, brother," Viola said, lowering herself to Evelyn's

bunk. A dim shaft of moonlight from the window fell across the front of Evelyn's nightgown, and Viola saw the crumbs. She brushed them into her hand and then licked them off. "Be careful. If Sister finds crumbs, we'll both get punished."

"Sorry."

Viola sat on the edge of the bed. "Finish now. Then I'll clean up the rest."

"Why are you being so nice?"

"Because that's what sisters do."

"But you weren't nice in the dining hall."

Viola looked off into the darkness. "I couldn't."

Evelyn didn't understand why, but that was just one more thing she didn't understand about this place or how differently her sister acted when they were alone. This sister. The one who would sneak her food at night, was the sister who always made Evelyn feel better for a little while. She poked Viola to get her attention.

"Are we ever going to get out of here?"

"I don't know."

"When I'm a mother, I'm not going to do this."

Viola frowned. "What?"

"Give my babies away."

"That's years and years away. You don't know what you'll do."

"Yes, I do." Determination pushed her upright. "I'll have a pretty house. Like Miz Beatrice. And three children. And a father. And a mother. And kittens who don't run away."

"Oh, brother."

Evelyn giggled. "You always say that."

Viola sighed. "You always say the silliest things."

"It's not silly. It's perfect."

Viola sighed again, then put an arm around Evelyn. "You're right."

"What do you wish for?" Evelyn asked.

"I don't know. I don't think about it much."

Viola paused for so long Evelyn wondered if she was going to say any more, then Viola pulled her into a tighter hug. "We have to think about now, Evelyn. How we are going to survive here in this place."

"Will you still take care of me?"

"When I can. But you have to learn how to take care of yourself."

A cold shiver of alarm ran down Evelyn's back. "I don't want to."

"You have to. I'm going to take care of myself, and that will mean that sometimes..."

The sentence trailed off as if Viola wasn't sure how to finish it, and then it hit. The reason Viola ignored her at dinner.

"I'll be good. I promise." But even as she said those words, Evelyn knew it wouldn't matter. Being good had not made her mother love her enough to keep her. It had not kept Miz Beatrice from getting The Cancer. And it was not going to make her sister choose her over what would help Viola most. But Evelyn didn't know what else to do but try.

4

REGINA – OCTOBER 1925

R egina finished her shift at Coney Island early and hurried home to wash off some of the odor of grease and chili that clung to her. She planned to go out for the evening, and it wouldn't do to smell like a hot dog. Two years now she'd been at the same job, living in the same tiny apartment with no bathtub and a tiny washbasin in the closet of a bathroom. Washing her hair in the kitchen sink was an ordeal she didn't undertake very often, and she would pass on that tonight, hoping a spritz of perfume would mask whatever odor might be lingering in her hair.

She looked around at the cramped space and sighed. She'd long ago given up on the thought of going to get her girls. That thought had plagued her the first few months after leaving them at the orphanage, but there was no way she could fit them into this apartment or her life here in Detroit. Not that they'd ever fit well in Milwaukee. Still, they were a family, and there were times Regina allowed a memory of a better time with them to cross her mind. Picturing the baby smiles, she'd feel a pang of sadness, but she never gave into the drag of the feeling.

The girls were better off without her, and she could always dull the pain of loss with another drink.

She put on the flapper dress she'd been lucky enough to find at the thrift store and headed out to Fatina's Bar. It was her favorite place for scoring a few dates, but the men she met were not keepers. They seldom came back more than once or twice. Men coming in and out of her life was a pattern that had started with Fred and continued with John, although John had not willingly deserted her. The accident that killed him wasn't his fault. It was the blinding rain and the narrow pavement that had him crash headlong into a Mack truck. Sometimes she wondered if she would ever find a man who would stay. Someone steady.

But enough of this feeling sorry for herself. Regina shook the thoughts aside and slipped onto a barstool, motioning to the bartender, Tino. He knew her usual and started drawing a mug of draft beer.

He came over and set the drink in front of her. "Looking good tonight, Regina."

The compliment was accompanied by a wink that stirred a bit of heat. Tino was dark Italian, gorgeous, with a well-muscled body that Regina longed to have pressed against hers. He never offered, but they played this little game every time she came in, which was often. She smiled at him. "Don't be such a tease."

Tino chuckled and moved down to serve another customer. Regina sipped the ice-cold beer, wondering if she should eat supper here—Tino's mother cooked the best pasta in town—or go home after finishing her beer. Looking around the room, she noted that there were not many people out on a Monday. Too bad. It had been a couple of weeks since she'd had a "friend" over, and she'd been hoping, but the pickings were slim tonight. Based just on looks, the man returning to the corner booth might have been a prospect, but her stomach roiled as a sour smell of his body odor trailed after him. She might be a little free and easy with her body, but she had standards. Not making her throw up was one of them.

Regina nursed her beer for a few more minutes. She'd about decided to go home and heat up the hot dog she'd brought home from work when the door opened and a man she'd never seen here before walked in. What a striking figure he was in a dark trench coat and brown Fedora with a blue feather. His shoes were so shiny she could use one of the tips for a mirror if he came closer. When he glanced down the bar, his gaze rested on her for a moment, and she gave him her best smile. Things were looking up.

The man walked over and slid onto the stool next to her. "Buy you a drink?"

"I don't know you."

"Henry. Henry Stewart." He smiled. "Now you know me. What are you drinking?"

"Beer."

"Beer? Pretty lady like you should have something nicer."

"I do like a good Scotch whiskey."

"Now you're talking." Henry motioned to get the bartender's attention. "Two glasses of your finest Scotch."

Regina tried to ignore the wink Tino delivered with the drinks. He knew her too well. Maybe she shouldn't try to walk out with this guy in the next fifteen minutes.

Henry took his glass and touched hers. "Salud." He took a generous swig. Regina took a much smaller swallow. It had been a while since she'd had the hard stuff. Wouldn't do to choke while trying to impress this guy. The booze slid down her throat, warm and easy, and she savored the woody flavor that clung to her mouth.

"What's your name, pretty lady?"

She hesitated just a moment. There was something about his smooth charm that made her wonder if she should back off. Finally, she shrugged and said, "Regina."

"Ah. A fine Italian name."

"My parents were German."

"Maybe so, but they gave you an Italian name. Do you know what it means?"

She shook her head. "Do you?"

"It means 'queen.' And quite appropriate I'd say."

Indeed, she did feel like a queen receiving his attentions, and it was nice not having to be the forward one. Some men were so dense you had to spell out what you wanted. This man was different. He seemed to understand. Did she dare hope for more than just a couple of nights of fun?

As if sensing her reserve, Henry pushed his hat back and gave her a long, appraising look. "Are you married?"

"God, no."

"You don't ascribe to the fine state of matrimony?"

Regina resisted the urge to laugh. He sure had an odd way of saying things. "It wasn't so fine in my experience."

Henry touched her cheek, the gesture so soft she wasn't even sure she felt it before he took his hand away. "Nobody should treat a queen badly."

Regina resisted the urge to pinch herself. Was this real? She was afraid if she blinked she'd wake up from a dream.

But she wasn't dreaming. Henry was real. This was real.

"Have you had supper?" he asked.

"No."

"Neither have I. Do you know a place nearby where we could get a bite?"

"There's always my place."

It took him so long to respond, she worried that she had been too forward.

"That is not a good idea for tonight," he said, touching her cheek again. This time, the touch seared her skin, and she felt a flush of heat. Oh God, he was a tease. "Anticipation will make it so much sweeter."

They went three doors down to a fancy Italian restaurant, where he said he could buy a dinner fit for an Italian queen. And true to his word, he did not go home with her that night. It took two weeks of meeting almost every evening before he satisfied that burning inside of her.

Two months later, they married.

Regina never told Henry about the girls, and she had brushed over the details about Frank, saying it was nothing. They had married in haste and quickly unmarried. She didn't know why she held back about her daughters. Well, actually she did. She didn't think Henry was like John, not wanting children, but she didn't want to take the chance that he would bolt. She was tired of the men in her life running out on her, and she was determined to make sure this one stayed. Even if it meant pretending. She was good at pretending, wasn't she?

5

EVELYN – DECEMBER 1930

E velyn pulled her brown sweater tighter against the frigid air in the long hallway. It was little protection against the cold that chilled her to the bone and turned her fingers blue. Viola had taken the sweater away from her after Evelyn pulled it from the donation bag first, then after Evelyn begged, gave it back. Evelyn was happy to have it, even though it was thinly woven and the cold air found its way in. This winter was harder than last year, and even the year before that. Sister Honora said it wasn't any colder outside. It was just that there wasn't enough coal to heat the whole building. The sleeping ward was so frigid that at night, all the children huddled under thick quilts still wearing their clothes.

The only warm spot in the entire building was the dining room, and that's where Evelyn was headed now. Viola should already be there.

All this week, Viola had finished her morning chores early and was first in line for lunch. In addition to having choice work assignments—she had been chosen to clean the altar in the chapel—Viola was allowed to attend classes in the afternoons.

Evelyn was not.

Two years ago, the good sisters had decided that there was something wrong with Evelyn's brain. She was slow. She was stupid. She was never going to be able to learn, so she might as well be doing chores all day. Those chores were still the worst a person could hope for, a lot of floor scrubbing, which left her hands red and made blisters on top of callouses.

Evelyn tried to pretend she didn't care that Viola had the lighter load, but sometimes, resentment reared its ugly head. Evelyn was sure that she could be as smart and as good as Viola if the sisters would just give her a chance. They were always impatient with her. Wanting her to give the answer to an arithmetic problem right now. Right this very second. Not letting her take the time she needed to come up with the correct answer. And she read too slowly. At least that is what Sister Marie said in front of the whole class.

It was no surprise that Evelyn read slowly and stumbled over the words when told to read aloud. Everyone in the class stared at her, including Sister Marie, impatience furrowing the brow under the white wimple. Having all the eyes in the room focused on her made Evelyn want to run away and hide. She was sure that everyone was poised to react the minute she made her first mistake in pronunciation. And, of course, the nervousness made the mistake come quickly.

The laughter followed.

Stepping into the relative warmth of the large dining hall, Evelyn saw several kids in line to pick up a tray and be served by Sister Magdalene, who stood behind the large metal pans ready to dole out portions of food. Evelyn had to walk the entire length of the line, passing by Viola, who was first, to get to the end and wait. Stepping into the line in front of her sister was not possible. That was an infraction that could get them both punished, and Viola was standing firm in her resolve to champion herself above Evelyn.

At every meal, the children had to stand in line until everyone had filed into the dining hall. Then Sister Honora would walk to the front of the room and lead the prayer before serving could begin. Lately, Evelyn had noticed that the food portions were dwindling along with the coal supply. Porridge used to be just for breakfast, but sometimes, now, they had it for lunch or for dinner. Sister Magdalene, who was in charge of the kitchen, said that come spring and summer, when they could plant a garden, the offering in the food line would improve. It's just that there wasn't enough money right now to buy all that the orphanage needed.

Viola had taken to eating with some of the other older girls, so Evelyn sat at a table with other eleven-year-olds and ate her bowl of porridge slowly. She wanted to linger in the dining hall as long as she dared, just to be warm for a few more minutes. She had to scrub the floor in the sleeping area this afternoon, and it would be colder there than anywhere in the building. But she couldn't put it off forever. She scraped the bowl for the last bit of food, then carried the empty bowl to the cart where they put the dirty dishes. Some lucky girl would get to wash those in the relative warmth of the kitchen.

After depositing the bowl, Evelyn went to the room off of the kitchen where cleaning things were kept and got a bucket and mop.

Once in the sleeping area for the girls, she first went to her cot and pulled out a cigar box from underneath. The box held a couple of pencils, some paper, a pretty rock she'd found last summer by the creek that ran behind the orphanage, and the spoon she'd brought from Miz Beatrice's. Her one connection to a happier time.

It also still held her mother's handkerchief, which wasn't a connection to a happier time, but something she treasured nonetheless. The cloth no longer held the sweet smell of her mother's perfume. That had long ago faded, but Evelyn didn't care. It had once belonged to that mysterious woman she longed to know.

Running a finger along the lace on the edge of the cloth, Evelyn thought about her mother. Where was she now? Did she ever think about her and Viola? Then she thought about Miz Beatrice. Had The Cancer taken her?

"What are you doing?"

Startled, Evelyn looked up and saw Sister Honora. "Nothing, Sister. Just—"

"You weren't sent here to do nothing."

"No, Sister. I will get to work right now."

"What do you have there?"

"Nothing... I..." Evelyn tried to drop the handkerchief into the box, but Sister Honora grabbed it. "Please don't take it. It's the only thing I have left of my mother."

Sister looked at the cloth in her hand for a moment, and Evelyn hoped.

"Your mother left you here, child. What should you care about a stupid handkerchief?"

The words punctured Evelyn's heart. "May I please have it back?"

Her plea was barely a whisper, but even that was ignored.

Sister held onto the handkerchief, and Evelyn slid the box back under the cot, tears burning in her eyes. She blinked the wetness back, not wanting to show weakness, and stood. Sister was still standing there, watching, and little prickles of alarm erupted on Evelyn's back. It didn't bode well when Sister stood like a statue, her eyes boring into Evelyn. "As your punishment for shirking your duties, you will not have supper."

Anger reared its ugly head, and Evelyn fought to control it. This was so wrong. She was not shirking. She worked hard, but she knew better than to voice any of her thoughts. Nothing was right or fair in this horrible place.

"You will also mop the boys' ward."

Evelyn forced the anger aside and nodded.

"Don't just stand there." Sister pounded her walking stick on the floor to punctuate her words. "Get busy."

Evelyn dodged around Sister and grabbed the mop. By the time she finished the floor in the girls' ward, the water was freezing and her hands were red and stiff from wringing out the mop. The supper bell had rung a few minutes ago, so this would not be a good time to go to the kitchen for warm water. Not only did she not want to see the other children eating, she didn't want to be under the scrutiny of Sister Honora, so Evelyn would finish with cold water. Pushing with the handle of the mop, she rolled the bucket along the uneven wooden planking of the floor into the boy's sleeping area, which was just like the girls' ward, only it smelled of sweat and something else she couldn't place.

As Evelyn mopped, she thought about what Viola had told her about how some of the children came to be here, and she wondered which boys had been left by their mothers and which had not. Viola had told her that some of the children had no mother or father. They were dead, and the children had no place to go, so they came here to St. Aemilian's. Evelyn wondered if knowing that your parents had no choice in leaving you made it easier to be here. When Evelyn had gotten old enough to understand that her mother chose to leave her, that realization had cut a deep fissure of pain that still hurt. Those first few years of ignorance had been better. She preferred not knowing what abandonment felt like.

Evelyn finished the mopping just in time to go to chapel for evening prayer. She knelt on the hard, wooden kneeler for an hour, shivering in the cold and hugging her freezing hands to her chest. All of the nuns sat in the first two pews, the children filling in behind, all facing the altar with the larger-than-life statues of Mary and Joseph on either side of Jesus on the huge cross. Sister Marie led the prayers, all done in Latin, and the children murmured responses, their voices blending together into a sort of chant. Often, Evelyn found the prayer time the best hour of the day. She could slip into the last pew and listen to the soft sound of the voices reciting the words in a low hum. She didn't know the words, but the rhythm always soothed her.

Tonight, however, she felt nothing but chilled to the bone and so hungry her stomach ached with the pain. She couldn't wait to go to the sleeping ward and crawl into bed with Viola. The normal rule was only one child per cot, but because of the extreme cold, the Sisters allowed the children to double up. The children could also get into bed with their clothes on, so Evelyn didn't take off her sweater or her shoes.

"You better not kick me," Viola said as they snuggled under the quilt.

"I won't. I'll be still."

Once everyone was settled, Sister Honora turned off the lights, and as darkness enveloped the room, the only sound in the room was the soft murmurs of children whispering to each other. When the murmurs slowly slid off into the deep breathing of sleep, Evelyn scooted closer to Viola's back, seeking all the warmth she could get. "Are you asleep?"

"Hush."

"I want to ask you something."

"I said to hush."

"It's important."

Viola rolled over and faced her sister. "What?"

"Why is there no more coal or food?"

"I don't know."

"Don't they tell you in school?"

"A few weeks ago, Sister said something about banks closing and people losing money."

"What does that mean?"

Viola sighed. "I don't know for sure. But Sister said people who used to help us couldn't anymore. It has something to do with a depression."

"What depression?"

"I don't know. Sister didn't say what that is."

"Will the people get the money back?"

"Oh, brother. When are you ever going to stop asking me all these questions? You're not a baby anymore."

Evelyn bit her lip to hold back the tears. Viola was right. They were no longer babies, but inside, Evelyn still felt like that child who had watched their mother walk away and didn't understand why. She felt like that child who believed if she was good and did what she was told, everything would be okay.

She closed her eyes and tried to drift off to sleep, and then she thought of something. What if she could get some money for the orphanage? Viola had told her that the silver spoon Evelyn had was worth money. Maybe she could give the spoon to Sister Honora to sell. Then there would be more coal and more food. And maybe Sister would smile at her and tell her she was a good girl. And everything really would be okay.

She let that thought carry her into sleep, and sometime later, a loud clanging woke her. Metal against metal in a rapid, staccato, ear-blasting beat. She sat up, trying to remember when she had heard that sound before. Then it came to her. The fire drills. Once a month, they practiced how to get out of the building in case of fire, but they had never had a drill at night. It was always done during the day. Sometimes, they would pretend it was night and go to the sleeping ward to learn how to get out. Was this a drill or the real thing?

Viola threw back the quilt and pushed Evelyn. "Move! We have to get out."

Evelyn tumbled off the cot and grabbed her box of treasures as the noise intensified and Sister Honora came into view, banging a washtub with a large metal spoon. "Make your lines and go out the way we practiced. DO NOT RUN! Grab your blankets and move quickly in an orderly manner."

"Is there really a fire?" Evelyn asked Sister.

"Yes. Now go."

The urge to run was strong, but Evelyn fought it down. Some instinct told her that if just one person panicked, everyone would. She clung to the box while Viola grabbed the quilt from the bed. They held hands and followed the line of girls out into the great hall. The acrid odor of smoke burned Evelyn's nose. Sister Magdalene stood in the middle of the great hall, directing the lines of children toward the front doors. The boys came from the other side, and the two lines moved in tandem. Two more Sisters were at the heavy oak doors and opened them so the kids could pass through.

Outside, the children huddled on the great expanse of lawn that was covered in several inches of snow that shimmered in the moonlight. Evelyn was thankful she had gone to bed with her shoes on, but still, her feet were cold, and she shivered under the quilt with Viola. The nuns stood in a line between the children and the burning building, but Evelyn could still see the flames that crawled up the side of the building like great orange and yellow fingers.

Several of the younger children had started to cry, and Sister Honora told them all to be brave. "Just be thankful we got out alive."

"How did the fire start?" Viola asked.

"In the kitchen," Sister said. "The cook left the stove door open for more heat. An ember must have fallen out."

Evelyn glanced at the fire again. It was amazing that one little ember could cause this inferno. Despite the efforts of the few neighbors who had come to try to stop the fire, it appeared that the flames would consume what had been her home for almost eight years. The side that held the kitchen was gone, and the greedy fire had moved across the front of the building. The buckets of water that people threw at the flames had no effect. What would happen now that the orphanage was gone?

After a few minutes, the people stepped back and dropped their buckets, leaving the fire to burn out. The groundskeeper, Mr. Mugliardi, ran up to Sister Honora, his breath fogging in the cold air. "Ach, what a tragedy. We tried our best."

"Yes. You did. And I thank you for the effort."

Kindness was not something Evelyn had ever seen in Sister Honora, and her response to Mr. Mugliardi surprised her.

"Were you able to call the authorities?" Sister asked Mr. Mugliardi.

"Yes, ma'am. People will be a'coming to take the youngsters to the empty building at the Lutheran's."

"It is very nice of them to let us use the building."

"'Tis for the children, ma'am. They said religion is no matter when it comes to helping the children."

Evelyn watched the tall, gaunt man stride away. Where was this other place where they were going? How far away was it? Would her mother be able to find them there? She clutched Viola's cold hand. "I'm scared."

"Me too."

But Viola didn't look scared. She had that same determined look Evelyn had seen so many times since they had been left here. The one that Evelyn had tried so hard to acquire for herself.

6

EVELYN – DECEMBER 1931

What was supposed to be temporary accommodations at the Lutheran Seminary dragged into another year. During the first few weeks there, Evelyn had learned that the building to which they'd been taken had been used to house young men preparing to be ministers. She had not known that other religions had seminaries. Of course, she didn't know much about other religions, but she knew about seminaries and seminarians. All of the children prayed for them during evening prayer every day. Sister Honora had told them all how important it was to pray for the men who were going to become leaders in the church.

When they'd first taken refuge in the old building, it was with great joy that they discovered the seminary already had cots and sheets and blankets. There was no food, however, so everyone's stomach growled with hunger for the first day until provisions could be brought in. Because everything had been lost in the fire, they had all worn the one outfit of clothes they'd escaped in for an entire week. At the end of that week, more clothes were donated, and Evelyn was so glad to be able to take a bath and put on something that didn't reek of smoke.

Almost a full year later, the fire had been overshadowed by the dwindling supply of food. And there had been no new donations of clothes for some time. The two dresses Evelyn had been given not long after the fire had fit her just fine back then, but she had since grown. In more ways than one. The good Sisters were quick to point out to the girls that their emerging breasts were of no use unless they were to have children. They were not to touch them, nor let anyone else touch them, especially a boy. Nobody would say why that rule didn't seem to apply to Sister Honora. Sometimes, Sister would come into where the girls were taking bahs. To make sure the girls were cleaning themselves properly, she would say. But then she might take a rag and start washing one of the girls, lingering a long time on the soft, rounded humps on the girl's chest.

Evelyn shuddered every time she heard the sound of Sister's approach. The Sister always came into the bathing area humming under her breath, as if to herald her arrival. The first time for Evelyn was the worst. The other girls looked away, hurrying to finish washing and get out as quickly as possible, leaving Evelyn alone with Sister. They knew what was going to happen.

So did Evelyn, and she had dreaded this moment.

Sister took the rag from Evelyn's hand and rubbed ever so softly across her budding breasts, not saying a word, just humming. Evelyn kept her eyes downcast, hating the fact that the rubbing made her nipples hard and sent a jolt of heat to her private parts. It was an odd mix of revulsion and... She couldn't put a word to the other emotion created by the unusual sensation down there.

When the rubbing stopped, Evelyn dared a glance at Sister's face. A smile lingered there, but it seemed wrong somehow, almost like a garish cartoon, and she did not meet Evelyn's gaze.

Evelyn waited several long minutes after Sister left before pulling her dripping, chilled body out of the bathing tub. She dried quickly and went to the neat pile of clothes on the bench. Sitting on top of her dress was the handkerchief Sister had taken from Evelyn so long ago. The sight stopped Evelyn's breath in her throat. She had mourned the loss of the handkerchief for several weeks after it had been taken, but in time, she had steeled herself against the pain. Compared to all the other losses in her life, this one had been insignificant.

Still, she reached out and took the soft cloth, holding it against her cheek and cried for the brief moment of happiness it gave her.

The following week, Sister came into the bathing area again when Evelyn was there. This time, Sister wore a smile that seemed more genuine, and a crazy thought flitted through Evelyn's mind. Did the smile mean Sister was happy to see her? Did Sister care? Had returning the handkerchief been some sort of gesture of apology for all the horrible treatment over the years Evelyn had been here?

"Thank you for the handkerchief," Evelyn offered, her voice cracking.

Sister did not respond, she merely motioned for Evelyn to finish undressing. Apprehension, mixed with an odd sense of expectation, came over Evelyn as the chill in the air raised goosebumps on her bare flesh. The emotions warred with each other as she tried to understand what was happening to her body. Sister reached out a hand and brushed her fingers across Evelyn's chest. Again, her nipples responded to the touch. It was wrong. Evelyn knew that. But it made her feel warm all over. Sister stepped closer to cup her hand around the tiny breast, and Evelyn wondered if this is what it felt like to be loved.

She had never felt the comfort of resting on a mother's bosom, or experiencing this kind of love, if that's what it was.

Today, Sister's touch felt different and it opened a well of yearning deep inside Evelyn. She wanted this comfort. This love. So she closed the short distance between them, reaching out to touch Sister the way she was being touched.

"Stop that," Sister said, slapping Evelyn away with a bruising blow to one shoulder.

Evelyn staggered back, slipping on the water from so many other baths that had puddled on the floor. She fell hard on her buttocks, causing a sharp pain to shoot up her back.

Sister glared at her. "You may never, ever do that again."

"But—"

"That is a nasty, sinful thing."

"But—"

"Do you understand?"

Evelyn didn't know if the truth would incite even more anger, so she kept quiet. She didn't understand. None of it. But she thought if she stayed down on the wet floor, perhaps Sister would not hit her again. She gave a brief nod, even though she wanted to shout, *why can you touch me and it not be a sin?*

Evelyn stood, silent as Sister started to hum and continued to rub Evelyn's body. There was no surge of heat anymore. Just a cold wave of anger and revulsion that made Evelyn shudder. Sister did not seem to notice. She hummed and rubbed for a few more minutes, then dropped the rag at Evelyn's feet and walked out.

Evelyn was so ashamed she didn't even tell Viola about what happened this time. By tacit agreement, none of the girls had ever said much about what went on in the bathing area. But Evelyn had talked to Viola after that first time. She wanted to know if Viola had felt the same sensations when it had been her first visit from Sister, but Viola had refused to talk about it.

For the next several weeks, Evelyn avoided the bathing area. She was still assigned to mop after baths were finished, and she was able to do a quick wash-up while she was alone in there. Keeping her clothes on, she quickly washed her face and stuck her head into the washtub to rinse the grime out of her hair. All of the girls had very short hair, cut once a month by another one of the good Sisters, so it only took a few minutes for Evelyn to dry her hair with a towel. Then she quickly mopped up the water and hurried out, hoping that Sister would not come in.

When Evelyn stepped into the hall, she almost collided with Maria. "Oh, sorry. Do you need something in there?" Evelyn gestured over her shoulder.

"No. Sister sent me to get the rest of the children. We're all to come to the dining area."

That was odd. It was mid-morning. They never went to the dining room unless it was for a meal. "Do you know why?" Evelyn asked as she followed Maria.

"Sister didn't say."

Even though Evelyn fervently hoped Sister would have good news to tell them, some instinct told her otherwise as she hurried to join the other children gathered in the cold dining room. Without the heat from the ovens that eased the chill and carried the comforting smell of food, Evelyn's sense of impending doom intensified.

After the last of the children made their way inside, Sister Honora strode stiffly to the front of the room and told all the children to sit down. For a moment, all that could be heard was the scraping of chairs across the wood planking on the floor, then silence. The children knew not to speak unless asked to do so.

"Children. This is most difficult news I bear today. As you know, God has sent us many challenges in recent years. The Great Depression..."

For a moment, Evelyn's mind wandered. Sister kept saying that, "The Great Depression," like it was something wonderful, but Evelyn didn't know what was so great about it. The last few years had been too often filled with days of being hungry and cold and miserable.

"...the orphanage will have to close."

Evelyn jerked her attention back to the good sister. What was that she said?

"We have made arrangements for some of you to go to work..."

Evelyn turned to Viola. "What is she talking about?"

"Shhh! If you weren't daydreaming all the time, you'd know."

"The orphanage will officially close in two weeks. We will meet with you individually to let you know where you will be going. That is all."

The silence that followed was so complete; Evelyn could hear the beat of her heart as it thumped against her ribs. This was worse than the fire. Much worse. And she wasn't sure she liked a God who would do this to them.

"What about Christmas, Sister?"

Evelyn looked around to see who had asked the question. It was Marie, and the look Sister gave the girl made Evelyn glad she had not asked.

"There is no money for food," Sister said. "How can you expect Christmas?"

Evelyn didn't care for herself, but she knew the younger children had been counting on something special for the Holiday. Last year, the fire had stolen Christmas. Now this? If only there was a way. Evelyn raised her hand. Did she dare say anything? "Um, excuse me Sister."

"What?"

"Perhaps if there was money. I mean... I have a silver spoon. I'd be happy to—"

"To what?"

"You could have it. Sell it and—"

Sister laughed, and the sound was anything but pleasant. "You stupid girl. You think that would help? One silver spoon will not bring enough money to buy even one present, let alone..." Sister let the sentence trail off as she gestured to the crowd of children. She shook her head and turned away. "Silly, silly girl."

Evelyn looked at the ground so nobody would see the tears that brimmed in her eyes and then ran down her cheeks. When would she ever learn?

———

So Christmas came and Christmas went with nothing to make the day special. Not even flowers on the altar for the Christmas Mass. There was nothing but porridge to eat for all three meals of the day, and Evelyn tried not to think of the roasted duck and potatoes they used to have on holidays. The next day, Sister Magdalene walked into the dining hall where Evelyn was cleaning the tables and tapped her on the shoulder. "Sister Honora wishes to see you."

"Should I finish washing the tables? There are only two left."

"No. She said to come at once."

"Yes, Sister." Evelyn went into the kitchen to dump the pail of water in the large steel sink. Rinsing the rag quickly and wringing it out, she wondered about the summons. Rarely were chores to be interrupted. Not for any reason. Therefore, Evelyn carried a great deal of concern with her as she hurried to the small room that Sister Honora had made into her office. It wasn't as well put out as the space she'd had at St. Amelians, but Sister had still managed to instill an air of officiousness. When Evelyn entered the room, Sister Honora motioned for her to sit on the wooden chair in front of the desk that was strewn with papers. Sister sat on the other side and was digging through the papers. She slid one out and looked up at Evelyn. "We have secured a job for you."

"A job? Where? Doing—?"

"Kindly do not interrupt. I will tell you all you need to know, and there will be no questions. Do you understand?"

Evelyn nodded, and Sister looked at the paper as she spoke. "You will be with a family in Milwaukee. They need a girl to care for the children and help with the household chores." Sister paused and made a notation on the paper in front of her. "The work is not dissimilar to what you have done here."

Evelyn swallowed the urge to ask about Viola. Where was she going? Were they to be separated? Or was it possible she would go to the same place?

"Regarding your time here." Sister paused and locked eyes with Evelyn. "You will not speak of it. Never. Not one word about anything. Is that clear?"

Evelyn swallowed hard and gave a small nod.

"Privacy in all matters is paramount." Sister emphasized each word with a hard tap of her pen on the top of her desk. "If we have nothing else, we have our privacy. Is that not true?"

Evelyn didn't know if Sister really wanted an answer, and did Evelyn have the courage to speak the truth? There had been no privacy since coming here. The nuns constantly watched the children. In the classes. In the dining hall. One of the Sisters would even walk through the sleeping area at night after lights out. Then there was what went on in the bathing area, but that, Evelyn decided, would never be talked about. It was too awful. Too shameful to ever be spoken about aloud to another person.

So instead of saying anything, Evelyn merely nodded again. She was getting good at nodding, even when she wanted to scream.

"That is all," Sister said. "You will be taken to your new home at the end of the week."

When Evelyn didn't move, Sister waved her hand toward the door. "You may go."

Evelyn stood and started toward the door, then turned back. She hadn't planned to. She'd planned to walk out silently like the obedient child she was supposed to be, but she needed to know. "Please, Sister? What about Viola?"

The glare was like being doused with ice water. "What did I just say about privacy, young miss? That is information that you do not need to know."

"But—"

"You may go."

Evelyn pinched her lips tightly together to keep from saying anything more and walked out.

————

On the day she was to leave, Evelyn stood by the cot with Viola. Her sister was leaving today too, but she still did not know where. They both had small suitcases open, packing their meager belongings. Evelyn looked over at her sister. "I don't want to go someplace without you."

"It's not up to us. Stop being such a baby."

"I'm not acting like a baby." Evelyn pushed her underwear

aside to make room for the cigar box with her treasures. "It's just that I don't want to be separated."

Viola stepped over and put her arms around Evelyn. "I know. I'm sorry."

Evelyn stood in the embrace for a few moments, then asked, "Will we be able to see each other?"

"I don't know. Sister said arrangements are confidential."

"She told me too. And I don't understand that." Evelyn pulled away from her sister, closed the suitcase, and latched it. "We should be able to know where the other person is. I don't know if I can survive without you."

"Don't be silly. Of course you can. You're stronger than you think you are."

Evelyn smiled at her sister, wanting to believe the words, but she didn't feel strong. She wasn't sure what it meant to be strong.

"Do you know what day this is?" Viola asked.

Evelyn shook her head.

"It's New Year's Day. A New Year. A new beginning." Viola smiled, but Evelyn couldn't tell if the smile was real or just put there to make her feel better.

Viola latched her suitcase, then picked it up and walked away, calling back, "Be safe, little sister."

Watching her sister join Sister Magdalene, who was going to take Viola to her new home, Evelyn choked on the tears she couldn't hold back. She wasn't crying for her sister. Viola would be fine. She was the strong one. Evelyn cried for herself. Now her mother would never find her. Viola didn't seem to care, but Evelyn cared. She cared so much it almost took her breath away.

7

EVELYN – JANUARY 1932

E velyn, wearing a faded housedress that someone had donated to the orphanage, stood on the porch with her satchel in one hand. Her other hand was gripped tightly by Sister Honora. They faced a door that was centered on the largest house Evelyn had ever seen—easily four or five times bigger than the one she'd lived in with Miz Beatrice. The porch wrapped around the front and one side of the house, and stately white pillars supported an upper balcony.

Sister rapped loudly on the door, and just moments later, footsteps approached. Then the heavy wooden door swung open to reveal a pretty young woman who smiled brightly. A small child, wearing short pants with a bib over a white shirt, peeked around the woman's full skirt. He looked to be about four years old.

"Mrs. Hershlinger?" Sister asked.

The woman nodded.

"This is the girl we spoke about last week." Sister pushed Evelyn a little closer to the open door. "She's a good worker."

"Yes. As you said on the phone." The woman stepped to one side. "Do come in."

Evelyn followed Sister Honora inside and saw the child scurry down the entry hall, his leather shoes clunking along the tile. He turned a corner and disappeared. "That's Jonathan," the woman said. "He's a little shy. Please. Come with me."

She led them into a front parlor that held several pieces of lovely furniture, the largest of which was a sofa covered in a floral print. The fabric was so shiny it could have been satin. Evelyn hesitated to sit on it even though the lady indicated that they could, but Sister had no such qualms. She sat quickly, pulled several papers out of a leather valise, and handed them over to the lady. "This is all the information we have on the girl."

"Evelyn, right?" The woman smiled at Evelyn. "That's a lovely name. My name is Sarah Hershlinger. That surname is hard to pronounce, so you may call me Sarah."

"Young girls are not allowed such familiarity," Sister said. "She will call you Mrs. Hershlinger or ma'am."

"Yes, ma'am," Sarah said, then winked at Evelyn.

That's when Evelyn decided maybe this wouldn't be so bad after all. On the way to this house, Sister had told her that this family had been lucky enough to hang on to their fortune during The Great Depression, and Evelyn was lucky as well to work here. Sister had said that she would have a room to herself, but Evelyn didn't know how that would feel. She hated being separated from Viola. She couldn't ever remember a time when they were not together, and this was going to be so strange. Sleeping alone. No warm body to snuggle up to when it was cold. Although maybe cold would not be a problem in this house. It was very toasty in this lovely parlor. She sat gingerly on the edge of one of the sofa cushions and put her little suitcase on the floor next to her feet.

"This is the agreement between you and the St. Aemilian's Home for Orphans." Sister pulled two more sheets of paper out of the valise. "You agree to provide room and board for the orphan girl named Evelyn Gundrum in exchange for house-keeping and childcare duties."

"We could pay her a small salary too."

"That is not necessary. The children do not work for money."

"Every young girl needs to have something in her pocket to spend on special things." Sarah smiled at Evelyn then faced Sister again. "Would that be a problem for St. Aemilian's?"

Sister hesitated for just a moment, getting that expression on her face that always made one tremble, and Evelyn was afraid Sister would insist on no payment. "Of course not," Sister said, her tone making it clear it was not perfectly okay. "That is between you and the girl."

Now Evelyn was sure she was going to like it here, and she was going to like Sarah. This was another side of Sister she had never seen before. Backing down to someone.

"If you will please sign both copies of the agreement," Sister said. "I'll leave one with you."

As soon as Sarah signed the documents, Sister took her copy. "Well. That concludes the business. If the girl gets sassy or gives you any problem, a good licking will set her straight."

"I'm sure it will."

The business concluded, Sister stood, and Sarah did as well, so Evelyn stood up too. Before leaving, Sister turned to Evelyn. "Mind your manners. There is no place for you to go if this doesn't work out."

A tremor of fear shot through Evelyn. "Yes, Sister."

"Very well, then." Sister Honora straightened her back and walked out of the room. Sarah hurried after her, but Evelyn didn't move. She was still locked in that fear. She couldn't imagine being out in the big city all alone. She tried to smile when Sarah came back, but she was shaking inside.

"Are you okay?" Sarah asked. "You are so pale."

"I'll do anything you ask." Evelyn couldn't hold the words back. "Please don't put me out."

"Oh, dear." Sarah took Evelyn's arm and guided her to a chair. "We have no intention of putting you out. We asked for a sweet girl like you."

"You did?"

Sarah smiled. "Yes. And I knew you'd be perfect."

Evelyn didn't know what to say in response. Nobody had ever talked to her like this lady did. And nobody had ever called her perfect.

After a moment, Sarah said, "Are you ready to meet the children? I think Jonathan probably ran to the playroom."

Evelyn picked up her suitcase and followed Sarah, who led the way to a room toward the back of the house. When they stepped inside, it was like entering a magical kingdom. A bold lemon-yellow paint brightened the room and shelves of red, blue, and green covered three walls. Some of the shelves held books, others were overflowing with small toys and puzzles. The fourth wall had tables and chairs on either side of a large window.

In the middle of the room was a dollhouse—a very large dollhouse. A girl with blond pigtails sat on the floor moving dolls from one room of the house to another. She looked to be a little older than Jonathan, and she wore a red dress with white ruffles at the neck and hem. Her legs were folded to one side, and shiny black shoes peeked out from the skirt of her dress. Evelyn marveled at how pretty the girl was.

"Abigail," Sarah said. "Please stand and say hello to Evelyn. She's the girl who has come to work here. You remember I told you about her last week."

"Yes, Mother." The girl scrambled to her feet and stepped closer. "Hello, Evelyn. We hope you will like it here."

"Where's your brother?" Sarah asked.

"Hiding in his fort." Abigail pointed to a corner of the room walled off with a tower of boxes.

Sarah laughed. "Abigail likes to play with her new toys. Her brother likes to play with the boxes they came in."

Given the choice, Evelyn would have enjoyed building something with the boxes too, but she kept that thought to herself. She couldn't tell if Sarah approved of what the boy was doing or not, and she didn't want to risk stirring any disapproval.

"Jonathan," Sarah said. "Come out this instant. Evelyn is going to be here for the foreseeable future, so you might as well be a gentleman and meet her."

Jonathan pushed one section of the boxes aside and stepped out. He had the same light brown hair as his mother and sister, but he had a little trouble looking at Evelyn.

"Hello, Jonathan," Evelyn said.

His response was barely a mumble.

"I like your fort," Evelyn said.

"You do?" Now he looked up, his blue eyes bright with excitement. "Want to play?"

Sarah chuckled. "Not now," she said. "She can play with you later. She needs to get settled in first."

Evelyn's room was up a long flight of stairs at the back of the house. The staircase was just off of the kitchen, so they stopped there first so Evelyn could meet the cook, Hildy, before going up the stairs. "All the servants have accommodations on this floor," Sarah said when they reached the top. "In addition to Hildy, we have Genevieve, the main housekeeper. You will be assisting her with chores."

"Yes, ma'am."

"Mr. Martinelli, the groundskeeper, lives in a small room above the stables, so there are no men on this floor."

The room that was to be Evelyn's was at the end of the short hall. "I must apologize. This is the smallest of the upstairs rooms," Sarah said, opening the door.

Evelyn couldn't imagine why the woman would apologize for the room. The space was adequate. In fact, it was more than adequate. The bed was narrow, but that left room beside it for a rug that looked like it would be very soft and warm on bare feet. A small maple desk stood under a window that had lovely white curtains swept back with gold ribbons, and opposite the bed was a tall bureau, also maple. There were so many drawers; Evelyn wondered if she could ever fill them.

"Oh, it's very nice," Evelyn said.

"Hildy cleaned the room for you yesterday." Sarah bustled in and checked the top of the desk for any dust. "But after this, it will be your responsibility to keep it clean and tidy."

"Yes, ma'am."

"Oh, please do call me Sarah."

"Yes, ma'am." Evelyn felt the heat of a blush on her cheeks. "I mean, I will try."

Sarah laughed. "You can put your things in the bureau. Mr. Martinelli must have forgotten to bring in the armoire. For now, you can hang your dresses on that peg in the corner."

"You wish for me to take off my dress?"

"What? No. I meant your other dresses."

"I have no other dresses."

Sarah looked shocked, but she quickly covered with a smile. "Oh. I see. Well, we shall have to remedy that."

And remedy that Sarah did. Within a month, the armoire in Evelyn's room held four new dresses, a long coat, and a jacket. In that same month, she had also settled into a comfortable routine. The work was almost like a vacation compared to the floor scrubbing at the orphanage that had left her fingers cracked and bleeding. Here, Evelyn dusted and ran the carpet sweeper in the downstairs parlor every day. Sarah liked to have it clean in case one of her friends dropped by. Evelyn also assisted the cook, chopping vegetables, peeling potatoes, and slicing meat very thin for the children, who ate many of their meals in the kitchen with Evelyn and the other servants.

The kindness was wonderful, but Evelyn worried that it might not last, so she was careful not to do anything that would change it to upset Sarah or her husband.

One day, after Evelyn had been there for coming on two months, Sarah announced that she was having a dinner party the following Saturday evening and asked Evelyn if she would like to help serve. "You can help Hildy bring out the dishes of food to the dining table and hold them for guests to take what they want."

"I'd like that," Evelyn said.

"Good. I'll get you a pretty white apron to wear over your charcoal dress."

That Saturday evening, Evelyn tied the apron around her waist and adjusted the pinafore top so the ruffles were not folded over. She couldn't wait to help Hildy and show Sarah that she could do anything that was asked of her.

"Here you go now." Hildy handed Evelyn a tray. "These are appetizers. Use these silver tongs to put one on each of the small plates on the table. Do you remember what I told you about all the plates and silverware?"

"Yes, ma'am. The little plate by the water glass is for this." Evelyn nodded to the tray in her hand. "It will hold bread too. Then I take it away."

"Okay. Good."

Evelyn went to the dining room, noting the smile that Sarah gave her, and carefully passed out the appetizers. She had tasted one in the kitchen earlier and didn't like it. Some kind of fishy stuff on a small cracker.

Everything went smoothly until Evelyn was helping Hildy with the main course. The platter with the large roasted turkey had been placed in front of Mr. Herschlinger to carve and serve, and Hildy was taking a large bowl of potatoes around to guests. Evelyn was following with a large boat of gravy, and when she tried to get between two seats to serve the lady on her right, the man on the left leaned too close and bumped Evelyn's arm. Gravy sloshed out of the boat and spilled down the side of the woman's dress. She immediately stood and used her napkin to wipe at the mess.

Evelyn froze for a moment then looked toward Sarah. "I'm so sorry. Please don't whip me. Please! I won't do it again. I promise I'll be good."

The words rushed out like a runaway train, and Sarah jumped up, moving quickly toward Evelyn. Evelyn backed up with the most terrified expression, stopping Sarah who looked at her for the longest moment. Then Sarah said, "Child, it's okay. It was an accident. We understand. Maribeth is okay." Sarah pointed to the guest. "See. She's fine. And she's not angry. I'm not angry. Please don't be afraid."

"Then you're not going to whip me?"

"Oh, dear God, no." Sarah crossed the space between them and took Evelyn in her arms, murmuring, "It's okay. It's okay. It's okay. You don't have to be afraid. Nobody here will ever whip you. I promise."

Despite the promise, Evelyn could not totally relax. She was extra careful with everything she did, the memory of the sharp whap of Sister Honora's stick never far from her mind.

On most evenings, Evelyn assisted the children with their baths, although Sarah sometimes did that herself, and there were daily walks around the property so the children could get fresh air.

The children were respectful and cooperative most of the time, and Evelyn enjoyed the walks. The chores were easy and left plenty of time to join the children in the playroom or in the parlor for reading.

Mr. Hershlinger was made of much sterner stuff than his wife, and Evelyn sometimes thought he was too much like Sister Honora, all stiff and formal and demanding. He was gone to his job in the city on the weekdays, sometimes staying overnight, and the evenings he returned to the country home it was always quite late. He preferred to dine only with his wife. While she waited for her husband, Sarah would often sit in the kitchen and visit while everyone else ate, snacking lightly on a piece of meat or a bit of bread. Sitting around the table like that always brought memories of meals with Miz Beatrice to mind, and Evelyn soon realized that Sister Honora had been right. She was so lucky to be here.

Weekends were special. On Saturdays, rain or shine or snow, the family would picnic in the large, white gazebo in the back garden, always including Evelyn. The picnics, with fried chicken, potato salad, and homemade bread, were delicious, and the children would romp on the grass, playing tag. It was all great fun, and even Mr. Hershlinger would lose some of his stiffness and laugh at the kids' antics. Occasionally, they would take the baskets of food and games to a nearby park where there were swings and slides to play on. Evelyn loved to swing, pulling herself up and away, imagining that she could soar into the sky.

Sundays, the whole family went to church in the morning. The servants were not required to go but could if they cared to. Evelyn liked going to Mass. She liked the solemnity of the whole experience. The cavernous room adorned with beautiful art. The grand music swirling out from the massive pipes and filling all the spaces. She even liked listening to the words in Latin. She didn't even try to follow along in the missal, preferring to just close her eyes and let the sounds come to her in a low, soft murmur.

After church, the family gathered for a large, fancy meal. It was the one day of the week when the children were allowed to eat in the dining room. Mr. Hershlinger preferred a more formal atmosphere for the Sunday dinners than at the picnics, so Evelyn was responsible for making sure the children behaved and used their manners. The children could only speak when spoken to, and Sarah often made a point to ask them a question, but only one.

Despite the stiff formality of the meals, they were always pleasant, and life was so much better here than at the orphanage. Sometimes Evelyn would pretend that she wasn't just a servant. She'd pretend that she really was a part of this wonderful family.

The days were always so full that Evelyn seldom had time to think about her mother or her sister. It was at night that she would wonder about them. Where were they? What were they doing? Missing her sister created a pain that stabbed like a knife in her chest, and she couldn't help but wonder if Viola missed her as desperately. The thought that she might not would always bring a new wash of tears, but Evelyn did her best to keep her sadness to herself. What more could she want besides the kindness she had found here?

8

REGINA – 1938

The tavern was lightly populated for a Saturday evening, but then, it was early hours. It would probably fill up after nine. Regina and Henry had started coming back here to the place where they had first met on a regular basis, and she especially liked to remember that wonderful evening that changed her life so dramatically. Even though they had been married now over ten years, Henry was still very romantic, and tonight, he had given her a single red rose to wear on the lapel of her coat.

She looked over at him through the haze of smoke that swirled through the room, riding the breeze created by the fans suspended from the ceiling. He smiled. His smile could melt her insides.

She set her mug of beer down on the table, took a deep breath, and then said, "I want you to find my girls."

Henry leaned forward as if he had not heard correctly. "What?"

"Can you find my girls?"

He held up a hand. "Wait. Go back. What girls?"

Regina could hardly get the words past the constriction in her throat. It was as if a large snake had wrapped itself around her neck. "My daughters."

"You have children?" He looked at her for a long moment. "Why didn't you tell me?"

"I was afraid."

"Of what?"

"That you would leave me."

Regina had been thinking about this for weeks, but it had taken her that long to get up the nerve to ask Henry. Now she watched him carefully for his response. Was he angry? Would he be the same as John and leave her? Henry took so long to answer that her fear increased. The palms of her hands were wet with sweat, but she still shivered in a sudden chill.

Henry took a long swallow of his beer and then set the mug on the table, matching it precisely with the circle of condensation that was already there. "I'm disappointed."

Regina wanted to ask why, but she was afraid to.

"You kept this from me? All this time?"

"I know. I know. I should have told you right away. But after John... when I told him about my girls... he didn't want them."

"How could anyone not want children?"

That question took her by surprise. And it stung a little. Was he judging her too?

In the years they had been married, Regina had told Henry little about Frank and John, carefully skirting around the fact that she had two daughters. It was probably shame more than anything else that had guarded that secret.

"Tell me about it, Regina. All of it."

So she did. Not leaving anything out. Watching him the whole time, looking for any sign of reproach. There was none.

"You kept calling them 'your girls.' What are their names?"

"Viola and Evelyn."

Henry took another pull on his beer, then said, "Have you had any contact since you left them at the orphanage?"

"Very little."

There was no response to that, and Regina drummed her fingers on the table in a light staccato. Henry's expression was unreadable.

He sighed, then asked, "Why now?"

"Why now what?"

"Why are you wanting to find them now?"

Regina thought for a long moment before answering. "Because I would like to see how they turned out."

"Is that all?"

"No." Tears burned in her eyes and she swallowed hard. "I want to tell them I'm sorry."

Henry reached out and stilled her hand with his. It was warm and comforting. "When did you last have news about them?"

"About six or seven years ago. The orphanage had to close. I don't know where the girls went."

"Didn't anybody tell you?"

Regina shook her head. "The last time I called, the head sister wasn't there. The one who answered the phone said she couldn't tell me anything about the girls."

After another long moment, Henry sighed and said, "Then we'll just have to find them."

That was not an idle comment on his part. He was a Detroit police officer, so he could ask the Milwaukee police for help as a professional courtesy. "I'm sure they can assist me in locating the girls."

"They aren't girls anymore," Regina said. "They're all grown up."

"I know that," Henry said. "But they were girls when you

lost contact with them. And they were girls when they went into the orphanage. And that is where some record of where they were sent later is likely to be found."

Regina finished her beer, torn between an eagerness to see her daughters and fear of what a reunion would be like. She was so quiet Henry finally nudged her arm. "Are you okay?"

"Yes. I think so. I mean, of course."

"It's going to take me some time to adjust to this. But I do like children."

Regina gave him a wan smile. "I know."

It took a couple of months, but finally, an attorney who had handled the work agreements for the children who had been at the orphanage found addresses for both girls. Henry had taken care of the correspondence between Milwaukee and Detroit at work, and he came home one day with the good news. He didn't even take off his coat and hat before handing it over to Regina, who was in the kitchen cooking their supper.

Regina looked at the information that Henry had taken from his colleague and written in his precise script on the back of an envelope. She didn't say anything for the longest moment. Just stared at the words and numbers that made up two addresses in Milwaukee.

Henry took off his hat and shrugged out of his coat. "If you would like to go there, I can take time off, and we can drive. We need a vacation."

"I don't know if I should just show up." Regina sat down at the table, not sure her legs would hold her anymore. She was numb. She hadn't expected that the detective would actually find the girls. "The last time they saw me was when I left them at the orphanage. Maybe they wouldn't want to see me."

"Maybe they will."

Regina gave him a small smile. "You are always so positive."

"One of us has to be." Henry put his coat over the back of a chair and went to the stove to turn the fire on under the aluminum coffee pot. "You want some coffee?"

Regina nodded. "Maybe I should send a letter first. Tell them I'd like to come to see them."

"You could do that." Henry got two white mugs out of a cabinet.

"Should I say in the letter a specific date we would come?"

"Sure."

Regina consulted the wall calendar hanging on the wall above the telephone. "What about in four weeks? I could mail the letter tomorrow. Do you know how long it takes for a letter to get there?"

"I don't know." Henry took mugs of coffee to the table. "Maybe a week?"

"Then we should wait to hear back from them."

"Come and drink your coffee." Henry sat down and waved her over. "I will see at work when I can get time off. Then we can set a date to leave."

"But I wanted to mail a letter tomorrow." Regina returned to the table. "Before I talk myself out of this."

Henry smiled. "Then we send another letter with the date later. We can afford two stamps."

Regina laughed. Henry always made her laugh.

———

Evelyn closed the book she was reading as Sarah came into the library. Jonathan and Abigail had books as well. This was the reading hour that was honored every day. The children needed no help with reading anymore. In fact, they had far surpassed Evelyn's reading ability and often helped her with words she didn't understand. Sarah walked over to where Evelyn sat in the comfortable Queen Anne chair that was her favorite. "A letter came for you," Sarah said, handing over a small white envelope.

"For me?" Evelyn couldn't remember the last time a piece of mail had been delivered for her here.

"Yes. It's postmarked Detroit, Michigan."

Detroit? Evelyn didn't know anybody there. Who on earth would have sent her a letter from so far away?

"Are you going to open it?" Sarah asked. "Or would you rather wait until you're alone in your room?"

"No. This is okay." Evelyn slipped a fingernail under the flap of the envelope and peeled it back. Inside was a single sheet of paper. She read the few lines of writing, blinked, then read them again. Tears welled in her eyes and one ran in a warm path down her cheek.

"Oh, dear," Sarah said. "Did you get bad news?"

Evelyn shook her head. "It's from my mother."

The children were engrossed in their books and not paying attention, but Sarah motioned Evelyn to go over to the other side of the room. They sat in two ladder-backed chairs that flanked a small table in the corner. "I thought you were an orphan," Sarah said. "All this time you worked for us and you never told us your mother was alive?"

"The subject of my mother has never been easy to talk about."

"I see." Sarah paused. "Do you want to share what's in the letter?"

Evelyn shrugged.

"Was it just the fact of hearing from your mother that made you cry?"

"Partially." Evelyn sighed. "She wants to come here."

"Oh." Sarah sat back in her chair. "Would that be a bad thing?"

Evelyn shrugged again. She didn't know if it would be a

bad thing or not. She didn't know how to feel about this. She was numb.

After a few moments, Sarah asked, "Why does your mother want to visit?"

"She's living in Detroit now. With a new husband. She wants us to meet him."

"Us?"

"My sister and me."

"You have a sister?"

Evelyn nodded. "Her name is Viola."

Sarah glanced over at the children who were still engrossed in their play, then turned back to Evelyn. "A mother and a sister? I am so surprised you could keep that a secret."

"Before I came here, Sister said we were not to tell the people we work for anything about our past or our families. She said that was private, and we should keep it private."

In the silence that followed, Evelyn wondered if Sarah was upset and quickly tried to cover. "Sometimes I wanted to tell you," Evelyn said. "You've been so kind and—"

"It's okay." Sarah waved the words away. "You were right to do as you were told. I was just surprised. That's all. I'd wondered why the Sister didn't give us more information about you, but I just figured if you were an orphan, there wasn't much to give."

Evelyn fingered the flap of the envelope back and forth and back and forth until Sarah reached out and stilled her hand. "What do you want to do?" Sarah asked.

"I don't know."

"Did your mother request a response?"

Evelyn nodded. "She wants to know where we could meet."

Sarah started to say something, then paused a moment, tapping a finger on her chin. Finally, the tapping stopped, and Sarah asked, "Do you know where your sister is?"

"No. Only that she went to work with a family somewhere here in Milwaukee."

"But your mother knows where she is?"

Evelyn pulled out the letter and read it again. "Yes. Mother said she has sent a letter to Viola as well."

"Then we shall find her too." Sarah folded her hands in her lap and lifted her chin. "And if you would like to see your mother and her husband, we can make appropriate arrangements."

"Then I should tell her okay?"

"Only if you want to. You should think about it."

"I will."

"Good." Sarah smiled. "And whatever you decide will be okay with us."

"Thank you."

"Why don't you go to your room now? I'll get the children ready for dinner."

"Oh, no. I couldn't. I should do my job."

Sarah patted the envelope in Evelyn's hand. "You need time to absorb this news. Go. I insist."

Overcome at the depth of Sarah's kindness, Evelyn thought her heart would burst into a million pieces. She so desperately wanted to jump up and hug Sarah, but other than a pat on a shoulder or the touch of a hand, there had been no signs of affection exchanged between them.

Evelyn stood. "Thank you."

Sarah touched her lightly on the arm, and Evelyn had to dash out of the room to escape her wild impulse. Once in her quarters, she sat at the little desk and pulled out the letter to read it again. Her mother had included a phone number. Should she call? Evelyn wasn't fond of the telephone and was glad that most of the time the housekeeper answered when the house phone rang. However, there had been one or two occasions when Evelyn had to talk to a caller, and she'd stumbled over her words. She hated feeling so unsure of herself that she couldn't respond to a simple call, but that was the horrible truth. No matter how much Sarah praised her, Evelyn could not forget the harsh words of Sister Honora that reduced her to tears and uncertainty. "You are a stupid child. You will never learn anything."

So she would not call her mother. In essence, it would be like trying to talk to that stranger who had called the other day.

Opening the desk drawer, Evelyn took out a sheet of the cream-colored stationery that young Abigail had given her last Christmas. Each page had tiny pink roses in the upper right corner. Abigail had been so proud of picking it out and paying for it with her own money. Positioning the paper just so on the surface of the desk, Evelyn took a pen out of the cup that held two pens and three pencils and began.

Dear Mother, Evelyn wrote, then stopped. Should she write "dear" or simply "mother?"

She decided to leave the salutation as is and thought about what to put next. She wasn't accustomed to writing or receiving letters, so she wasn't sure how one should begin. Her mother's letter had started with, "I hope this letter finds you well," but that didn't seem like the right thing for Evelyn to say. She wasn't sure she could write that and really mean it. She had carefully packed away any thoughts of her mother some years ago as they were always so painful. This request, coming as such a shock, had shaken the box of memories, and horrible feelings threatened to spill out.

Evelyn took a breath and tried to push those feelings aside. All she had to do was write a simple response. She could do that much. Several more minutes of internal debate about how to word the letter followed, after which Evelyn decided to just tell her mother she was welcome to come for a visit and to please let them know what date to expect arrival. Then she sealed the letter and took it downstairs. Letters to be posted were always left in a shallow silver tray on a small table in the entry for Mr. Hershlinger to pick up and take to town. Evelyn had often seen envelopes there that had been written by Sarah, and sometimes one or two that were written by Hildy or Genevieve, but this was the first time Evelyn was to use this informal courier service.

The thought of what might come of the letter exchange brought a mix of excitement and apprehension. She couldn't even imagine what it would be like to see her mother after so long. She still pictured her as that pretty woman who had come in the nice car, but that pleasant image had been blurred with the passing of time. Would they even recognize each other?

———

After dinner, when the children had gone to their rooms and Evelyn was helping Hildy clean up the kitchen, Sarah came in. She asked Evelyn to wait when Hildy finished and went to her room. Then Sarah asked if Evelyn had come to a decision regarding her mother.

"I told her she could come."

"Good. We will do our best to make her welcome."

Evelyn wasn't sure how she felt about that, but Sarah did not give her much time to think about it. "I was trying to figure out how we could find your sister, and I thought a direct approach would work best. Your mother knows Viola's address, so perhaps we could ring her up."

Evelyn almost dropped the stack of plates she had just picked up. "Call my mother?"

"Yes. If she put her telephone number in the letter."

There was a number in the letter, but again, the thought of

using the telephone made Evelyn's palms sweat and her heart race. "I don't think I could. Perhaps you might?"

Sarah raised a finger to her chin. "I don't know if your mother would appreciate a stranger making such an inquiry."

"I see."

"But I could try another avenue. I do love trying to solve a mystery. That is much more fulfilling than needlework."

Evelyn smiled. She was well aware of how much Sarah disliked the usual activities that women engaged in.

Two days later, Sarah came into the playroom where Evelyn and the children were seated at one of the tables, coloring books and crayons spilled across the surface. Evelyn liked to color with Jonathan and Abigail, and they were delighted when she would draw a cat or a bunny on one of their pages. Today, she was helping Abigail draw a bunny. "Evelyn," Sarah said, touching her on the shoulder. "May I have a word?"

Evelyn rose from her chair and followed Sarah out into the hall. "Is something wrong?"

"No. I just wanted to tell you that I have located your sister."

"Oh." The surprise was so complete it made Evelyn's knees tremble, and she leaned against the wall to steady herself. She had not expected this to happen so quickly. "How?"

"It wasn't very hard. My attorney helped find the information on the family where your sister works."

"Have you spoken to her?"

"I thought that might be something you would like to do first."

"Is she far away?"

Sarah shook her head.

"Oh." To think she had been close all these years. Evelyn had made herself not even consider the possibility of seeing Viola again. It was the only way she could be somewhat happy here. Sister Honora had always been so quick to remind the children, "It doesn't help to moon over something you cannot change."

So, like her feelings about her mother, Evelyn had carefully packed away her feelings about her sister. They were like little treasures kept in a box that was never opened. Until today. "When can I see her?"

"Whenever you would like. You can have an entire day to get reacquainted."

"What is her address? I should post a letter."

"I think perhaps you should overcome your reluctance to use the telephone." Sarah smiled and thrust a paper into Evelyn's hand. "Here is her number."

Evelyn glanced at the table that held the phone.

"Go ahead," Sarah urged. "I'll leave you to it."

Sarah went into the playroom, and Evelyn stood rooted to the floor for several long minutes. Then she took a breath and walked over to the phone. She lifted the receiver and the operator greeted her. "May I help you?"

"Yes. I would like to place a call."

"The number, please."

Evelyn read the numbers that were written on the scrap of paper.

"One moment, please."

Evelyn switched the phone to her other hand, and wiped her sweaty palm on her skirt. Then she heard another voice. "Hello."

"Hello. I would like to speak to Viola Gundrum please."

"This is Viola. Who is this?"

Evelyn sank into the chair, thankful that it was always there by the telephone table. "This is your sister."

"Evelyn?"

"Do you have any other sisters?"

It took a moment, but then Evelyn heard a chuckle from the other end of the line. "I can't believe we are talking after all this time." Viola said. "How did you find me?"

"The lady I work for used her attorney to investigate. I can tell you all about it when we meet." The thought of seeing her sister made Evelyn wish it could happen right now. "But first tell me about where you are working and how you have been."

"This isn't a good time to talk," Viola said. "I have a light workload on Thursdays. Could you possibly come here day after tomorrow? We could visit then."

Viola was so abrupt, Evelyn wondered if perhaps she didn't care for the phone either.

"Evelyn?" Viola prompted.

"Oh. Yes. I'm pretty sure I can come. What time?"

"In the afternoon. About three?"

"Okay. Give me the address."

Evelyn picked up a pen and carefully wrote the information on the little pad of paper on the desk and then said good-bye. She hung up, excitement quickening her breath. Her sister. She was finally going to see her sister.

9

EVELYN – 1938

The day of the visit, Evelyn elected to take the bus to the address where Viola was living. Sarah had offered to have their driver take her, but Evelyn preferred it this way. As the bus rumbled along the street, lurching every now and then when it hit a pothole, she wished it could go faster. She leaned forward in her seat as if that could hurry things along. The night before, Evelyn had hardly slept as she anticipated this visit, images of a joyful reunion playing through her mind. She had sorely missed her sister's companionship and strength and was eager to reconnect.

Sarah had helped Evelyn find the street on a city map and figure out a bus route. It was not complicated, and Evelyn got off at the bus stop that was three streets from where Viola lived. Walking along in the early spring sunshine, Evelyn noted the unkempt yards in front of houses that looked as if the flowerbeds and shrubs needed some attention. Paint peeled from a few of the houses, and one had shutters that were all askew. The only pleasant thing about the walk was the warm sunshine and the tulips that had popped up in some flowerbeds. She carefully checked addresses until stopping in front of a frame house that was only slightly better kept than its neighbors.

Evelyn went to the door and rang the bell. As she waited for the door to open, her heart thumped against her ribs like a bird trying to escape a cage. When finallyViola stood there, Evelyn was speechless. Her sister was so beautiful. And so grown up. And so opposite of Evelyn. Sarah often told her that she was pretty, but Evelyn had a hard time believing it. She never felt pretty, or competent, or self-assured. That little voice in her head kept repeating all the negatives the Sisters had showered her with. "You're stupid. You're homely. You will never amount to anything." She always tried to quiet the voice, but it was persistent.

Viola stepped out and embraced Evelyn, the hug reminding her that the love was still the same. Evelyn felt so warm and safe with her sister's arms around her, she hated for the contact to end so they could go into the house. Following her sister through a narrow entry and past a parlor, then a dining room and into the kitchen, Evelyn thought how tragic it was that all these years they'd been so close and didn't know it. They didn't speak as they walked along, and Evelyn sensed a tension in her sister that she had missed at first embrace. The kitchen that Viola led her to was cramped, and this house was so different from Sarah's, Evelyn wondered whether Viola was well taken care of here. The meager decorations she'd seen in the dining room and parlor as they passed made her think that this family was poor. Maybe poorer than Miz Beatrice had been.

Evelyn struggled to find something to say, now wishing that she'd let Sarah accompany her. Sarah was always so good with handling uncomfortable moments and finding cheerful conversation.

"I can't visit for long," Viola said, motioning for Evelyn to take a seat at a small table.

"Do you have someplace to be?"

"No." Viola walked to the stove where an aluminum coffee pot sat on a fire. "I'll have to cook supper in a little while."

"Oh." Evelyn wasn't sure what else to say. At the Hersh-linger household, a guest would be invited to stay for supper. It was clear that this house ran differently, and again, Evelyn wondered if the owners were kind to her sister.

"Would you like some coffee?"

"That would be nice." Evelyn took off her gloves and put them on the table, creating a stark splotch of white on the deep red Formica. "I'm so glad mother put us in contact again. I've missed you."

"I missed you too." Viola turned off the heat under the coffeepot and poured two cups. "I hope you don't mind reheated coffee."

"Not at all."

Viola served a small plate of sugar cookies with the coffee, and Evelyn nibbled on a cookie before asking, "Do you like it here?"

"I have to work very hard." Viola shrugged. "But not as hard as I remember you working at St. Aemilian's."

"You remember?"

"Of course I do. I hated the way the Sisters made you scrub the floors every day."

"You never said anything. Why didn't you ever say anything?"

"What good would it have done?" Viola sighed. "It wouldn't have changed anything."

Evelyn fiddled with her spoon, turning it over and over. "All that time, I thought you didn't care. You seemed so pleased to have the easier load."

"I wasn't pleased. I was thankful."

"Is there a difference?"

"Of course. I smiled and was cheerful so the Sisters would say I was such a good, pleasant child. And they rewarded me. You were such a sad, dour little thing, and I think they liked picking on you."

"I didn't know any other way. I couldn't pretend to be happy."

Viola took a sip of her coffee, then set the cup down. "But look at you now. The first thing I noticed when you came to the door was your smile. You weren't just pretending?"

Evelyn chuckled. "You're right. I am happy."

That reminder made Evelyn realize that in some ways her life and her sister's had been reversed. She paused with a cookie halfway to her mouth to consider how she felt about that. Except for the fact that she could never be pleased with another's misfortune, she would be content with the reversal.

"Have you heard yet when Mother is coming?" Viola asked.

"No. I'm waiting for another letter." Evelyn took a bite of the cookie. "What about you? Have you received any more correspondence?"

"Just the one."

"What do you think about seeing her after all this time?"

Viola shrugged. "She's still our mother."

Evelyn picked up crumbs with a finger. Bringing an image of her mother to mind stimulated emotions she'd worked hard to suppress. The reason she never let memories of her mother surface was because they dredged up anger at being abandoned. She and Viola used to share that anger, along with the cot at the orphanage, but now, Viola seemed to have forgotten. "A mother doesn't leave her children," Evelyn reminded her.

"That was a long time ago. And we are no longer children."

"Does that mean we should just forget all about our past?"

Viola sighed. "What good does it do to think about it? It's better to forget about it all and look to the future."

"What good does it do to pretend it didn't happen?" Evelyn didn't know if she could forgive or forget.

"I haven't forgotten. Nor am I pretending," Viola said, her dark blue eyes flashing. "Circumstances change. People change. At least some people change."

"What does that mean?"

"You still whine." As soon as the words were out, Viola put a hand across her mouth as if she could pull the words back.

Viola looked as stunned as Evelyn felt. This was not the reunion Evelyn had expected. While she would never be as strong as her sister, she was not a tearful child anymore. And remembering how their mother had let them down was not whining. How could Viola even suggest that they forget about all those horrible years in the orphanage? She started to rise. "Perhaps I should go."

Viola reached across the table to stop her. "No. I'm sorry. It's just that—"

"Viola!" A stern-faced woman bustled into the kitchen casting barely a glance at Evelyn before continuing. "The bathroom needs to be cleaned. Little Betha got sick. And then you should see to your other chores."

"Yes, ma'am," Viola said. "This is my sister. Evelyn. I told you about her the other day."

Evelyn wasn't sure what surprised her the most, the uncertainty she heard in her sister's voice or the coldness of the woman who just barely nodded before scuttling out of the room.

"I'm sorry." Viola stood and grabbed the dishes off of the table. "Truly. I didn't mean what I said before. Really."

"I remember how you hated it when I cried."

Viola offered a smile. "Yes. I tried so hard to make you strong."

"You were always the strong one."

"I'm not so sure about that." When had Viola changed? She had never been cowed before. Not even when being disciplined. She would stand firm in front of Sister, not flinching when the strap connected. Not letting a tear escape. And now in some ways she was like a timid little mouse.

Mrs. Martin came to the kitchen doorway. "Viola!"

"Yes, ma'am. I'm coming." Viola turned to Evelyn. "I wish we could visit longer."

"I understand." Evelyn picked up her gloves and stood. "Can I help clear?"

"That would be nice."

Evelyn carried the plate of cookies to the counter and set them where Viola indicated. Then she got her coat from the back of the chair and shrugged it on. "Mrs. Hershlinger, Sarah, the lady I work for, said we could have a dinner at her home when Mother and Henry come. Would that suit you?"

"I shall have to make my own arrangements to meet them," Viola said. "Mrs. Martin needs me here every day."

"Oh." Evelyn took a breath to cover her disappointment. "Then perhaps we could all meet someplace close to here."

"It would be best to wait and see when they are coming. Then make plans."

"If you'd like." Evelyn pulled on her gloves.

"I'll see you to the door."

"No need. Perhaps you should tend to the child."

Viola nodded. "Yes. Thank you." She gave Evelyn a quick hug and accompanied her to the hall. Viola turned in one direction, and Evelyn walked to the front door alone.

10

EVELYN – APRIL 1938

E velyn stood on the porch looking toward the road. Henry and her mother were to arrive today. A late spring snow had fallen overnight, but Mr. Martinelli had cleared the drive and front walk that morning, and the early afternoon sun was quickly melting any remnants of white left on tufts of new grass. Still, Evelyn shivered.

Over the past few days, Evelyn had thought a lot about all that had changed since she had been left on the doorstep of the orphanage with Viola. Of course their mother hadn't literally left them on the doorstep, but that's how emotion served it up, and emotions were so strong now, spilling out of the corner of her heart where she had shut them away. Anger, sadness, disappointment, and more than just a touch of shame. What had been wrong with her and Viola that their mother didn't want them? Surely, if they had been good enough, their mother wouldn't have deserted them. Right?

And now, she'd added apprehension to the emotional mix.

She was worrying the cuticle on her thumb with her forefinger when Sarah stepped up beside her and put an arm around her shoulder. "It will be okay."

"What if it isn't? I have no idea what to say to her."

"I'll help." Sarah moved her arm to Evelyn's waist and gave a little squeeze.

That was reassuring as a car turned off the road and started into the circular drive leading to the house.

Evelyn's breath caught in her throat.

The car that carried her mother ever closer was bright red and glinted in the sunlight, but everything else about the moment was so much like that day so long ago on Miz Beatrice's porch that Evelyn lost what little composure she had scraped together. The years melted away like that morning snow, and she was that little girl again with trembling legs and tears stinging her eyes.

Sarah gave her another squeeze. "We will have a nice visit. You'll see."

Nodding, Evelyn took a breath and stiffened her spine. She could handle this reunion.

Sarah invited the company in, and during the bustle of hanging coats on the hall tree and formal introductions, Evelyn stayed in the background and watched. Her mother appeared calmer than what Evelyn remembered of her at Miz Beatrice's. Happy even. Henry Stewart was a smaller man than she expected. Somehow, her vision of a police officer was taller and more imposing. Even Mr. Hershlinger might be stronger than this man who stood in the entry holding his brown Fedora in one hand, his other touching Regina on the small of her back. It was actually barely a touch, but there was a connectedness to it that Evelyn was familiar with from the novels she read. To Evelyn, stories about people who loved each other were worth the struggle to make out the words.

Sarah urged Evelyn forward with a gesture. "Why don't you

take your company into the parlor? You can have some privacy there."

Evelyn tried, but she couldn't keep the panic from showing in her eyes. It was easy to be resolved when she didn't have to move or to speak. Sarah patted her shoulder and gave her a look that said, "It will be okay."

Regina and Henry sat on the settee, and Evelyn took the Queen Anne chair across from them. Her fingers plucked at the fabric of her skirt. She'd dressed up for the occasion, wearing a lavender blouse with lace and pearl buttons and a gray skirt with gathers at the waist. A black sash accented her narrow waist.

"You have grown into a very pretty young woman," Regina said after a few moments of painful silence.

"Thank you."

Another long silence followed, then Henry cleared his throat. "It is nice to finally meet you. Your mother speaks of you often."

"Really?" Evelyn shot a glance at her mother. She thought she was long past caring if her mother even thought of her anymore, and the surge of hope that Henry's words created took her by surprise.

"Well of course. I didn't stop caring just because..."

She seemed unable to finish and Evelyn wondered why. Was it a lie? She knew people often said one thing but meant another. This was something else she had picked up from reading. How people might pledge a loyalty that didn't exist. But she didn't know how to recognize any duplicity in the midst of a real conversation. She was glad when Sarah came to the doorway to inquire as to whether anyone would like something to drink. "Perhaps some hot tea?"

"Yes. That would be lovely." Evelyn stood. "I'll go help Hildy."

"But..." Sarah tried to stop Evelyn's dash from the room, but the young woman swept past her without a pause. Sarah offered a smile to Regina and Henry. "We'll be right back with the tea."

"What's wrong?" Sarah asked as she walked into the kitchen where Evelyn was putting China cups painted with yellow roses on a serving tray. Hildy stood at the stove minding the tea kettle.

Evelyn glanced over at Sarah. "It's even harder than I thought."

"Of course. There have been too many years apart and much you have not yet shared."

"But still..."

"But still what?"

"She's my mother." Evelyn wiped at a tear that had crept down her cheek. "I should feel something."

Sarah put an arm around Evelyn. "Don't worry about feelings right now. Think of this as meeting a new friend. Take time to get to know each other and try to forget the rest."

That was so much like what Viola had said, yet Evelyn felt this was more like advice than an indictment.

The tears came in earnest now, and Sarah pulled a handkerchief from her pocket and handed it over.

Hildy came over with the teapot. "Everything a'right, Mum?"

"Yes, Hildy. Evelyn just needs a moment to compose herself."

Hildy set the pot on the tray Evelyn had been preparing and shook her head. "Odd business this."

"Yes. I quite agree," Sarah said, then urged Evelyn to move. "We should get back before they wonder if we went to China for the tea."

The bit of humor is what Evelyn needed. She smiled as she

picked up the silver tray and carried the tea things out to the parlor, where she set the tray down on a side table. Careful not to spill, despite the tremor in her hands, she served the tea before putting the plate of scones on another small table near her mother and Henry. Then she sat down opposite them with her cup. Sarah sat next to her on the matching Queen Anne chair, and they all sipped and smiled in awkward silence, the only sound being the soft clink of china against china as a cup was set down on a saucer.

Evelyn was searching for something to say when Sarah finally broke the silence. "Did you have a good trip?"

"Yes." Regina reached for a biscuit from the tray. "We stopped in Chicago and visited a club that had very nice jazz music."

"I read in a newspaper that there are a lot of gangsters in Chicago," Sarah said. "Were you concerned?"

Henry shook his head. "I think they can smell a cop."

Evelyn wasn't sure what he meant, but Sarah laughed, so maybe it was a joke. Evelyn smiled to be polite.

"You are still planning to stay for dinner, aren't you?" Sarah asked. "Hildy has outdone herself with the pot roast."

"That's very kind of you," Regina said. "But we were hoping to go see Viola first. I understand from her letter that she will not be able to join us for dinner."

Evelyn had been disappointed when she found out that the Martins would not let Viola have the evening off. It would have been so much easier to get reacquainted with their mother if Viola could be here to take some of the attention. As it was, Evelyn felt like a doll on display as her mother and Henry stared at her. They would glance away when Sarah spoke, but their gaze would quickly return to Evelyn.

"Is your other daughter expecting you at a specific time?" Sarah asked.

"We were to call when we arrived," Regina said. "We were hoping to be able to use your telephone."

"But of course." Sarah stood. "It's in the hall. I can show you."

Regina looked over at Henry. "You go."

Nerves made Evelyn's knees tremble as Henry walked out with Sarah. Whatever was she to say to her mother?

"He had the number." Regina broke into the tense silence. "I didn't."

"Oh."

Regina took another bite of the scone. "This is very good."

"Yes. Hildy is an excellent cook."

"Do you like it here?"

"Yes. It's very nice."

It was a relief when Henry and Sarah came back in. To Regina's questioning look, Henry said, "Viola could not get away. She would like to meet us tomorrow."

"Where?"

"She suggested the hotel."

"Then you will stay and share our meal this evening," Sarah said.

"We wouldn't want to impose," Regina said.

"Not at all. We had extended the invitation and prepared. You must be hungry after your travels."

"Yes, thank you," Regina said.

"I'll tell Hildy to be ready to serve the dinner as soon as Mr. Hershlinger arrives home from work."

"Should I see to the children?" Evelyn asked.

"No, dear. Hildy arranged for her granddaughter to come and help with dinner for the children."

"How many do you have?" Henry asked.

"Two. Abigail and Jonathan. Would you like to meet them?"

"That would be nice."

"Lisa can bring them out while I confer with Hildy."

The wait for Mr. Hershlinger's arrival was helped along by the children. Evelyn was proud of how well-mannered they were with her mother and Henry, and she was also pleased to see how much Henry seemed to enjoy their company. She wondered briefly if he was a father. Surely her mother would have said so in the letter. Then she had a sudden realization. She didn't even know how long her mother and Henry had been married. It would be rude to ask, but curiosity was strong. Luckily, Mr. Hershlinger came home before she gave in to the impulse to inquire, and they moved to the dining room.

Evelyn had only been in the main dining room on occasions when her help was needed to serve guests for a special dinner or to tend to the children on a Sunday. Today, it felt very strange to be seated at the great oak table that was set for five and to be served by Hildy, although the wink that she was given along with her plate of roast beef eased her discomfort just a bit.

Sarah and her husband kept the conversation lively through the meal, talking about the children and inquiring about Regina and Henry's life in Detroit. Regina didn't say much, but Henry shared the story of how they first met, and Sarah seemed delighted. "It's almost like a story one of the Bronte sisters could have written."

Evelyn nodded in agreement. She could easily see Henry as a character in one of the love stories she had read. He was charming, and handsome, and had a clever wit. She wondered how much he knew about the circumstances that had landed her and her sister in the orphanage. Perhaps Regina had told him why Evelyn's father had left. Had she shared all the family secrets? Did he know all the bad things and love Regina anyway?

"Since I care nothing about those romantic stories," Mr.

Hershlinger said, "I would like to know more about your work with the police, Henry."

As the conversation focus shifted to the men, Evelyn speared a piece of roasted potato, but she couldn't eat. Her emotions seemed to be all gathered in her throat, making swallowing almost impossible. Thankfully, nobody said anything about the fact that she pushed the potatoes and carrots around without eating them, except for Hildy, who gave a tsk, tsk, as she cleared the dinner plates.

After the meal, they moved back to the parlor for dessert. Mr. Hershlinger had offered brandy and cigars in his study, but Henry had declined. Evelyn thought that a bit odd. When the Hershlingers entertained, the men normally separated themselves after dinner, preferring the alcohol to coffee.

Today, Hildy served peach pie and coffee, and after they were all settled, Henry cleared his throat, looked at Evelyn, and said, "We were wondering if you would consider coming to Detroit to live?"

What? Move? Evelyn was frozen in shock for a moment, her fork halfway to her mouth. Then she looked at her mother, wondering if this was something that she wanted. Was this part of the plan all along? If so, they must have discussed it. But why did he ask and not her? And shouldn't it have been asked in private?

The room was heavy with silence and Sarah put a hand to her throat. "Oh my," she said. "That is a considerable request."

"Of course," Henry said, turning to Sarah. "We just want her to think about it."

Still stunned, Evelyn waited for her mother to say something. Anything. Evelyn certainly could not even consider such a drastic change if her mother didn't want her. Then another more troubling thought occurred to her. If her mother did want this, why now, after so many years?

When her mother still did not speak, Evelyn dropped her fork back on her plate and turned to Henry. "What did you have in mind?"

"In mind?"

"Yes. In what capacity am I to live there? Do you need a housekeeper?"

Henry shook his head quickly. "No. No. That's not why I asked." He looked to Regina. "That isn't what we were thinking, was it?"

"No, of course not."

Finally, words from her mother's mouth, but not words of encouragement. Still, it was a beginning.

"Where would I stay?" Evelyn asked. "What would I do?"

"I... we were hoping you would stay with us," Henry said.

Evelyn glanced at her mother, who nodded. Was the message in that nod to be trusted? Did Evelyn dare give in to the hope that it could be? "I don't know what to say."

"You don't have to decide right now," Henry said. "Your mother and I know that this is probably not what you expected."

"No. It isn't."

"Perhaps Evelyn could consider the request and give you an answer before you return to Detroit," Sarah said. "Then she could make the move later if that is her choice. That way, it would be at her convenience, and ours. We would have to find someone to assume her duties here."

Sarah reached over to lightly touch Evelyn's hand. "Does that plan suit you?"

Evelyn nodded, not trusting her voice at the moment. She couldn't even put a word to this jumble of feelings that were getting more and more tangled. She was afraid if she pulled one out, they would all tumble out in one great clump, like the yarn sometimes did when they were rolling a new skein.

Regina and Henry seemed satisfied with the plan as well, and finished their coffee and pie quickly, saying they were tired from their drive and would like to go to the hotel. Mr. Hershlinger bid them goodbye and went to his study. Sarah and Evelyn walked Henry and Regina to the door, where they all shook hands. Evelyn could not imagine hugging either of them and was so relieved when they made no move to embrace her before stepping out.

After closing the door, Evelyn turned to Sarah, tears in her eyes. "What am I to do?"

"Right now. Nothing." Sarah took her by the arm and led her back to the parlor. "I think you should have a glass of sherry and go to bed. You have had quite an emotional shock."

"But I've never had sherry before."

"Good. Then it won't take much to help you sleep."

11

REGINA – APRIL 1938

H enry set his beer down on the small table in the hotel bar where they were waiting to meet Viola and nudged Regina. "You're very quiet tonight."

"Just thinking."

"Worried about your daughter?"

Regina had to stifle an urge to chuckle. Which daughter did he mean?

He put an arm around her and pulled her to his shoulder. "Everything will be just fine."

"Will it?" Regina took a big swallow of her beer. "What if they don't want to come?"

"Then life will go on. The way it always has."

"You wouldn't care?"

"Of course I care." Henry picked up his mug and mopped the puddle of condensation with his napkin. "You forget I'm the one who suggested this trip."

"I didn't forget."

"I know, it's just—" Henry stopped abruptly, and Regina

followed his gaze to a lovely young woman who had just stepped into the shadowy bar. She paused in the doorway and looked around, and Regina noted the black dress with a white collar that Viola had told them she would be wearing. Regina nodded toward the woman. "That might be her."

Henry nodded and then stood to catch the woman's attention.

When she faced them fully, there was no doubt in Regina's mind that this was Viola. She looked so much like a nineteen-year-old Regina she couldn't be anyone else's daughter. Nerves fluttered in Regina's stomach as Viola acknowledged Henry's wave and headed to the table, taking off her black gloves along the way. Henry pulled out the third chair for her, but instead of sitting right away, she walked around and gave Regina a brief hug.

Regina was so shocked at the embrace she didn't know what to say. She was expecting the same reserve they had found in Evelyn, but Viola seemed relaxed and her smile was warm. When they sat, Regina watched the light play across her daughter's features, marveling again at how they favored each other.

"I'm glad you could meet me here," Viola said. "I so rarely get away from work."

"Would you like a drink?" Henry asked. "Or should we go straight to the restaurant?"

Viola settled back in her chair. "I wouldn't mind a whiskey sour."

Regina was a little surprised. Was nineteen a legal drinking age? When Henry gave the waitress the order, she took it without comment, so perhaps it didn't matter here.

"Did you have a nice visit with Evelyn?" Viola asked.

"Yes," Regina said, then waited while the waitress put the

whiskey sour on the table and then left. "She works in a lovely home."

Viola picked up the drink and took a swallow. "She told me about it when we visited. She seems happy there."

Regina nodded, then took a sip of her beer to cover her discomfiture. Evelyn did seem happy where she worked. And that was the problem. Would she be willing to leave everything she had here? And was it even fair of her and Henry to ask? Just because Regina was feeling guilty for abandoning them those many years ago? Regina set her beer down before it slipped out of her shaking hand. Henry touched her elbow. "Are you okay?"

"Yes. Yes, I'm fine." She took a breath and looked at Viola. "Tell us about your work."

"I clean and cook and look after the children."

"Do you enjoy that?" Henry asked.

Viola shrugged. "The children are nice. Two little girls."

"What about the parents?"

"Mr. Martin is gone a lot. He travels for his job. Mrs. Martin... she's... rather a harsh taskmaster."

"That's too bad," Regina said.

Viola shrugged again. "It's still better than the orphanage."

Regina grimaced when Viola said the word. It was such a stark reminder, but to her surprise, Viola reached across the table and gently touched Regina's hand. "Don't be upset. I'm long past the anger."

The weight on Regina's shoulder shifted just a bit. "That's good to hear."

Viola nodded and they drank in silence for a few moments. Then Henry caught Regina's eye and raised an eyebrow. Regina was sure that he was asking silent permission to make the same request to Viola that they had made to Evelyn the day before. When they had discussed this during the long drive from Detroit, Regina knew she would not be able to find the courage to make the request herself. Regina nodded.

"Viola," Henry said, getting her attention, "I hope this isn't too soon to be asking. But would you consider moving to Detroit with us?"

She glanced from one to the other, then settled on her mother. "Why would you want me to do that?"

It wasn't the response that Regina expected, and she turned quickly to Henry. "Well..."

Henry patted her hand. "I think your mother was hoping that the three of you could be together."

Viola faced her mother. "Why now? Are you ill?"

Regina quickly shook her head. "Maybe we could... be a family."

Viola sipped some more of her drink and let a long moment of silence stretch between them. Then she asked, "Is Evelyn going?"

"She hasn't decided yet," Regina said.

"What about you?" Viola directed the question to Henry. "Why do you want us to come to Detroit?"

"This isn't something that we just suddenly decided," Henry said, exchanging a glance with Regina. "We discussed it for several days. And since I never had a family. Well, I thought why not?"

"Take time to think about it," Regina said. "We can wait for your answer."

"Deciding won't be hard," Viola said. "I'd be happy to get out of the place where I am now. But it would take time to work out the arrangements."

"For us too," Henry said. "We'll have to look for a bigger place—"

"You want us to live with you?"

"Of course."

"I don't mean any disrespect. And I don't mind the idea of being together again. But I'm an adult, and I would prefer to live on my own."

"I see."

Henry seemed at a loss for anything else to say, so Regina said, "We understand. I'm just happy you are willing to consider the move."

———

Evelyn sat on the small settee in the playroom with the children on either side of her, reading *The Cat Who Went To Heaven* aloud. Even though both children could read better than Evelyn, they never made fun of her. Maybe because the children couldn't read much at all when Evelyn had first come, and they had all learned together. Evelyn had been surprised when Sarah had said she wanted her to take care of the first few years of lessons with the children. Evelyn didn't feel qualified, but Sarah had insisted, so Evelyn read with the children and taught them some numbers. She had always been better at numbers than words. And Sarah had been satisfied with the progress the children made until Abigail turned eight, and that's when a nanny was brought in to teach history, geography, and music.

This year, Jonathan had turned eight and would now start taking his lessons with the nanny. Still, both children liked to sit with Evelyn and listen to her read. And Evelyn loved having the warm bodies nestled next to hers. The children were growing up so fast. At times like this, she imagined that she could someday have a home and a perfect family of husband and wife and two adorable children.

"Evelyn?" Sarah stepped into the room. "There's a phone call for you."

"Me?" Evelyn hadn't even heard the phone ring. But then she rarely listened for it.

"Yes. I believe it is your sister."

"Oh. Okay." Evelyn closed the book and stood. "Did she say what she was calling about?"

Sarah shook her head. "She just asked to speak to you."

"Will you come back and finish the story?" Jonathan asked.

"Yes, I'll—"

"Why don't I read to you," Sarah said. "Evelyn may be more than a little while."

Evelyn walked into the hall and picked up the receiver. "Hello."

"It's Viola."

"Yes. Sarah told me. Did you have a pleasant dinner with Regina and Henry?"

"It was very nice."

There was a pause as if Viola couldn't think of what to say next. Evelyn couldn't either. Talking on the phone was so strange. Like the other person was there but really wasn't because you couldn't see her.

"Listen," Viola finally said, "have you decided about moving to Detroit?"

"Oh. So they asked you too?"

"Yes."

Another long pause, then Viola said, "So?"

"They said I could think about it." Evelyn put a finger to her mouth and bit a piece of cuticle that was hanging loose. "Did you, uh, decide?"

"Yes. I mean, maybe. There really isn't anything for me here. Well, except you."

Evelyn smiled. It was good to hear that.

"So if I say yes. Will you?"

The plea was unmistakable, and Evelyn was torn. This was the scariest thing she'd ever had to decide. What had happened to her up to this point in her life had been decided for her. There had been no choices.

"Do I have to answer now?"

"No. But soon. I think it would be a grand adventure to go to another city. And you always wanted Mother to come back for us, and now she has."

"I stopped wishing for that a long time ago." Viola was quiet for so long Evelyn wondered if she'd hung up. "Viola?"

"Yes."

Evelyn heard a deep sigh, then Viola continued. "If you don't want to come to Detroit for yourself. Or for Mother. Can you do it for me? I really want to do this, but I don't want to lose touch with you. We've just found each other."

Even though they didn't agree about some things, Evelyn didn't want to lose Viola either. "Okay. I will think about it and let you know soon."

"Not more than a couple of days. Promise?"

"All right."

So four weeks later, Evelyn was packed and ready to make the move to Detroit. Sarah had been of tremendous help in making the decision. She'd told Evelyn that she thought Henry and Regina were sincere in their desire to make some kind of family unit. And family was the most important thing in life. Even though Regina and Henry did not feel like family, Viola did, and maybe if she gave it a chance, she would one day feel as close to Henry and Regina as she did to Sarah.

Evelyn took the small suitcase off her bed and went downstairs. Her other belongings had been shipped a few days before, so she only had one bag to take on the train. She stepped into the parlor and sat on the settee for a moment, thinking of all the years and all the events that had happened in this wonderful place. A tinge of sadness tugged at her heart as she stroked the satin upholstery. She would be leaving part of her heart in this home with these people.

"Oh, there you are." Sarah came into the room. "Are you ready?"

Evelyn stood. "Yes."

"I am not riding to the train station with you," Sarah said. "I hate tearful goodbyes."

Evelyn nodded, trying her best to hold her tears back. She lost that battle when Sarah rushed over and embraced her, whispering in her ear, "We will miss you."

"I will also miss you." Evelyn clung to Sarah for a full minute before pulling away and turning to take the first step into the unknown.

———

The first few weeks that Evelyn and Viola were in Detroit, they stayed with their mother and Henry, but they were cramped in a small apartment with one bedroom and another smaller room that barely held a twin bed and a bureau. Viola slept on the couch until she got a job at the Book Cadillac hotel in downtown Detroit and moved into the downtown YWCA, but there were still too many people for such a tiny space. Henry had looked for a bigger apartment that they could afford, but those efforts fell short. Partly because of the fact that the job at the Coney Island her mother had arranged for Evelyn didn't work out. Evelyn despised the work: the grease, the smells, and the manager said she was too slow, so she was fired after a month.

"We needed you to be able to contribute," her mother said

when explaining why they could not afford to move. "I'm sure you understand."

Evelyn did understand, and she certainly didn't want to be dependent on Henry and her mother. While they were both pleasant enough, especially Henry, Evelyn did not feel any kind of bond forming. The mother/daughter reunion just wasn't happening, not like those tender moments she sometimes saw in a movie or read in a book. She'd hoped, but then again, hoping was so fruitless. If she'd learned anything in her seventeen years on this earth, it was to hope for little; that way, the disappointment would not be so great.

Viola tried to get Evelyn a job at the hotel, but there were no openings, so she started looking for something else. She applied at a few stores as a clerk, but with no experience, she was turned away. She'd about given up hope when Henry came home one evening and told her that he'd heard of a couple that was looking for a housekeeper. "My captain said his younger brother, an attorney, had just lost the woman who had worked for them. I mentioned you might be interested."

Evelyn had hoped to not have to settle for this type of work again, but she didn't know what else to do. "I suppose I could."

"The couple is John and Vivian Gardner. I could take you over to meet them."

So he did, and a few days later, Evelyn started working for them. They were nice enough people, but nothing at all like Sarah and her husband. Here, the line between employer and employee was firmly drawn, and Evelyn missed the familiarity she had had with Sarah. Sarah had said that she could keep in touch, but Evelyn hesitated, not sure if she really meant it. Perhaps it was best to close that chapter of her life. Evelyn was getting quite good at closing chapters.

One nice thing about where she worked is that the home was just a couple of miles from where Henry and Regina lived, so they could still see each other often. When she'd first arrived in Detroit, she had tried to call Regina "Mother," mostly because Viola wanted her to. But it just never felt right, so in recent weeks, Evelyn had gone back to using her mother's name when referring to her. The change had gone basically unnoticed by Regina, so Evelyn was comfortable with her decision.

The Gardners had two school-age children, Elspeth, seven and Gerald, ten, and Evelyn was to get their breakfast and walk them the half mile to the school in the morning then meet them at 3:30 to walk home. In between, she had cleaning and laundry to do every day, as well as dinner to prepare. The work was no harder than at the Hershlinger household, but the circumstances were so different it was hard for Evelyn to adjust. She was never allowed to eat with the family or enjoy time with them after dinner. How fortunate she had been to be able to share books and television and games with Sarah and Abigail and Jonathan during those pleasant evening hours before bedtime. She had never truly understood how fortunate she was until now.

Every weekday, when Mr. Gardner arrived home for supper, Evelyn had to go to her little room off the kitchen and read or listen to the radio. She tried to enjoy the quiet time alone, but the room always felt so confining. There was hardly room to walk more than ten steps between the narrow bed, a three-drawer bureau, and a ladder-back chair that was so uncomfortable she could only sit for a half an hour to read. Another inconvenience was how close her room was to the door leading to the garage. Anytime someone went in or out of the garage, the hinges on the door would emit a high-pitched squeak that pierced her eardrums. Last week, she'd found some sewing machine oil and squeezed some on the hinges. It was blessedly quiet for a few days, but then the squeaking resumed.

Today, she sat in the chair while tears rolled down her

cheeks. She had tried to hold them back. Tried to tell herself it would get better. She did the right thing coming here to Detroit. But her heart was not convinced. Most days, Evelyn missed Sarah and the children so fiercely she thought she might not be able to stand it. And she wondered if she would ever have anything so good again.

12

EVELYN – APRIL 1940

On her way to the pantry to get some flour, Evelyn heard faint strains of music coming from the garage. She needed the flour to get started on the cake she was going to bake for Easter Sunday, but she had a few minutes to spare, so she detoured and went out to the garage, hoping to find the young man she'd met a few weeks ago. When she stepped out, she was pleased to see him sitting on an overturned milk can, guitar resting on his knee. "I heard you singing."

He looked up. "Yeah?"

"It was nice."

"Thank you."

Evelyn didn't know what else to say.

Russell Van Gilder was working with his uncle down the street. His uncle, whom he referred to simply as Hoffman, had a small tool and die shop, and Russell had come to Detroit from West Virginia to learn the trade. He was renting the garage from the Gardners to have a place to work on his car. He'd nodded to the dismantled Model T. Evelyn didn't know if it was the soft southern drawl or the smile that had made her heart go all aflutter. Although it could have been his eyes. The purest crystalline blue she had ever seen, and when he smiled, they seemed to flicker with mischief.

They were flickering now.

"I should let you finish," Evelyn said, starting to turn away.

"Stay if you'd like. Is there a song you'd like to hear?"

Evelyn shrugged. She listened to music on the radio, but her mind couldn't come up with a single song title.

"How about 'Tea for Two?'" Russell strummed the guitar to life again, then softly started to sing. His voice was true and pleasant to the ear, and Evelyn thought she could stay here forever and listen. Of course, that was not possible. She had to start the cake in a little while. But for now, there was the music.

The way he looked at her when he sang "Me for you, and you for me," she wondered if he was sending a message. The warmth of a blush touched her cheeks and she glanced away, telling herself not to be silly. They were just words in a song.

He finished, paused for a moment, then started, "On a hill far away, stood an Old Rugged Cross..."

Evelyn listened, entranced, as he sang the whole song. She recognized it as a hymn, but she had never heard one like it in the Catholic Church. "That was beautiful," she said when he finished. "I'm not familiar with it."

"Don't you go to church?" He grinned at her. "It's a popular hymn."

"I go to the Catholic church. Our songs are in Latin."

"Kind of hard to follow the words that way, isn't it?" He smiled when he said that, so she smiled back and said, "I don't think we're supposed to."

Russell put the guitar in the open case at his feet. "Why not?"

"I don't know." Evelyn thought for a moment about the music at church. She knew that most of it was Gregorian

Chant. They had learned that at the orphanage. But she had never thought about why the words were never in English. She did always like the way the music sounded, so soft and soothing, but nothing at all like the song she had just heard. The story of that cross was so tender and sad it had brought tears to her eyes. She'd never felt that way in church.

Russell clicked the guitar case closed and stood. "Need to get back to work."

"Yes. Me too."

"Maybe I can sing for you again sometime."

Evelyn ducked her head as a blush warmed her cheek. "I'd like that."

Inside, Evelyn went to the washroom to splash cool water on her face before going into the kitchen to make the cake. The way her body was reacting to being near Russell was tantalizing, but also scary. She had never felt that kind of heat in her privates before. Not even when Sister Honora rubbed and rubbed her there because she was dirty. That's what Sister told her when she found her looking at her private place. Evelyn had just been curious, but Sister said it was bad to touch, to look, or to let anyone else touch. When Evelyn dared ask how come Sister could touch it, she'd received a harsh smack on the mouth that made her lip bleed. She didn't ask many questions after that.

Evelyn dried her face and folded the towel before hanging it neatly on the rack. Mrs. Gardner did like things to be neat.

———

Russell wiped his greasy hands on a rag already stained with oil and grease, and then he closed the hood of the old Model T and picked up his guitar again. He slowly began to strum a few chords, thinking about Evelyn. Evelyn. He said it aloud, liking the way her name rolled off his tongue. It was so lyrical he thought he could write a song about Evelyn.

When he'd first rented the garage from the Gardner's, he hadn't intended to also make it a place to play music. But then it was quieter here than at his uncle's house where his cousin's children ran in and out of rooms and down the halls with loud whoops and laughter. Here, the children were more sedate, possibly saving the noise for when they were taken out to the park. Most of the time, that was done by Evelyn. He knew that because he'd seen her walking with the children a few times late in the afternoon as he came up the street from his uncle's.

Each time he saw her, Russell knew that Evelyn was different from some of the other women he'd been attracted to. Women that he had just been with for sex. There was a purity about her that both warned him off and challenged him.

He had had his first taste of what glories lay between a woman's legs when he was just a boy of seventeen. Priscilla, a neighbor whose husband had left her with two little children had invited him over one evening on the pretext of needing his help with fixing a broken window. The window was indeed broken, but when he finished boarding it up and told her that he would return later with a piece of glass to finish the job properly, she had invited him to stay for a cup of coffee.

After he had taken a seat in the spindly wooden chair at the kitchen table, he'd been shocked when she took a flask from the top shelf of a cabinet and added a generous amount of whiskey to each of the coffee cups. He'd had also been shocked a little later when she'd taken his empty cup and put it on the counter and then took him by the hand to lead him into her bedroom.

That summer, he'd had fixed many things at Priscilla's house, and she had taught him what pleasured a woman.

He would like to pleasure Evelyn.

———

Saturdays were Evelyn's days off, and she often went to visit her mother and Henry in their little apartment. Viola would sometimes come too, and that made the visits livelier. It seemed like Viola was always happy, and she often had funny stories to tell about the people at the hotel. Today, however, they were all meeting at the hotel bar to hear a vocal duo that was scheduled to perform. Viola had heard them at a bar in Hamtramck a few weeks ago and said they were very good.

Viola went to bars often since they had come to Detroit, and Evelyn was a bit dismayed at her sister's drinking. She could still remember how Viola talked about their mother coming home drunk and how much Viola had hated the sour smell of alcohol and the too-loud declarations of love that sounded so false. When Viola shared that in soft whispers under the blanket in the orphanage, they had both vowed never to do the same.

The one time Evelyn tried to remind Viola of that vow, her sister had laughed it off. "We were kids. We're grown up now. You should come with me sometime."

So Evelyn had agreed to this evening, but she didn't know what to expect. Walking into the dim room heavy with smoke, Evelyn didn't see her sister at first. She did notice that several women at tables were smoking cigarettes and thin cigars along with their male companions, and Evelyn raised an eyebrow in shock. According to Emily Post's book on proper etiquette, it was considered poor taste for a lady to smoke, especially in public. Only certain types of women indulged in that activity and a "lady" did not. But maybe ladies did not come to bars. Evelyn had read the book in hopes that it would help her get past some of her social ineptness, but she feared it might have just made her a bit judgmental.

Spotting her sister at a far table, Evelyn wound her way through the crowd and joined her, feeling a bit dowdy in her black dress with the white lace collar. Viola wore a red dress cut a bit low in the front and gold earrings that sparkled in the candlelight. "Your dress is very pretty," Evelyn said.

"Thank you."

"Are Regina and Henry coming?"

"No. She isn't feeling well. He's staying home to take care of her."

Evelyn sat down. "Anything serious?"

"No. Just a late winter cold."

"The children I tend are sick too. Mrs. Gardner was reluctant to let me take my day off today."

"How did you convince her?"

"I told her I would quit." Evelyn smiled at the memory of the surprise on her employer's face and then the permission.

"Ah. My little sister has a spine after all."

Evelyn warmed to the compliment, pleased to have Viola's approval, and was disappointed when the waitress stepped up to the table, spoiling the moment. "What can I get you?"

"Uh..." Evelyn realized she had no idea what to order. Gracious.

"Give her one of these," Viola said, raising her glass. "And bring me another."

"What is it?" Evelyn asked.

"Whiskey sour."

"I've never had whiskey before."

"Then it's time you did." Viola laughed, and Evelyn couldn't help but join in. She was here to have a good time, so why not?

The drink had a pleasant, tart taste, almost like lemonade, and Evelyn decided it was quite good. She had another as the York Brothers finished their first set with a song called "Detroit Hula Girl." Everyone in the bar clapped and cheered, and Viola even stood and did a little hula, making the people at nearby tables applaud. Evelyn felt the heat of embarrassment, yet a part of her was tempted to dance as well. The room seemed oddly tilted and she felt like she was moving with it. Still, she couldn't remember feeling this good since coming to Detroit. She smiled at her sister and patted her arm when she sat back down.

When the band stepped off the stage, the lights in the room brightened. Evelyn realized that she was not going to be able to hold her water until she returned home, so she leaned toward Viola and asked, "Does this place have a powder room?"

"This way." Viola stood and started threading her way around tables.

As they neared the bar, Evelyn saw Russell on one of the stools. She paused just a moment. "Russell?"

He turned and smiled. "Evelyn."

She loved the way her name sounded when he said it. Almost musical.

Viola nudged her and nodded toward Russell. Evelyn got the message. "This is my sister, Viola."

Russell glanced at Viola, then looked again. Of course, Evelyn thought. Why wouldn't he look at what Viola was displaying?

"You ladies enjoying the music?"

"Oh, yes." Viola flashed a smile. "It's quite good."

"Russell plays music." Evelyn wasn't sure what prompted her to say that. Maybe because she didn't like the way Viola was looking at him and just blurted something as a distraction. "But not like what we heard tonight."

"What do you play?" Viola asked.

"Mostly old songs and hymns my daddy taught me."

"Maybe you can sing one for me sometime."

"I'd like that."

A little surge of resentment told Evelyn that even though they had never gone out together, she had started to think of Russell as hers. She hadn't talked to him in the garage in the past couple of weeks, but she'd heard him out there singing on two occasions. Rather than disturb him, she'd stood at the door and listened, pretending he was singing for her. He had a rich, mellow voice, and she thought he was every bit as good as the professionals they'd heard this evening.

Evelyn tugged on Viola's arm and sent her a silent message when their eyes met.

"You'll have to excuse us, Russell. My sister has to see a man about a horse."

"What?" Evelyn didn't mean to let the word burst out like that, but it appeared to have a mind of its own.

Viola chuckled and flashed another smile at Russell as she moved away. She leaned in to whisper to Evelyn, "I heard a woman staying in the hotel say that about needing to use the facilities. I thought it was funny."

Evelyn didn't think it was funny. Her face burned with embarrassment and, yes, a bit of anger still. Once they were inside the small bathroom with one commode behind a curtain, she turned to Viola, who had walked to the mirror. "Please don't embarrass me like that again."

Viola turned to face her. "Did you want me to tell him you had to pee?"

"Don't be crass."

"Don't be such a fuddy-duddy."

Evelyn went behind the curtain and relieved herself and then walked over to the sink where Viola still stood, refreshing her lipstick. The color was a bold red to match her dress. Evelyn watched her sister while she washed her hands. Viola really was a beautiful woman. She didn't even need the makeup she so generously applied. She could attract any man she wanted.

Evelyn wished she could be more like her sister, carefree and able to laugh and flirt. It was obvious Viola had been flirting with Russell, and Evelyn hoped it would not happen again. She had met him first and thought he felt a spark of attraction too. But tonight, Viola had overshadowed her. She'd always done that, and most of the time, Evelyn had not cared. However, tonight she cared. She wanted Russell to notice her, but she could not even consider trying to vamp the way her sister did.

When they got back to the main area, Russell was gone, and Evelyn was disappointed not to be able to talk to him again. Yet she was also a bit relieved. Now Viola couldn't flirt with him, and those two might not ever see each other again, which would be just fine with Evelyn.

———

Another week passed before Evelyn saw Russell again. Then one afternoon as she was headed to her room for a short break before starting preparations for supper, she heard the music from the garage. Instead of staying on the other side of the door to listen, she opened it and stepped out. Russell paused for a moment to give her a smile and then resumed the song. It was a sad song. Something about an old man and a clock that stopped when he died. When the song ended, she said, "That was so nice. But a bit sad too."

"It's called 'My Grandfather's Clock.'"

"Was it really?"

"Really what?"

"Your grandfather's?"

Russell gave a little laugh. "No. It's just another song my daddy taught me."

"Did your father teach you all those other songs I heard you sing?"

"Ah, you've been listening again."

"Yes. I... I like music."

"What else do you like?"

The way he said it, with a little smile and that glint in his eyes, Evelyn thought her legs had turned to butter. She leaned against the doorframe to keep her balance. "I like books, and..."

She couldn't think of anything else, so she shrugged, hating that she was so tongue-tied. He'd probably think she was stupid, just like the good sisters. When the silence became painful, she started toward the door. "I should go."

Just before closing the door, she heard him call out, "Do you like movies?"

"What?" She poked her head back in and saw that he was smiling.

"I wondered if you like to go to the picture show?"

"Oh." She took a moment to stop the flutter of her heart. "Yes. Yes, I do. Very much."

He put his guitar down and stood as if his next question needed the formality. "Would you consider going to the picture show with me?"

Evelyn could barely stammer a response. "Yes. I... I would like to."

"My aunt told me there's a new movie with John Wayne at a theatre downtown. You like John Wayne?"

"I think so. He's a cowboy, right?"

Russell chuckled. "He's an actor. But he plays cowboys."

"Of course. How silly of me."

"Not silly at all." Russell stepped closer and touched her arm. "Will Friday be okay?"

His fingers were light on her arm, but they raised goose-bumps where skin met skin. Evelyn took a breath to still her heart and quiet her nerves. "That will do fine."

"I'll ring you up tomorrow to say what time," he said, then paused for a moment. "Are you allowed to take calls here?"

"As long as they're brief. And not too frequent."

"Alright then. I'll phone tomorrow."

Evelyn stepped back into the house, cradling her arm.

———

Friday night, Russell called for Evelyn promptly at six. She had fretted all afternoon about what to wear, wishing in a way that she had clothes as daring as her sister. If she was even brave enough to wear something like that. The words of warning from the good sisters about what happens to girls who are loose in their dress and manners still rang loudly in her mind. She wondered at how quickly Viola had forgotten. Or did she just not care?

Evelyn opened the door of the small closet in the corner of her bedroom and selected a blue dress the color of the summer sky. It always made her feel pretty. It had a full skirt that swirled just a bit when she walked and little pearl buttons on the bodice. She wore white gloves and a white bonnet, and Russell smiled when he saw her. She hoped it was a smile of approval.

They didn't take the Model T Ford that Russell was working on in the Gardner's garage. Not much progress had been made, even though Russell had spent some time on it, but he spent more time with his guitar. "This is my uncle's car," Russell said, opening the passenger side door on the Buick Roadmaster for her.

The car had soft leather seats and a fresh, clean smell. "It was kind of him to let you use it," she said, sliding into the seat.

"My uncle's a good man." Russell slid behind the wheel and cranked the engine to life.

Thankfully, it was not far to the theatre as conversation came in fits and starts. After inquiring about his family and his job, Evelyn didn't know what else to ask him, and he seemed equally at a loss. That mischievous charm from their encounters in the garage was missing now, and she saw him pull at his tie as if it was too tight. Evelyn sincerely hoped they would get past this unease soon.

Walking into the Fisher Theatre was like entering the great room of a mansion, and the sight took her breath away. The theatre lobby was open and spacious with plush carpeting and walls of gray and white marble. Looking up, Evelyn saw a grand chandelier suspended on a heavy chain from the center of the ceiling, which was also covered in marble in a lovely mosaic pattern. The chandelier sparkled with what looked like a thousand lights that glinted off the mirrors on one wall. This was the kind of place she read about in books where characters lived in beautiful homes with ballrooms large enough for a hundred people to dance and not step on any toes.

Evelyn waited while Russell acquired tickets then followed him up the staircase where a young man in a dark suit and white shirt escorted them to their seats. Evelyn tried not to gawk, but the gilded cornices and red velvet drapes on the box seats that lined the walls were stunning. "How do people get into those seats up there?" Evelyn asked in a whisper, pointing to the wall to their left.

Russell laughed. "See the curtains? The people step through them from a hall in the back."

"Oh."

"I guess you haven't seen box seats before."

"No." Evelyn glanced at him and smiled. "I've never been in

a place like this before."

"I never was either. Until I came here. My aunt brought me shortly after I came to town. She thought the hick from the hills needed some culture." He chuckled. "Back home, our little movie house is very plain."

"So is the one I went to in Milwaukee."

"You're from Wisconsin?"

"Yes. That's where I was born."

"Oh." Russell shifted in the seat to face her. "Is your family there?"

"There's no family left there. My sister and mother live here in Detroit."

"What about your daddy?"

"I know nothing about my father." Despite her efforts to modulate her tone, the words came out with an edge to them.

"Sorry," he said. "Didn't mean to pry."

She sighed. "And I didn't mean to be so short. If you would like to know the truth. My father left when I was a baby. I have no memories of him."

He glanced away for a moment, then back to her. "I'm lucky then. To know my daddy. Even though he doesn't live with my mother anymore."

"Oh." Evelyn found this odd bit of connection between them interesting. "Are they divorced?"

He shook his head. "Separated. He lives in a rooming house in town and my mother lives on the home place across the river and up the hill." He laughed. "Mountain really. You should see it sometime. Almost a mile to the top, with streets running around it."

Was that an invitation? The idea of visiting his home town with him did hold a great deal of appeal. "I must admit I've never seen a mountain. Except for pictures of course."

Before he could respond, the lights dimmed and the stage

curtains opened to reveal a large white screen, at least twice the size of the screen in the theatre Evelyn had gone to once or twice in Milwaukee. The lights along the wall dimmed, and then Evelyn heard a whirring noise from behind. A picture came to life on the screen and music surrounded them.

Evelyn was soon so engrossed in the movie she forgot to worry about what impression she might be making on Russell. She worried about the passengers on the stagecoach as they made their way to the New Mexico territory, and she liked the character that John Wayne was playing. He wasn't on the side of the law, but he was a good guy, and oh, so handsome. When the Indians attacked the stagecoach, Evelyn clutched Russell's arm, and he put his other hand over hers. She didn't want to move after that. The contact felt so good.

When the movie ended and the lights in the seating area came up, Evelyn was a little disappointed. The story could have gone on forever. And she sure hoped that the Ringo Kid and Dallas got together and stayed together.

"Did you like the show?" Russell asked as they stood to file out with the rest of the audience.

"Yes. Most of it, anyway. Except for the shooting."

Russell smiled and took her elbow to guide her into an opening in the stream of people coming up the aisle. "I don't like that either," he said. "It bothers me to see anything get killed."

That admission surprised Evelyn. She thought all men liked to hunt and kill animals for food or for sport. That's what the men who were guests at the Hershlinger's often talked about, and even Mr. Hershlinger had his annual trip to Montana to shoot elk.

The drive home was mostly silent, but unlike the trip to the theatre, this was a comfortable silence. Occasionally, Evelyn heard Russell humming softly and saw him drumming his fingers on the steering wheel. When he noticed her glancing at him, he smiled. "The music in the movie was very good."

"You remember it?"

He nodded. "You don't?"

She shook her head. "I don't think everyone hears music the way you do."

He laughed. "My daddy said that to me once."

"He was right. You have a special talent."

Keeping one hand on the steering wheel, Russell reached over with the other to take her hand. The touch was electric, and Evelyn took a breath to steady her heart. "I wanted to be a singer," he said. "But everyone said I should learn a trade. Be able to earn a living."

Evelyn took another breath and found her voice. "Don't singers earn money?"

He laughed again.

"What about those men who sang at the hotel bar that night?"

"Sure. They were paid. And were lucky to be in a class joint like that. But most places singers go to are smaller bars or clubs. The pay hardly covers expenses to be on the road."

"I had no idea." Evelyn gazed out the front window, watching the lights of oncoming cars grow big on the windshield then fade as the cars passed. Then she looked at Russell again. "Did you ever sing in one of those bars?"

"A few times. Even played on the radio a couple of times with a buddy of mine. We both thought we could hit the big time. Be rich and famous."

He took his hand off of hers to negotiate a turn, and Evelyn was disappointed when he didn't put it back. She wondered if she dared to tell him of her dream of being an actress. The first time she'd gone to a movie show and saw Top Hat she fantasized about going to Hollywood and being a movie star like

Ginger Rogers. But maybe sharing that with Russell was a reve-
lation better saved for another time. If there was going to be
another time.

At her house, Russell got out of the car and came around to
help her out of the car. Then he walked with her up to the front
door. If he tried to kiss her, would he know that she had never
been kissed before? Her fingers shook as she searched in her
small evening bag for her key. When she found it, she carefully
inserted it into the lock, lest she drop it. Then she turned to
him. "Thank you for taking me," she said. "I had a very good
time."

"I did too." He leaned in and softly touched her lips with
his, looking deep into her eyes as he pulled back. "Was that
okay?"

Evelyn wasn't sure what he meant by that, so she said
nothing.

"The kiss? Was that too forward of me?"

She shook her head. The kiss had been quite nice.

"Then I'd like to do it again." He touched the back of her
head to draw closer, and the kiss was more intense this time,
making a fire burn deep inside her belly.

She pulled back this time, a bit breathless. "I should go."

Russell nodded and waited on the porch as she unlocked
the door and stepped in. She saw him still standing there as she
closed the door.

She leaned against the wood, heat still pulsing through her
body. It was like every nerve ending was on fire, and that place
in her privates, the one that had responded to the touch from
Sister, was throbbing now. Would it be wrong to let Russell
touch her there?

"Sins of the flesh are the worst sins of all." Evelyn could
hear Sister Honora's voice in her head.

There was the answer.

13

EVELYN – JULY 1940

E velyn had never kept company with a man before, so she was never quite sure how to refer to Russell when she talked to her mother or to Viola. Was the proper word "suitor?" Or was there a new word in these modern times? When she'd read Charlotte Brontë's *Jane Eyre,* she'd liked the term suitor. As if the man might suit the woman, like a certain style of clothing, and she was quite certain that Russell suited her. She often found excuses to go out to the garage when she knew he was there working on the car or practicing music, and he'd taken her out every Friday night now for almost two months. Did she dare think that they might be a couple?

This Friday night, early in July, they were at the Fox Theater to see Babes in Arms, and he had his arm around her shoulders, his hand just brushing the top of her breast. Even through the cloth of her dress, she could feel the contact and was becoming more comfortable with the feelings that touch aroused in her. After that first night and that first kiss, she'd quieted that nagging voice in her head, pushing it away and creating a barrier in her mind to keep it at bay.

For the most part, the barrier worked.

Last week, when Russell had taken Evelyn home after dinner, they didn't go to the door right away. He'd turned off the car engine, then turned to her, leaning in to touch her lips with his. Still holding the kiss, he'd unbuttoned the top few buttons of her dress and slipped his hand inside. If not for the kiss, she might have pushed his hand away, but passion overcame reason. And the barrier was intact.

Remembering that evening brought a hint of that heat again, and Evelyn shifted in her seat. Russell leaned close and quietly asked, "You okay?"

"Yes," she whispered back, but she wasn't really sure. While part of her wanted this man to do to her what the lovers did in the romance novels she read, she had to admit the prospect did terrify her.

Evelyn shook the thoughts away and settled back to enjoy the movie. She did so love to get lost in a story as it unfolded on the screen.

When the movie was over, they went to an Italian restaurant for a late dinner. Russell ordered a beer to go with the spaghetti and Evelyn had a glass of red wine. It was so sweet and tasty she had another, wondering why she had waited so long to have alcohol like every other adult. Even though it made her a little woozy, she liked the mellow feeling.

Later, parked outside her house, Russell turned off the car engine and lights. Moonlight bathed the interior of the car with a white light that lit the planes of his face as he turned to her. There didn't seem to be any need for words. She could see his intent in his eyes so she let him kiss her fiercely and bare her breasts. When he touched one nipple with his lips, like he was tasting her, she thought she would explode. Then he lifted her skirt and slipped a hand inside her panties. To that place that was on fire. That place that the good sister had said nobody should touch. But Russell's touch felt so good.

"Evelyn, can we finish this?"

She leaned away from him for a moment. "What do you mean?"

"I want to be in you. Feel how hard I am." He took her hand and placed it on the front of his pants. *So this is what a man feels like.* She knew the basics of the male anatomy but had never seen a grown man's penis, nor felt one. When she had bathed Jonathan, she did glance at his privates now and then, even though the warning about sins of the flesh from Sister rang clearly through her mind. Jonathan had a small, soft penis and looked nothing like she imagined this one beneath her hand would look like.

Evelyn tried to clear the fog from her brain. "I don't know how... I've never..."

"You're a virgin?"

"Yes."

He didn't say anything for a moment, then asked, "Do you want to?"

She paused even longer, then said. "I don't know. I think so... but how... where?"

Russell started the car and pulled away from the curb. "Not here. Not so close to where you live."

Evelyn buttoned her dress while Russell drove for a few blocks and came to a street that was very dark. It had houses on one side and what looked like a park on the other. "Come on," he said, opening the car door.

"Into the park?"

"No. The back seat. It's wide enough for us. Almost like a bed."

Russell eased her down on the back seat and undid the buttons on her dress, then pushed it off her shoulders, taking her bra straps with it. The night air was cool, even for July, and it felt good when it swept across her bare skin. For just a moment, she worried that he might not like to touch the place beneath her breast where sweat had gathered, but that worry was forgotten in the heat of his next kiss.

Then she thought of nothing as his passion grew more intense, and he hurriedly pulled her panties down. His fingers brushed over the place where she was burning up and the pressure of his finger was like being touched with a lightning rod. Then he fumbled with his pants, and she felt something else touch her. "Are you ready?" he asked in a soft whisper in her ear. "I'll be easy."

Despite those words, and as much as Evelyn thought she wanted this, it hurt when Russell pushed into her, but pleasure accompanied the pain, creating an odd mix of sensations.

Now that the act was over, he was still inside her, and that felt nice. As did the soft kisses on her neck, but suddenly, the image of Sister Honora shaking her finger to punctuate her lecture about bad girls broke through the barrier Evelyn had erected to keep them out. Oh my God. What had she done? Was she now a bad girl? She didn't realize she was crying until Russell wiped a tear from her cheek. "I'm sorry if it hurt. I didn't mean to."

Evelyn didn't know what to say. She couldn't tell him why she was crying. Not now while he was still on top of her, warm and firm and gentle with his kisses. Then he shifted so he could zip up his pants, and she swiveled to sit up, careful to stay on the towel he had put beneath her. At first, she'd been so grateful he had something to protect her skirt from the mess, she didn't think of anything else. But now, she wondered about his being so prepared. Was it just a coincidence that he had a towel in the car, or did he do this with lots of women?

Evelyn hated having those thoughts, but she couldn't help

it. Guilt and a bit of disappointment were driving her. Something was still burning inside her, like a kettle boiling that would soon erupt if the lid was not taken off. The act, she didn't know what else to call it, hadn't been like the scenes in stories where the couple languished in mutual satisfaction. She didn't feel sated. Oh, how she loved that word and imagined what it would feel like, but she wasn't feeling that tonight. She fumbled on the floor until she found her panties and slipped them on, pulling the towel out at the same time. Even in the dim light from the moon, she could see the dark stain of her lost virginity. She held up the towel. "What do you want me to do with this?"

"Here." He took it, folded it, and stuffed it in the corner of the seat. "I'll get rid of it before I return my uncle's car."

Now what? Evelyn smoothed her hair and put her hat back on. What had just transpired was such a monumental thing to her. Did it have the same importance to him? She was trying to figure out what to say, but he spoke first.

"I'll take you home." Russell got out of the backseat and held the door for her.

Evelyn bit her lip to keep from crying. He sounded so... so... distant. Was that the way all men were afterward? Or did it mean he was one of those her sister had warned her about? The ones who would sweet talk a woman just to have sex and then disappear. She kept her face averted as she slid into the front seat so he wouldn't see the worry.

The drive back to her house was short, but the silence in the car could have stretched for miles. It was not the companionable silence they'd come to enjoy on other occasions, and Evelyn wondered what Russell was thinking. Was he disappointed? Was there something wrong? Should she ask? What should she say when he walked her to the door?

Turned out, there wasn't time to say much of anything. Instead of lingering like he often did, he gave her a nice, gentle kiss then quickly said goodnight and turned to leave. The kiss was reassuring, but the abrupt departure left her shivering in a cool breeze.

Inside, Evelyn went to her room just off the kitchen, glad for once that her bedroom wasn't upstairs with the family. She threw her hat on the bed and took off her dress, checking carefully to see if it had gotten stained. Nothing. Thank God. She grabbed a robe and clean underwear and went to the bathroom to clean up.

As she expected, her panties had blood on them, but not any more than she sometimes had when her monthly started without warning. She rinsed the panties in cold water, then washed herself, noting that she felt a little tender in her private parts. As she took care of cleaning up, she couldn't shake the image of Sister Honora and her accusing finger. All the lectures about sin and sex whirled through her mind, and she scrubbed harder, trying to still the harsh voice.

She never should have said yes to Russell. She could blame her weakness on the wine, but the truth was, she wanted this. She wanted to make him happy. And she wanted to see what it would feel like to make love. *Oh my God. I've sinned terribly.* Maybe if she went to confession... Well, no maybe about that. She would have to go to confession for fear of dying in the state of mortal sin. And maybe if she remained pure after that, God would not send a lightning bolt to strike her dead. She should do that. Resist the sins of the flesh until Russell married her.

For he would. She was sure of that. Despite the roiling emotions she was experiencing, she convinced herself that they now had a commitment. She also told herself that he was not like those other men. He was a true gentleman, and a gentleman did not deflower a virgin without the intent of making her his bride.

There could never be another man for her.

When a week passed and Russell didn't come by, Evelyn's firm belief started to weaken. She tried not to worry but couldn't help but wonder if she'd been a fool to let him have his way.

Then one day, she heard the music in the garage and ran out in her eagerness to see him. He sat on a stool, playing a slow, melodic tune on his guitar. He looked up and smiled, and the doubts vanished like the morning mist when touched by the sun.

Evelyn knew she should be coy. That's the way women were supposed to act, but she couldn't hold back. "I'm so glad to see you."

He strummed a few more chords, then winked at her. "Me too."

She leaned against the fender of his car and listened as he finished that song, then started another. When he finished, the notes sliding off into silence, he set the guitar down. "I've got good news."

"What?"

"I have a gig at the Cadillac Hotel. Your sister introduced me to the man who arranges the entertainment."

Evelyn was stunned. She had no idea that he'd seen Viola. When had that happened? Last weekend when he didn't take her out? Evelyn didn't want to leap to any conclusions, but she couldn't help it. Insecurity was in control. Did he? Would he?

He was looking at her so expectantly; she knew she had to say something. "When is it? Your performance, I mean."

"Next Friday. Can you come?"

"I don't know..." She let her words fade.

Russell stood and walked over, touching her cheek with his fingertips. "I thought you'd like to."

"I would." She tried to get some excitement into her voice,

but she couldn't shake the thought of him and Viola together, and her enthusiasm was dampened.

He stepped closer and slipped his fingers into her hair, brushing her lips with a kiss at the same time. Her body did not listen to her mind, and she leaned into the kiss. Passion ignited them both, and Russell's hands were urgent as they slid down her back and buttocks. The burn started deep inside and seemed to call out for the hardness he pressed against her.

Russell broke the kiss. "I saw the family leave earlier. We could go inside."

"No." Evelyn didn't intend the response to be sharp but realized it must have been when she saw him wince.

"A bed would be better than the back seat."

"Yes, but..."

"What?"

Evelyn took a step back. "I can't. We can't. It's wrong."

Russell wiped a hand across his face. "What about...?" He made a vague gesture, but she knew what he meant. What about last time?

"I gave in to temptation." She hesitated then finished. "But it was a sin."

"A sin?" He shook his head. "A sin is something bad. Something ugly. What we did wasn't ugly."

"No, it wasn't ugly, but it wasn't right. What we did is supposed to be saved for the marriage bed."

He shook his head. "Geez! Just how religious are you?"

That question surprised her. She raised one eyebrow and shrugged. "I don't know. Average?"

"I'm way below average. I believe in God but not church."

"What?" Evelyn looked at him with eyes wide. "There is no God without church."

He took a few steps away, then turned back. "Where was God before churches were formed?"

Evelyn bit her lip. She didn't have an answer for that, and after her initial shock wore off, she realized it was an interesting question. She'd never thought about God outside of Mass. According to Sister, that was where people went to meet Him, and Mass was always in church. "If you don't go to church, how did you learn all those hymns you play?"

"My daddy played organ in the Methodist church. When I was a kid, we went all the time. And my whole family loves to sing. The church songs are what most of us know."

"Would you ever go back to church?"

He didn't answer for the longest moment, then gave a slight shake of his head.

Evelyn didn't know how to respond to that. She didn't know all the rules of the church when it came to marriage, but she remembered being told to find "her own kind." What a quandary. She wasn't sure she could give up on Russell, especially not after having given him her most precious gift.

She had to make sure he was her husband someday. The fact that he wasn't a Catholic was a complication. They couldn't marry in the church, and she didn't know if that would mean she could no longer receive communion, but she'd have to figure out what to do about all that later. Right now, she knew she had to go back inside before she gave in to the temptation he was offering with that crooked grin and glint of longing in his deep blue eyes.

———

Friday night, Viola came to drive Evelyn to the hotel for Russell's performance so she wouldn't have to take the bus. Recently, Viola had learned how to drive and purchased a used Chevrolet Standard.

Sliding into the passenger seat, Evelyn took note of the slim black dress her sister wore. Her dress tonight had a bit of a scooped neck, but that was as close to sexy as Evelyn could get. "You look very nice," she said as Viola pulled away from the curb.

Viola glanced over with a smile. "You do too."

Evelyn had hoped to ride to the hotel with Russell, but the other day, he'd told her that he had to be there early to set up. It would be better for her to come later for the show, so she wouldn't be bored sitting alone while he was getting the sound equipment in place. Still, she'd dressed as if they would be on a date, wearing a pale lavender sundress with a wide white sash. Even though Viola's words had sounded sincere, Evelyn worried that her sister found her dowdy in comparison. Then she shook that thought away. It didn't matter what her sister thought. It only mattered what Russell thought of how she looked, and so far, she'd never heard a word of complaint from him.

"It was very nice of you to arrange this opportunity for Russell to perform," Evelyn said as Viola pulled the car into a parking space at the hotel.

"He deserves it. Have you heard him sing?"

The question stumped her for a moment, and Evelyn was glad for the distraction of getting out of the car and walking toward the hotel entrance. She'd told Viola about how she and Russell had first met and his singing in the garage. Did her sister not remember? Or was there something else in the question? Had he sung for Viola the way he did for her? Is that what he did those evenings when he didn't come to the garage?

Evelyn shook her head, trying to scatter those thoughts to the wind. She needed to stop obsessing about what Russell did when she didn't see him. It wasn't any of her business, even though she longed to know so she wouldn't have to wonder. Wondering always led to such wild imaginings. She followed

Viola inside and they worked their way through the crowd to find a table.

At the front of the room, Russell, dressed in dark brown slacks and a cream-colored shirt that was open at the neck, checked microphones and speakers with another man. Evelyn thought about going up to greet him, then decided not to. Maybe Russell didn't need an interruption. Once everything was set, he sat down in a chair and put his guitar across his knee. The other man grabbed the mic and smiled out at the audience. "Welcome to the Cabaret at the Cadillac Hotel," he said. "We've had a lot of talent cross our little stage and are proud today to introduce you to a singer from the hills of West Virginia, Russ Van Gilder. This is his first appearance here, but he's played in clubs in his home state and even had a gig on the radio. So let's give him a warm welcome."

A few people stopped talking and clapped, but others ignored the emcee. Conversations buzzed in the background as Russell strummed a few chords then started to sing. He opened with "Is it True What They Say About Dixie," which was a jazzy tune that stilled some of the audience, then he sang a couple of silly songs that made people laugh. That got the attention of most of the crowd, and folks were silent as he continued the set. Evelyn was glad that the people started paying attention. She couldn't imagine how it would feel to be up on a stage trying to entertain and have people talk over the music.

The next song started with a few slow strums on the guitar, then Russell started to sing, "You made me love you. I didn't want to do it..."

As he sang, he looked directly at Evelyn's table, and she swore her heart swelled. The warmth of a blush tingled on her cheeks, and she turned to see if Viola noticed. Her sister was staring at Russell, a smile lighting up her face. Evelyn glanced back at Russell and wondered if he really was looking at her or Viola.

Evelyn dropped her gaze and took a quick swallow of her drink. She tried to talk herself out of the surge of jealousy. She was being silly. Then she looked at Viola again. Her sister was leaning her chin on her hand, and the smile had widened.

Evelyn had to get out of there.

Inside the lady's restroom, she went behind the curtain around the commode and took a few deep breaths to calm down. Why was she even letting herself think there was something between Viola and Russell? It was wrong to jump to a conclusion like that. Why was she always so quick to assume the worst?

Evelyn sat on the closed toilet seat for a few moments, using tissues from her purse to wipe the tears from her cheeks. She took another deep breath to still the pounding of her heart, and then she heard the door to the restroom open.

"Evelyn, are you in here?"

It was Viola.

"Yes." Damn. "I'll be out in a minute."

Evelyn heard the sound of water running, then Viola said, "You were gone so long, I was worried."

"I'm fine." Evelyn stepped around the curtain and walked to the sink area, trying her best to smile and look normal.

Viola glanced at her sister. "Your makeup is all smeared. Here, let me fix it for you." She reached into her evening bag and pulled out a compact. Then she stepped closer to Evelyn. "Have you been crying?"

For a moment, Evelyn couldn't formulate an answer. Should she say yes, and then explain why? She gave her head a slight shake. She hated confrontations. She was always the first to back down when faced with possible conflict. But to hell with it.

"You do know Russell is mine."

"What?"

"We've been going out. And made some commitments to each other." Evelyn blushed at the thought of exactly what kind of commitment they'd made in the backseat of his car.

"I don't see a ring on your finger."

"Nothing is formal... yet."

"I see." Viola turned to the mirror and checked her lipstick.

Evelyn took a deep breath then blurted, "I always hated it when you took things from me."

Viola sighed. "What things?"

"The best desserts. The newest sweater."

Viola snapped her purse closed and faced her sister. "My God, that was years ago. And I gave the sweater back, didn't I?"

"Yes." Evelyn hesitated for a moment. "When you were tired of it."

Nothing was said for a moment, and Evelyn wished she could just stop, turn the clock back to an hour ago, and get out of this mess. She was never good at holding her own in an argument. Viola glared at her, and Evelyn wasn't sure what her sister was thinking. Then Viola flipped her hair off her shoulder and lifted her chin. "Well, let's just see what Russell decides, shall we?"

"Have you been... seeing him?"

"Well, I had to see him to arrange this, didn't I?"

"You know what I mean."

"Yes. I know what you mean. And the answer is yes. We met and had a drink."

Evelyn couldn't believe it. Her dream was unraveling like an old sweater. "Is that all?"

Viola didn't answer. She just smiled and walked out.

After waiting a moment for the new rush of tears to stop, Evelyn wiped her eyes and walked through the crowd to their table. Viola looked up and gave her a broad smile as if they had not just had harsh words in the restroom. Evelyn sat down, glancing at the stage where Russell had just stepped up to do his last set, but the magic of the evening had been shattered, like broken glass. Like broken dreams.

14

EVELYN – SEPTEMBER 1940

Another month had passed so quickly that it took a while for Evelyn to realize she'd missed her monthlies. Twice. This morning, she'd opened the drawer for a clean pair of panties and noticed her belt for her sanitary pads in the corner of the drawer. That's when that feeling of dread hit and twisted her stomach into a knot. She'd never missed a month. Not once since that day when she was fourteen and "became a woman" as Sarah had put it. Sarah had helped her with supplies as well as a candid talk about what the monthly "visits" were all about and what would stop them. Only two things. Pregnancy and the change of life. Since Evelyn was much too young for the change, that only left one possibility.

Evelyn dressed quickly and raced out to the kitchen to check the calendar, trying to remember the exact date of her last period. Near as she could recall, it was early in July. Maybe right around the Fourth? And that had been almost two weeks before she let Russell have his way with her. The guilt over what she had done was not as strong if she thought of it in those terms. It also helped if she didn't think about the wanton way her body had responded that warm July evening.

It was now the middle of September. Well past the time she should have started her monthly. She stood there staring at the numbers in the little squares wondering what on earth to do. Other than slither down to the floor and cry. She should tell Russell, that's for sure, but how? When? How would he react? They'd only gone out three times since that evening he played at the hotel about a month ago, so she wasn't as sure about their possible future together as she had been. And she wasn't sure if that was because he was busy with work, or busy some other way. Always those doubts that came like unwanted guests.

When they were together, Russell respected her wishes about sex. He would ease off the heavy kissing and touching when she asked him to. Not that she always wanted him to. Her body seemed to have other ideas than her morality did, but she'd never told him that sometimes it was hard for her to tell him to stop. Although she had almost given in the last time he tried to convince her that they could visit the back seat of his uncle's car again, and God would not deem it wrong. The way her body responded to his touch, she was sorely tempted, but she'd made a promise to God, and one did not break promises to the Almighty on the whim of passion.

Evelyn turned when she heard footsteps and saw Mrs. Gardner, who furrowed her brow and asked, "Something wrong?"

"No... I..." Evelyn took a breath to compose herself. "Do you need me for something?"

"I wondered if you had started dinner."

"I was about to."

"Good." Mrs. Gardner pursed her lips. "Are you sure you're okay?"

"Yes... I'm..." Evelyn turned and pulled a skillet out of the drawer under the stove to brown the onions for a ham and potato casserole. "I should get on with the cooking."

"Very well."

Today, Evelyn had the evening off, so after she prepared the meal for the family, she'd go to Henry and Regina's for dinner. They had made plans the week before, and Viola would also be joining them. The sisters were finally on speaking terms again after the argument at the club. Viola had called a few days later to apologize for how she had acted and to assure Evelyn that she didn't have any designs on Russell. Evelyn so wanted that to be true that she accepted the apology.

Evelyn put the casserole into the oven and told Mrs. Gardener when it would be ready. Then she quickly got her coat and purse and walked to the bus stop. It was a pleasant fall evening, and Evelyn enjoyed the cool breeze that brushed across her face. It was refreshing, easing the turmoil in her head. She didn't know what to do about this devastating situation. Maybe she could talk to Viola tonight about it. Find some way to have a few minutes of privacy. She had to tell someone, and she certainly did not want to tell her mother. Not yet.

———

"Are you ready?" Henry walked into the small bedroom where Regina sat at the dressing table. "The girls will be here any minute."

"They're hardly girls anymore, Henry."

"I know." He walked over and nuzzled her neck. "But I like the sound of that. 'The Girls.'"

"You're being silly." Regina fastened the clip in her hair, and met his eyes in the mirror. "Did you stir the soup like I asked?"

"Your humble servant obeys." He stepped back and gave her

a sweeping bow, then stood and looked at her reflection in the mirror. She had such a serious expression. "What is it?"

"I don't know." Regina sighed and set her brush down on the vanity top. "It's just..."

"What?"

"You always get so giddy when my daughters come over."

Henry frowned. "I'm happy to see them. Is that wrong?"

Regina broke the reflected eye contact but did not turn to face him. He touched her lightly on the shoulder. "Are you not happy to have them here?"

"Oh, no. It's not that." Now she turned and looked up at him. "I just wonder if they're happy they are here."

"Of course they are. They could have gone back to Milwaukee months ago if they weren't."

"I know."

"Then why are you worried?"

"I just feel so unsure. Especially with Evelyn. She can be so distant at times."

"She's just quiet and reserved." He took her hand and pulled her toward him. "It has nothing to do with you."

"Or maybe everything. I'm the one who walked away from them."

Henry took a step back. Long ago, Regina had told him the basics of why she put the girls in the orphanage, but she'd never revealed how she felt about that. He'd never asked as he thought it best that he not. If she ever wanted to tell him, she would. Was this the time? He looked into her eyes, in search of an answer in the pale blue depths. Regina said nothing, not even with a look or a gesture.

"Are you worried that Evelyn is still angry?"

Regina nodded.

"You should talk to her."

"No." Regina pulled away from him and walked toward the door. "I need to check the soup."

Henry watched as she left the room, her full skirt billowing behind her. He never could get accustomed to her walking away from this sensitive subject.

When Evelyn and Viola arrived, they gathered around the table and Henry brought out the large tureen of vegetable soup with chunks of beef. Regina had purchased some pumpernickel bread that they slathered with butter. As they ate, Viola provided plenty of stories about the people who were guests at the hotel. The anecdotes were funny and kept everyone entertained, but Henry noticed that Evelyn was a little quieter than normal. She was sitting just to the left of him, so he leaned close. "Is everything okay?"

"Yes."

"You've hardly eaten."

Evelyn picked up her spoon and scooped a piece of carrot but still did not take a bite.

"Is there something wrong with my soup?" Regina's question came from across the table, and Evelyn looked up.

"Uh, no," Evelyn said. "It's just... I'm not... um..."

Suddenly, she jumped up and ran to the bathroom. Henry looked to Viola. "Is your sister sick?"

"I don't know. She seemed fine when we first arrived."

They all resumed eating, but when Evelyn didn't come back in a few minutes, Regina started to get up. Viola held up a hand to stop her. "I'll go see if she's okay."

———

There was a soft knock on the door, then Evelyn heard her sister ask, "Can I come in?"

Evelyn splashed cold water on her face and pinched her

pale cheeks to bring back some color. The horrible bout of vomiting had cast an ashen pall on her face. Even though she had flushed the toilet, a sour smell permeated the room, and she knew there was no way she could hide what had just happened. She couldn't prevent Viola from coming in, either. There hadn't been enough time to lock the door as Evelyn raced to get to the bathroom in time.

Another knock. "Evelyn?"

"I'll be right out."

"I'm coming in."

"No. Don't."

But the words were too late. The door opened, and Evelyn turned from the sink to see her sister. A progression of expressions moved across Viola's face. First a flash of distaste in reaction to the awful odor, and then puzzlement as she obviously tried to figure out the sickening smell. Then an awareness that made Evelyn glad she did not have to say the words.

"I'm guessing it isn't the flu," Viola said.

Evelyn nodded, then her legs started to shake, so she sat down on the toilet seat.

"Oh, my." Viola stepped the rest of the way into the bathroom and closed the door. "You're sure?"

Evelyn nodded again. Viola didn't speak for a few moments, then she started to laugh.

Evelyn looked up, shock momentarily replacing her fear. "You think this is funny?"

"No." Viola put a hand to her mouth to still the laughter.

"Then why are you laughing?"

"Because, dear sister, I'm pregnant too." Using both hands, Viola smoothed the fabric over her stomach, and Evelyn saw the slight bulge.

For a moment, Evelyn couldn't speak. She didn't even want to think it, but she momentarily flashed on the times she'd seen

Viola flirting with Russell. Surely they... She couldn't even finish the thought. Then she swallowed hard and asked, "Who's the father?"

"Some man I met."

"Some...?" The rest of the words got stuck in Evelyn's throat.

"What's wrong?" Viola asked. "Surely you are not judging me." She finished with a pointed look below Evelyn's belt.

"No. I'm... I'm just surprised, that's all. I didn't even know you were seeing anyone."

Viola smiled. "I see lots of people."

There was something in the smile and the words that made Evelyn squirm just a bit. She still had such a hard time with Viola's disregard for all that they had been taught about the things between a man and a woman. Especially that it should be one man and one woman forever. Not...

She tried a weak smile, and when that didn't work she asked, "Have you told Regina yet?"

"No. Have you?"

"Oh, God no. You're the first one."

"I'm honored." Viola checked her hair in the mirror, giving the ends a finger-comb. "Do you know who the father is?"

"What a silly question. Of course I know."

"You're certain?"

The question sounded like an accusation, but still, Evelyn nodded. This is not what she expected. She'd been hoping for some kind of guidance from her sister. Not more confusion. And certainly not these questions that felt like accusations.

"Everything okay in there, girls?"

It was Henry.

"We're fine," Viola called out. "We'll be out in a few minutes."

"Okay then."

In the silence that followed, Evelyn heard his footsteps receding, soft clumps as he went back down the hall.

Before Evelyn could say anything, Viola spoke up. "I'm not sure I'm going to have this baby."

"What?" At first, Evelyn couldn't imagine what Viola meant. How could she not...? Then the realization dawned at the same time Viola continued.

"I found out about this woman who takes care of things." Again, Viola ran her hand across the bulge in her tummy. "It would make everything so much less complicated. We could go together, and the problems would go away like that." Viola snapped her fingers to emphasize the last two words.

Evelyn couldn't find her voice. It was as if everything inside her froze. The thought of not having the baby had never crossed her mind. When she looked toward the future, the picture in her mind was always of her and Russell and their child, living that happy-ever-after life. Plus, it would mean killing the baby. Isn't that what happened when people had an abortion? "I don't think I could do that." Her voice was soft, barely a whisper over the ice in her throat.

"I said don't judge me." Anger flashed in Viola's eyes. "You think it's easy for me to consider it?"

"I didn't mean..." Evelyn let the rest of the words fade as she shook her head. She wasn't sure, but she hoped it was not easy. She wasn't sure about so many things about Viola. This grown-up sister was so different from the big sister who had helped Evelyn negotiate those difficult years of childhood. What she had seen as strength back then had turned into... ? What? She couldn't even think of how to describe her sister now. Some of that strength still showed through, but there were other things that weren't so admirable.

"Why not tell the father and get married?" Evelyn asked.

"Then you wouldn't have to..." Her mouth would not cooperate and say the words. Kill your baby.

"Is that what you plan to do?" There was just a hint of a smirk in the question.

"Yes. I'm sure Russell will do the right thing."

"Russell?"

"Yes. It's his baby. He's..." The rest of the words choked her as the strangest look crossed her sister's face. Evelyn couldn't stop the thought or the outburst. "He's not... Please don't tell me—"

"Of course not." Viola gave a little laugh as if the possibility was absurd. "I lied. I don't know who the father is."

"Oh."

The word just hung there for a moment.

"You're shocked."

"I just... I mean, I never—"

"Of course not. You were always Miss Perfect. Evelyn the saint, always trying to win the favor of the sisters."

Now Evelyn was beyond shock. How could they have such different views of the past?

"I was never perfect," Evelyn said, again in a voice barely above a whisper.

They stood and looked at each other in a silence heavy with incrimination, and then another voice intruded. "Evelyn? Viola?"

This time, it was Regina on the other side of the bathroom door.

"Coming." Evelyn stood and roughly brushed past her sister. She opened the door and stepped into the hall.

"Are you okay?" Regina asked.

"Yes. I just had a little upset to my stomach. I'm fine now."

"Coming down with the flu?"

"No. I don't think so. But I do think I should go home."

Viola didn't follow them out of the bathroom, which was fine with Evelyn. She didn't know if she could maintain the façade of normalcy if she had to face her sister and hug her goodbye. She grabbed her coat, hugged Regina and Henry, and left, declining his offer to drive her home. He was so kind she was afraid she would break if she didn't get away.

It was a short two-block walk to the bus stop. Lampposts were haloed by streetlights, and she stepped in and out of the lights and shadows without a thought to safety. She was still trying to sort out all her thoughts and feelings about the confessions in the bathroom. That could almost be a title for a story in one of those true romance magazines Viola liked to read. She had tried to interest Evelyn in them, but they were a little too... well... trashy for Evelyn.

Evelyn sat on the bench to wait for the bus, the cool evening breeze tossing the ends of her scarf, her emotions in turmoil. She couldn't shake that little fear that kept rearing up and rattling her to the bone. Could it be possible that Russell and Viola had...? She shook her head. *Stop it. He loves you. He said so, didn't he?*

But he hadn't. That was the horrible truth. She'd imagined it so many times she had come to believe. And now, she would imagine her dream of the perfect home and the perfect family coming true.

15

EVELYN - OCTOBER 1940

They were sitting at a table covered with white linen, lit by only a candle. The flame sparkled against the crystal wine glasses set in front of them, and Evelyn wondered if she dared to hope that Russell had brought her to this fancy restaurant to ask her to marry him. She hadn't yet told him about the baby, even though another month had passed and there was no longer any doubt. But she didn't want to trap him. If he proposed first, there would be no trap.

She hadn't told Regina and Henry yet, either. Although she could have when Viola announced her pregnancy last week. It might have been easier to do it then, and they could both share the shame of being unmarried and pregnant, but Evelyn was so relieved that Viola had decided to keep the baby that she let the opportunity slip by. And if Russell proposed, and they got married, there would be less shame to endure. Somehow, marriage put a stamp of approval on a pregnancy, even if the baby was born just a few months after the ceremony.

A waiter, wearing a fancy black coat with a white ascot,

stepped to the table and poured a dark red wine into Russell's glass. Amused that he didn't seem to know what to do, Evelyn covered a smile with her fingers. The waiter discreetly whispered to Russell that he could now taste the wine and indicate his approval of the choice. After the tasting was completed and Russell nodded, the waiter poured wine into her glass and then stepped away. Evelyn raised her glass and took a small sip. The wine was sweet.

"This is very nice," Evelyn said, setting the glass down and glancing around the restaurant. In a far corner, a gray-haired man in a tuxedo sat at a small spinet piano, playing a sweet soft song.

"A guy I met at a club told me about it," Russell said, drawing her attention back. "I thought you'd like it."

Just like that time in the garage, impetuousness overrode any effort to be coy, and she asked, "Are we celebrating something?"

"Yes. I have news."

Oh. Since a proposal could hardly be news until after the fact, this obviously wasn't what Evelyn had hoped for, but before she could ask about the news, the waiter came back to inquire if they were ready to order. Flustered, Evelyn could hardly read the menu. She hated that her nerves always seemed to interfere with her ability to read. She always flashed back to her childhood when she'd been told she was too stupid to ever learn anything. She looked over at Russell and asked if he would order for her. He seemed pleased by her request and told the waiter that they would each have the prime rib, roasted potatoes, and sugared carrots. When the waiter retrieved the menus and stepped away, Evelyn took a sip of her wine then asked about his news.

"I've got an opportunity to go on the road and perform."

Oh my God. "But... What about your job? Your uncle?"

"He said I can take six months. See if I can get anywhere. If not, I can come back to his shop. Finish learning the tool and die trade."

"You already talked to him about it?" Evelyn hated the hint of a whine that had crept into her voice.

"I had to. I couldn't just up and leave."

"What about me? When were you going to talk to me about it?"

There was that whine again, and it seemed to push Russell back in his chair. "I'm talking to you now."

Evelyn fought the panic and fear that were churning in her stomach as she tried to make his news somehow fit with hers. And what about hers? Should she tell him? Could she tell him?

He reached across the table and took her hand. His was soft and warm and comforting. "Could you be happy for me? This is something I've always wanted."

"It's just such a surprise."

"It was for me too. This producer, Tom Ferrill, heard me play at the hotel last month. That's when he started talking to me about this."

Last month? That meant that the whole time that Evelyn had alternated between agonizing over the pregnancy and fantasizing about a wonderful life with Russell, he had his own fantasy that was obviously closer to reality than hers. And why didn't she know he had played at the hotel again? Was there some reason he hadn't told her? Did that reason have anything to do with Viola?

Evelyn was grateful for the distraction of the waiter bringing their dinner plates to cover the roiling emotions that hit her now and the tears that filled her eyes and threatened to spill free.

"I won't be gone the entire six months," Russell said after

the waiter left. "Some of the clubs I'll be playing are close enough that I can come home in between dates. And they aren't all set up yet. Tom is still getting the schedule set for the last three months of the tour."

"So you'll be finished by March?"

"With the first part. Then if—"

"The baby's due in March."

"We might book another six—" Russell dropped his fork and the sound of it clattering against the China plate resounded in the sudden silence like a gunshot. "Baby? What baby?"

Evelyn hadn't planned to tell him this way. But there it was. "I'm pregnant."

Russell sat back abruptly, letting air out in a loud whoosh.

"I'm sorry. I didn't mean for—"

He held up a hand to silence her. "Just give me a minute."

Evelyn sat still as he rubbed a hand across his face, then reach out to take a big swallow of his wine. Finally, he said, "What do you intend to do?"

At least he didn't insult her by asking if the baby was his. Evelyn chased the small English peas around her plate for a moment, then looked up at him. "I don't know. This is obviously a complication for you."

He didn't say anything for the longest time, and she blurted, "I could... have it taken care of. Viola knows—"

"No. No. No." He leaned forward to take her hand. "You can't do that. Just give me some time. I'll figure something out."

———

True to his word, Russell took care of things. He did the honorable thing and told her they could get married. It wasn't the romantic proposal she'd been hoping for, but at least it had been a proposal, and here they were at the courthouse.

Evelyn still hadn't told Regina and Henry about the pregnancy. She wasn't sure why, exactly. Maybe because she didn't have the closeness with them that invited confidences. If they hadn't guessed already, considering the quickie marriage, they'd figure it all out in a few months when the baby came "early." So maybe she didn't have to tell them at all.

She hadn't even planned to have them at the ceremony today, but Viola had insisted after Evelyn asked her to be a witness. "She is our mother," Viola had reminded her. "I'm sure she'll be hurt if you don't invite them."

Now they were standing in the hallway outside the judge's chambers, waiting to be called in. Like the proposal, this wasn't the wedding Evelyn had dreamed about. Instead of being in a beautiful church, they were in a drab county courthouse with gray walls and metal benches. She was in a simple blue dress under her gray coat with the red collar. The only thing of beauty was the small spray of yellow daisies Russell had given her earlier when he picked her up for the ride to the courthouse.

Russell's uncle was there to act as the other witness. Hoffman was a tall, stern man, and in his black suit and top hat, he reminded Evelyn of Abraham Lincoln. He was pleasant enough, if a bit aloof, and Evelyn suspected that he did not approve of her or this hasty marriage. Convention obviously kept him from expressing that aloud, a consideration for which she was immensely grateful. The moment was strained enough. With Viola so obviously pregnant now. With Regina appearing ill at ease. With the smile on Russell's face looking so forced.

Evelyn was sure her smile was lacking too. The only one who looked relaxed was Henry. But then, Evelyn had never seen him uncomfortable since they'd first met.

Finally, they were called in to stand in front of Judge McCorkle, a man with a full head of silver hair and a pleasant smile. His clerk handed him the papers, and after glancing at them, he looked at Evelyn and Russell. "Don't look so frightened," he said. "This is a happy occasion."

The comment drew a few laughs, and Evelyn relaxed just a bit, trying to mask the fear that Russell was only doing this because. Of course, the judge didn't know The Because. He told them to hold hands and then had them repeat the marriage vows. Russell didn't hesitate or stumble over the words, so maybe he did mean them. Evelyn did her best to keep her voice from wavering, feeling a thump of her heart as she said "to love, honor, and obey until death do us part." There was no doubt about the veracity of those words. She did love this man, and it seemed right that she would honor and obey him.

They exchanged rings, simple gold bands, and just moments later, Judge McCorkle pronounced them man and wife. Russell kissed her, and the contact was reassuring. There was meaning in his lips and a tinge of passion, so maybe her fears were unfounded. The earlier strain could just have been from nervousness. After all, neither of them had been married before. This was going to be okay. It had to be okay. Maybe it could even be better than okay. She finally had someone to love her and take care of her. And they could make a good home together. She just knew it.

Outside on the courthouse steps, Evelyn clung to Russell's hand, only letting go when her mother and Henry stepped over to offer a hug and words of congratulations. Plans had been made for everyone to go the hotel where Viola worked for a fancy celebration dinner. Viola had arranged for a corner of the hotel restaurant to be reserved for the party, and she'd also gotten a discount on the bridal suite.

Dinner consisted of large servings of beef bourguignon, baked potatoes, and asparagus almandine. It was fancier food than Evelyn could ever remember eating, and she was eager to try something new, but after a couple of bites, she was unable to continue. The meat sat heavily in her stomach, and she hoped she was not going to be sick. The extreme nausea she'd experienced the first weeks of her pregnancy had more recently eased, but a wave could still hit her at any time. Especially when she was on edge. But then everyone seemed a bit on edge. Her mother kept giving her questioning looks. Hoffman fidgeted in his seat, as if he'd rather be any place but here. Viola filled awkward silences with too much babble, and the sound of her voice grated on Evelyn's nerves.

Between the main course and dessert, presents were given. Henry and Regina gave them a bottle of champagne. "For celebrating later," Regina said. "Had you told us sooner, we would have had time to acquire an appropriate gift."

The comment stung just a bit, and Evelyn looked away from her mother. Henry turned and smiled at Evelyn. "It's okay, though. We're happy for you and Russell. And once you are settled in your own place, we can bring you something special."

"Thank you," Evelyn said, relieved that he had broken the tension.

Hoffman slid a card across the table to Russell, and when he opened it, a hundred-dollar bill fell out. Oh my. Evelyn's opinion of the man shifted. Maybe he wasn't so cold after all.

"Hoffman, I don't know what to say." Russell slipped the money back into the card.

"Perhaps 'thank you?'" It was said with a smile, and everyone chuckled.

Then Viola handed a box across to Evelyn. "This is also for celebrating later."

Evelyn felt heat crawl up her face as she pulled a red lace nightgown out of the box. At least she thought it was a nightgown. She had never seen one so skimpy. It drew appropriate comments from the men and a tsk from Regina. Evelyn quickly put it back in the box and closed the lid.

"And now, a toast to my little sister and her new husband," Viola said, raising her glass of wine. "May your love always be as strong as it is today."

Glasses clinked and wine swallowed, and then it was time to go. Hugs were exchanged with everyone, except Hoffman who was more formal. He shook Russell's hand and gave Evelyn a nod and a smile before leaving. Once the guests were gone, and she was free to go upstairs with Russell, Evelyn was relieved. Still, she was nervous about what they would be doing once they were alone in the room. Certainly it would be better than that first and only time in the car, but her lack of experience bothered her. She didn't want to disappoint him and make him regret the marriage before it had even barely begun.

"Are you ready?" Russell asked.

She nodded, and they gathered the presents and headed upstairs.

When they reached the room, Russell unlocked the door, and before she could step inside, he swept her up in his arms and carried her in. "My sister reminded me that this is the tradition," he said.

"Oh." She waited until he put her down then continued. "You never told me you had a sister."

"I have three."

"Just sisters?"

"I have a brother too." He shrugged out of his suit coat and draped it across the bed.

"Have you told them about me?"

"Of course. I called to tell them about the wedding." He walked back to her and put his arms around her. "They couldn't make the trip up considering the short notice, but Mother said to bring you down so they can meet you."

147

Getting a sense that his family approved made Evelyn smile, and she liked the feel of him holding her close in his arms like this. That eased the cloud of uncertainty that had been drifting in and out since he'd said he would marry her. She wanted him to love her the way she loved him. Not just be doing a duty. And there was that little fear about him and Viola that was so hard to shake. When Viola had offered the toast, Evelyn had wondered about the look they exchanged.

Russell cupped her face in his hands and kissed her. It was a tender kiss, yet urgent, and she felt the heat spread from between her legs, through her belly, and into her breasts. He pulled back, breathless. "I'll get our things."

She'd forgotten about the presents they'd put down to open the door and realized that the door was still ajar. Thank goodness nobody had passed in the hall while they were locked in that kiss, and thank goodness she had a moment or two to get control of her body. She had never reacted with such force before and wondered if it was because now the sex was sanctioned. She wasn't even going to think about the fact that the marriage wasn't sanctioned by the church, since she'd married before a judge and not a priest, but it felt legitimate to her.

A bottle was nestled in a bucket of ice on the small table that sat between two occasional chairs upholstered in a rich red and gold tapestry pattern. Evelyn walked over to look at the note that was propped between two goblets. The note read: *Enjoy your night. Love Vi.*

Russell had stepped up beside Evelyn and he read over her shoulder, then gave a chuckle. "Your sister knows how to have a good time."

Evelyn wished she could laugh along with him, but his comment stirred up that fear again.

Russell touched her cheek. "What's wrong?"

"Nothing."

He didn't speak, his blue eyes brimming with such emotion, and she blurted, "I do love you so much."

He smiled. "I know."

More silence, then his smile turned into a grin. "Are you going to put on that pretty red thing Viola gave you?"

Evelyn took a breath to keep from reacting to her sister's name again. She hated that Viola seemed to be a third party to this relationship. She looked up at him and said, "I brought something else, but if you'd rather...?"

She let the words fade, and he said, "I'd rather you wore nothing."

A blush heated her face. "I bought it special. That's another wedding night tradition. The bride should wear something new."

"Then please do."

Evelyn hung up her coat in the little closet by the door, then took her small suitcase that Russell had brought up earlier into the bathroom. She pulled out the white silk negligee, touching the softness of the fabric to her face. She didn't deserve to wear white. Not according to another belief, but that was a taboo she was willing to ignore. When she'd seen the silk and lace negligee in Hudson's department store, she'd splurged and bought it. It cost more than any one item of clothing she had ever purchased, but it was an extravagance she thought she deserved for this event that was changing her life so dramatically.

Stepping out of the bathroom and hearing Russell gasp, Evelyn knew she had made the right choice. This gown, made of cloth so soft it hugged her body like a warm caress, suited her more than the scraps of lace that made up the one Viola had given her. She didn't know if she could ever bring herself to wear it.

Russell had removed his tie and unbuttoned his white dress

shirt, and when he took her in his arms, she could feel the heat of his body and the thump of his heart through the thin fabric of his undershirt. "You're beautiful," he said, kissing her lightly and fingering the gown. "How long do you need to wear that?"

She laughed. All worries lost in the magic of the moment.

16

EVELYN – JANUARY 1941

E velyn wished Russell was here with her. She felt so awkward with the weight of her pregnancy pulling her forward. She shouldn't have worn high heels, but she'd wanted to be dressed up for Viola's wedding, so she'd put on her good black shoes and her best maternity dress under the gray coat that could hardly button over her stomach. They were at the same courthouse where Evelyn and Russell had married, but a Justice of the Peace was officiating today. Viola was so far along it looked like she was going to burst right there, but she looked happy.

Glancing at the man her sister was marrying, Evelyn hoped the happiness would last. Lester Franklin was tall with a craggy face and dark hair cut very short. He was a long-haul truck driver, and when Viola had first talked about him, she had seemed glad that he would be gone for long periods of time. Evelyn found that odd. If you were in love, wouldn't you want to spend every moment you could together? She certainly missed Russell those weeks that he was on the road with his little band.

Russell had met two guys who played at the Cadillac one night, and they'd teamed up after playing a few times together. Gus played bass guitar, and Lindy played drums. "They're great," Russell had told her when he shared the news of the band forming. "We have a better chance of making it as a trio than I do as a single."

That did make sense, but a secret part of Evelyn didn't want them to succeed. She believed their life would be better if he worked a regular job and stayed home, but she wouldn't tell Russell that. The music was important to him. His whole being lit up when he was singing, whether in their living room or on a stage. The dreamer in her understood his desire, and sometimes, she toyed with the fantasy that he would become rich and famous. But that was all it was, a fantasy. No matter how hard she wished, or he wished, it probably would not happen, and they needed to face life with practicality, not fantasies.

"Hey." Her sister's voice pulled her out of her reverie. "It's time to go in."

Evelyn pulled her bulk off the bench where she had been sitting with Henry and Regina, and they all filed into the chambers where the ceremony would take place. The clerk and the Justice of the Peace tactfully ignored the fact of Viola's obvious pregnancy, handling the ceremony and the paperwork quickly and efficiently. It lacked the warmth Evelyn remembered from her marriage, and she felt sorry for her sister as she signed as one of the witnesses. Henry signed as the other, and then they were done and out the door.

There would be no family celebration. At least not right away. Since he was scheduled to drive out tomorrow, Lester had made it clear that he wanted his new bride all to himself this day. So when the bride and groom left for their wedding night, Henry and Regina drove Evelyn home to her little one-bedroom apartment. It was the apartment Russell started renting shortly before they married, and despite the size, Evelyn was quite pleased with it. It was her first home, and she wanted to make it special. In addition to knitting and crocheting things for the baby, she had made doilies for the end tables and antimacassars for the large upholstered chair that once belonged to Hoffman and was stained from his hair tonic.

A small sofa was the other piece of furniture in the living room, fronted by a coffee table that had been a gift from Henry and Regina. Evelyn had made a runner for the table out of a pretty piece of blue satin, and a crystal bowl sat in the center.

The other end of the main room housed the kitchen area, with the sink and stove and refrigerator against the wall. A small table with a Formica top was pushed into the corner with two chairs.

"Would you like some coffee?" Evelyn asked when Regina and Henry made no move to leave.

"If it's no trouble," Henry said. "We were expecting to take the new couple out for a dinner, so we are at a loss."

"Let me take your coats, and then I'll put the coffee on."

"I would be happy to take care of our things," Regina said. "If you don't mind, that is."

"Okay." Evelyn shrugged out of her coat and handed it over. "You can put them all on my bed."

Regina took the coats and disappeared down the hall. Henry followed Evelyn into the kitchen area and watched as she put a flame under the coffee pot. "This was fresh this morning," she said. "I hope you don't mind the reheat."

"Not at all. May I get the cups?"

Evelyn nodded and opened the cabinet that held the cups and saucers. Henry arranged three on the small counter and waited. "Lester seems like a nice enough chap," he said just as Regina joined them.

"Hardly," she said.

"You don't like him?" Henry asked.

"No. He reminds me of this fellow I once knew. Just a little on the sleazy side, and he lied to me all the time. I don't know why I stayed with him as long as I did." Regina stopped as if suddenly realizing she had said too much.

Evelyn glanced at Henry and saw that he was just as shocked as she was. Then this crazy thought flew through her mind. "Was that man my father?" Evelyn kept her voice calm and level, but her heart was pounding.

"Oh, no." Regina said quickly. "It was someone after... but before..."

Regina was obviously struggling, but Evelyn did not want to rescue her. Obviously, Henry did. He walked over and took her in his arms. "Hush now. You don't have to explain yourself."

Evelyn looked away, not wanting to be a party to this. She did want her mother to explain herself, but she was polite enough not to insist. She poured the coffee and invited them to sit in the living room. The rest of the visit was strained, and Evelyn was glad when they left. That meant she could stop pretending to have a nice time. She could also get out of the clothes that were too tight and put on the robe she liked to wear around the house. And she could ease her aching feet into slippers.

As she changed clothes, she thought about what her mother had said. About Lester and about the man her mother had been with. Briefly, she wondered just how many men there had been between her father and Henry. To think there had been more than one was scandalous, so Evelyn chased that thought away, thankful that her mother had ended up with Henry. He was kind, and she had to admit that she was growing quite fond of him. She felt more comfortable with him than she did her mother, and a few months ago, she'd been surprised by the realization that she wasn't sure she'd continue to visit their home as frequently if not for him.

———

Late one afternoon, Russell surprised Evelyn, walking in the door with a big smile, his guitar in one hand, satchel in the other. He'd been playing at a club in Grand Rapids and there was one more week to go, so she had no idea why he'd come home. If something was wrong, he wouldn't be smiling, so it couldn't be bad news that he was bringing in with the January cold. She put her crocheting aside and, with a great effort, pushed herself, and her large belly, off the couch. She waddled toward Russell. "Are you finished with your shows in Grand Rapids?"

He leaned forward to give her a kiss and then said, "No. I have to go back. The club was booked for a private party tonight, so the owner gave us the night off. I told the guys I needed to come see how you're doing."

"That was nice. Did they come too?"

Russell shook his head. "They stayed. I have to go back tomorrow."

Evelyn hid her disappointment by turning and heading to the kitchen. "Do you want something to eat? I have some left-over stew."

"I am hungry. I'll put my things up."

Evelyn turned on the light in the kitchen and opened the Frigidaire to get the bowl of stew. Then she pulled a pot out of the drawer under the stove and lit a burner, stepping back when the gas whooshed into flame. No matter how many times she did that, the sudden burst of fire always scared her.

Russell walked into the kitchen, the sleeves of his white shirt rolled up to his elbows. He sat down at the small table that was against the opposite wall from the stove and rubbed his hands together. "Got any coffee?"

"I'll make some. It'll just be a minute." Evelyn set the pot of stew to heat and picked up the aluminum coffeepot. While she prepared the coffee, she asked, "Are you doing good with your music up there?"

"I guess. People come to hear us. The club owner is pleased with the crowds."

"That's nice." Evelyn stirred the stew, which was now starting to bubble, and got a bowl out of the cabinet. One good thing about this very small kitchen. Things were really close together, so she didn't have to move much. She reached over and pulled a spoon out of the drawer under the counter, then she served up the stew.

"Thanks," Russell said, taking some crackers out of the Saltine tin on the table.

While he ate, Evelyn waited for the coffee to perk and then poured him a cup. She got a glass of milk for herself before joining him at the table. "I'm glad you came home."

He put his spoon down. "Everything okay? With the baby and all?"

"Yes. I think he's healthy and strong. He moves around a lot."

Russell smiled. "You think it's a boy?"

Evelyn shrugged. "But maybe if I say 'he' enough it will be true."

Russell chuckled, then dug back into his supper.

When he finished, he sipped his coffee while Evelyn cleaned up the kitchen, then he stood and led her by the hand to their tiny bedroom. There was a double bed pushed into one corner and the cradle for the baby on the other wall next to the bureau. Those were the only pieces of furniture that would fit in the room, but the size of the space didn't matter. This was their room. Their place for communicating without words, and Evelyn always felt so secure in his love when they were intertwined. "I've missed you, and this," he said, brushing his lips against hers as he ran a finger across her breast.

"Me too. But we must be careful for the baby."

"Is it okay?" he asked, pulling back a bit.

"Yes. Just not as..." she stopped, not sure how to say the rest. The doctor had been straightforward in telling her that intercourse should not be energetic, but the thought of saying that to Russell made her cheeks red with embarrassment.

"It's okay. I'll be careful."

Thankful that he figured out what she had not been able to say, Evelyn closed her eyes and gave herself over to the delicious sensations of being undressed, then lifted and put on the bed. There, Russell made slow, gentle love to her.

Afterward, as they lay together in the warmth of the quilt and their love, he kissed her, and then lay back on the pillow. "I wish I could just stay here."

"Why don't you?"

"I have responsibilities. To the guys. To the club owner."

That stung just a bit, but Evelyn didn't want to ruin the moment by asking him what about his responsibilities to her.

They were quiet for a few more minutes, and Evelyn thought he had gone to sleep, but then he asked, "How's your sister? She have her baby yet?"

"Not yet. It could be any time though."

"Did she move back with your mother?"

"No. She got married."

Russell turned to face her. "Married? When did that happen?"

"Two weeks ago."

"Who's the guy?"

"His name is Lester."

Russell flopped back down. Evelyn wished he wouldn't ask any more questions. She didn't want to talk about Viola and the wedding anymore. But Russell obviously did. "Is he a good man?"

"I can't say. I only met him once before."

"She deserves a good man."

Something in the way Russell said that was irksome. As if Viola was somehow above other women who might not be as special. "Every wife deserves a good man," she said, not hiding her irritation.

"Okay. Don't get all riled up on me." Russell reached over and drew her close. "I didn't mean anything by what I said."

Evelyn settled her head on his shoulder and sighed. She hated when these little twinges of jealousy cropped up. Maybe that would all stop once Viola and Lester were settled as a family. Evelyn fervently hoped so.

"I'm sorry I missed the ceremony," Russell said. "I could have come if I'd known."

"She planned it at the last minute. And I lost the paper that had the number of the club. I couldn't call you."

"The operator could have helped you."

"I know. But then I couldn't even remember the name of the club. The operator said there were lots of clubs in Grand Rapids. She couldn't try them all looking for you."

Remembering how flustered she'd been in her attempts to contact him, finally giving up in frustration, a few tears escaped and ran a warm path down her cheeks. Russell kissed one. "It's okay. Don't cry."

"I can't help it. I'm so stupid."

"Don't say that."

It was a command, not a statement, and Evelyn pulled back to look at him. His cheeks were red. "Are you angry?"

He gave a slight nod.

"At me?"

"Not you. What you said. And I didn't mean to raise my voice." He swiped a hand across his cheeks, squeezing his lower lip. "It's just that word."

"What word?"

"Stupid. My daddy told me never to call someone stupid."

"But you didn't. I did."

"Doesn't matter. It still stirs my dander," Russell said. "And you say it too much about yourself."

"It's not just my opinion. You know that."

"Yes. I remember what you said about the orphanage. But you need to quit saying it. You are not stupid. You're actually very smart."

"I am?"

"Of course you are."

That was a shock. Even when she'd first told him about what the sisters said about her, he hadn't countered their assessment of her intelligence. He'd offered a few words of concern that they could be so cruel but had said little else. At the time, Evelyn hadn't even been sure the full impact had penetrated his consciousness. How much did a man remember of what was told to him after having sex? That seemed to be the time she wanted to talk, and he indulged her, but before tonight, she'd never been sure if he really listened.

It was nice to know that he sometimes did. She snuggled closer. "Thank you."

"For what?"

"What you said."

"I meant it." He trailed a finger down her arm, then across to her breast. He teased the nipple, which immediately peaked in response. "I mean this too."

Evelyn turned her face to his, reveling in the kiss, the touch, and the feeling that everything was perfect.

17

EVELYN – MARCH 1941

E velyn felt like she had been in this labor ward for days. It had only been hours, but they were the longest and most painful hours she'd ever experienced. Each contraction that tore through her felt like someone was ripping her insides out with a garden rake. Evelyn tried to be brave, to hold back the screams, but they erupted despite her best efforts. A nurse stepped up to the bedside and put a soothing hand on Evelyn's forehead. "There, there. It will all be over soon."

"Not nearly soon enough." Evelyn forced the words out between teeth clenched against the agony. Then the intensity of the contraction slowly ebbed and the nurse wiped the warm puddle of perspiration from Evelyn's face.

"Just think," the nurse said, "when this is over, you will have a lovely baby to cherish."

The nurse meant well. Evelyn was sure of it, but right at this moment, she wasn't sure the end result would be worth the pain.

Another contraction started to build, and Evelyn tensed her body against it. Maybe she could hold it back before it became unbearable, but as it crested, pounding her body like waves pounding a beach, she knew she could no more hold this back than she could move the moon.

Soon the pain consumed her, and Evelyn was only vaguely aware of being moved, rolling down the hall on a gurney and being transferred to a hard metal table. She had only seconds to register how cold the table was before another contraction seized her, obliterating every other sensory input. Then a voice penetrated the fog of pain as another contraction crested. "Push now, Evelyn. Push, push, push."

Gritting her teeth, Evelyn did her best to comply, but it hurt so bad down there. It felt like a bowling ball was tearing her apart.

She wasn't aware of easing off her efforts until the voice called out again. "Keep pushing. Don't stop. We're almost there."

"Damn." Evelyn pushed again, and then felt a flood of wetness before the blessedness of no more pain. The contrast from one moment to the next was so dramatic she almost wished she could relive it, just to experience that profound relief once more.

———

Evelyn's eyes fluttered open, and for a few moments, she couldn't figure out where she was. Then she remembered. The ride to the hospital, the hours of terrible pain, then the blessed relief. "Russell?"

"I'm here."

She felt a touch on her hand and turned to see him. He was smiling. "Am I okay?"

"Yes."

"The baby?"

"Yes."

"Did you get your boy?"

Russell shook his head.

"Oh, I'm sorry."

He leaned in and gave her a kiss. "Don't be. It's okay. Maybe next time."

As much as Evelyn hurt all over, she didn't want to think about next time, but she couldn't help but smile when he winked. He was a charmer.

"How long have I been asleep?"

"A couple of hours. The doctor said you need plenty of rest."

"Have you seen her?"

Russell nodded and smiled again. "In the nursery. She was sleeping too."

The curtain around the bed was pushed aside and a nurse bustled in, her white uniform crisp and bright. "Sir. I'm going to have to ask you to leave. We're bringing the babies out in a few minutes."

"I can't stay?"

"No, sir. Hospital rules. Nobody can be on the floor except the mothers and the staff." With that, she turned and walked off, leaving the curtain partially open.

Russell leaned in again and kissed Evelyn. "I'll be back tomorrow after work."

Through the opening in the curtain, Evelyn could see the other side of the maternity ward where several beds jutted out from the wall. Only two were occupied. She remembered that she'd been brought here when her labor started last night, and the cries she heard from someone further down on her side of the large room were undoubtedly from other women struggling to bring new life into the world.

Evelyn had never imagined it would be so hard.

She reached down and touched her belly, now much flatter, glad that the whole ordeal was over. Well, that birthing part anyway. Motherhood was just beginning.

The nurse came through the opening in the curtain, holding a bundle wrapped tightly in a pink blanket. "Here's your little girl," she said, handing the baby over to Evelyn.

Oh my. She was so small. And so light. She felt like nothing in Evelyn's arms, and a terrible fear seized her. What was she to do with this baby? She'd never even been around something this small and fragile.

"You have to hold her head like so." The nurse adjusted Evelyn's arm to cradle the baby's head. "Don't let her head wobble."

"Wobble? Will she break?"

The nurse smiled and shook her head. "Babies are stronger than they appear. You won't break her. Unless you drop her, but I don't see that happening."

The nurse may have meant that as a joke, but it struck fear deep into Evelyn's heart. What if she did drop her? "Oh my God. I can't do this."

The nurse took Evelyn's hand and squeezed gently. "Yes, you can. Every new mother has these fears with the first one. And first babies have been surviving for centuries."

Evelyn looked at the tiny face nestled in the blanket and touched one rosy cheek. It was so soft, like nothing Evelyn had ever touched before. The baby turned her face to the touch and the nurse said, "She's ready to eat. You're lucky that she is not a screamer. Most babies are yelling for their first meal."

"What do I do?"

"Your gown opens in the front. Just help her find your nipple."

Baring her breast was a little embarrassing with the nurse standing right there, but Evelyn complied. "Will she—?"

The question wasn't even fully formed when the baby latched on to Evelyn's nipple with a surprising strength. The nurse smiled. "See. She knows just what to do."

Evelyn pulled in a quick breath. "I'm glad somebody does."

"After a few minutes, let her suckle on the other breast."

Having the baby attached to her like that brought a mix of pain and pleasure. The pleasure was not unlike what she felt when Russell fondled her breasts, and she could feel that same tingle in her privates his caresses aroused. A need. A calling out. How strange that would happen now when she was so sore down there.

"Has your mother helped you prepare for this?" the nurse asked. "Told you what to expect?"

Evelyn shook her head, then quickly before the nurse could inquire more said, "My sister just had a baby. We're learning together."

The nurse straightened the sheet and blanket at the foot of the bed. "We'll send a New Mother booklet home with you. That will give you some information. Now, if you are settled, I'll go tend to the others."

"Thank you."

After the nurse left, Evelyn looked down at her baby, who now had her eyes open. They were the deepest blue. Evelyn wondered if they would lighten and look like Russell's or turn hazel like hers. Viola had told her that babies were born blind, but Evelyn was not so sure about that. This girl-child was looking at her so intently Evelyn was sure she was looking into her very soul.

Watching the baby nurse, Evelyn was overwhelmed by this miracle of life. Nine months ago, there was nothing but passion, and now this. Slowly part of the uncertainty slipped away and was replaced by a warm feeling that was almost overwhelming in its intensity. Evelyn wondered if this was what she had heard called mother's love. Whatever it was called, it was the most delicious feeling, and Evelyn wanted it to last forever. She wondered if her mother had felt the same surge twenty-two years ago. But perhaps not. How could anyone feel this depth of love and then just walk away?

———

Late in the afternoon the next day, Russell came in humming a tune. Evelyn smiled. It was always great to hear him humming or singing as that was a clear indication of how happy he was. He leaned over and kissed her, then started to sing, "Nita, Ju a a nita."

He stopped singing. "What do you think?"

"Of what?"

"The name. Juanita. I thought it might fit our dark-haired beauty."

Evelyn didn't know what to think. They had not discussed names yet. "Is that Spanish?"

"I'm not sure. I heard Al Jolson singing it on the radio at work today, and I liked it." Russell sang a little bit more of the song, then grinned.

"You really want to name our baby Juanita?"

Russell nodded, the grin still in place.

Evelyn still wasn't sure, but she had not seen him this happy in months. Not since he'd quit playing at clubs after Grand Rapids. How could she refuse? "Can I pick the middle name?"

"Sure, but think about your middle name."

Evelyn burst out laughing.

"Louise. It goes well," Russell said. "Juanita Louise."

They were interrupted when Regina peeked around the partially open curtain. "May I come in?"

"Sure." Russell moved closer to the head of the bed, and Regina stepped in.

"Congratulations," she said, giving a nod to Evelyn and then Russell.

"Thank you." Evelyn felt like the excitement of a moment ago had gone behind some unnamed cloud. "We were just discussing names."

"Oh. Have you picked one?"

Evelyn hesitated so Russell said, "Juanita."

Regina took a moment to consider, then said. "Pretty. But very unusual."

"Yes, but Russell likes it."

"Do you?" Regina asked Evelyn.

"Of course."

There was another moment of awkward silence, and then Regina said, "What about a middle name?"

"Maybe Louise," Evelyn said.

"Really?"

Evelyn wondered about the look of surprise that crossed her mother's face but didn't get a chance to verbalize a question before Regina said, "That's my middle name."

Evelyn gave a little gasp, and Russell took her hand. "Is something wrong?"

"No," she said. "I was just surprised, that's all." She looked at her mother. "I didn't know we shared a name."

Regina fidgeted with the scarf at her neck. "When you were born, I was hoping..."

She let the sentence fade, and Evelyn waited for Regina to continue. When she didn't, Evelyn asked, "Hoping for what?"

Regina dropped her hand away from the scarf. "That maybe if we were connected by name, it would make a difference sometime in the future."

"Well it didn't, did it?"

Regina touched her hand to her mouth, as if to hold back words. Russell was stunned into silence, and part of Evelyn wanted to take the words back. Another part of her liked the discomfort they had caused her mother. She knew it was wrong to feel that way, but she couldn't control feelings that had gotten so out of control since the pregnancy. Before, she'd been better about keeping the feelings at bay and not giving voice to these caustic remarks, but more recently, they escaped without warning.

"I'm sorry," Regina said, turning away. "I'll be going."

"Wait," Russell said. "I'm sure Evelyn didn't mean—"

"It's okay." Regina turned and gave him a slight smile. "She's entitled. And I do want to go to the nursery to see the baby."

After Regina left, Russell turned to Evelyn. "Why did you do that?"

She shook her head. "I don't know."

"Someday, you're going to have to get over your past."

He said the words softly, but they still cut deep. Evelyn turned her face away from him as tears swam out of her eyes. Tears, like her emotions, seemed out of control of late.

"Hey," he said, touching her shoulder. "Don't cry. I didn't mean to upset you."

She patted his hand but didn't respond.

"Visiting hours are now over." The nurse stepped partway into the room. "You'll need to leave, sir."

"Okay. Just a minute." He leaned over and kissed Evelyn on the cheek. "I'm sorry about what I said. I love you."

It took a few minutes after he left for the words to sink in. He'd said he loved her. He'd only implied that before in song, or in kindness, but never out loud. She let the words wrap her in comfort. It didn't matter what her mother did or didn't do. Evelyn and Russell and this baby were a family, and she would not do to this child what had been done to her.

———

The first night home from the hospital, the baby cried off and on all night, and Evelyn was frantic. Was something wrong with her? Russell got up and staggered sleepily over to where Evelyn was sitting in the rocker, trying to soothe the red-faced baby. "Here. Let me take her."

Evelyn handed her over, surprised when Juanita quieted when he put her to his shoulder. He jostled her slightly and started to hum, which soothed her even more. After a few minutes, Juanita fell asleep, and he put her back into the cradle where she continued to sleep.

"Thank you," Evelyn murmured. "I didn't know what to do."

"I helped Mother with Anna when she was born. She was a fussy baby too, and music was the only thing she'd respond to."

"I don't think I'm going to be a very good mother."

"If it wasn't the middle of the night, I'd argue that point. But I'm too tired." He kissed her lightly. "You'll be just fine."

Evelyn sat in the chair for a bit longer after Russell settled under the covers on their bed. She was so glad he was home in the evenings now. Shortly before the baby was born and bills started piling up, he'd taken a job at a small tool and die shop in Detroit. Russell had said it was time he accepted the responsibility of being a husband and father, providing for his family. He also said he had no regrets about giving up the music, but Evelyn knew how disappointment could fester deep inside. She'd had plenty of experience with that. She just hoped that his disappointment wouldn't eat away at him until it hardened him.

As the days and weeks passed, Evelyn slowly gained more confidence in caring for the baby. It helped that Juanita started sleeping for longer periods at night, so Evelyn wasn't totally exhausted every day. And Russell did what he could to help in the evenings. In some ways, it was looking like Evelyn's fantasy of the perfect family could become reality. They only needed a pretty house instead of this small apartment.

One day, when they sat down to a supper of boiled vegetables and ham, Russell looked at her and said he'd like to take a trip to see his mother. "I can take a week off work in June."

Evelyn put her fork down and swallowed the bite of meat she was chewing. She didn't know how far it was to West Virginia, but she knew it was a long trip. He'd told her once before that it took over twelve hours to drive. "That would be a long drive for a short visit."

"Yes." Russell helped himself to another helping of the potatoes. "But I'm anxious for everyone to meet you and Juanita."

Evelyn remembered what Russell had told her about the odd living arrangement his mother and father had, but he'd hardly talked about them since. He'd called his mother to tell her about the wedding, then again about the baby, but there had been no other contact. Telephone calls were expensive.

"Tell me a little more about your family," Evelyn said, curiosity overriding her reticence to pry. "Are you close?"

"Sure." He shrugged. "Mother and Daddy still get along despite living separately."

"If I can ask, what do you think about that?"

"What do you mean?"

Evelyn took a moment to formulate a question. "Does it bother you that they are not together?"

He shrugged again. "A little. It's been hard on Mother. And I hated to leave when she needed my help."

"Then why did you?"

"It was her idea. She didn't want me to go into the mines. I thought I could get a job at the glass plant, but she insisted that I come work with Hoffman. She said it would be better pay up north."

"Is it?"

Russell laughed. "I think so. But since I never worked in the factory down there, I won't ever know."

Evelyn smiled and concentrated on eating for a few minutes, then asked, "Do you think they will ever reconcile?"

"I don't know, and I don't ask. That's their business." He took another bite of a potato, then raised his fork. "Listen, I know you are curious, but don't bring this all up when we visit."

"Well, I wouldn't." Evelyn took a swallow of her water. "I understand that it's private business."

He nodded and resumed eating.

The prospect of the trip was exciting, and Evelyn spent several weeks preparing. She made a couple of new dresses for her and the baby and picked up two suitcases at a thrift store. In the days before they were to leave, she washed and ironed and carefully folded the clothes to pack.

During all the preparations, Evelyn grew even more eager to meet Russell's family, despite her worry that they might not like her. Russell assured her over and over that they would. "They couldn't not like the woman I married," he told her one night.

His affirmation had made her smile, but she was still apprehensive. She had never even spoken to his mother, and now she was going to spend several days in her house?

18

EVELYN – MAY 1941

One good thing about the long car ride to West Virginia was the fact that the movement kept the baby quiet. Juanita only woke up when the car stopped, which didn't happen often enough to suit Evelyn. Not that she wanted the baby to be awake and crying to eat again, but the seats in the car were hard and uncomfortable. Every bump in the road made her tailbone ache. Plus, she thought Russell was driving much too fast. He'd told her he had to so they could make good time, which is also why he didn't want to stop until he needed gas. Every stop cost precious minutes, so it was better for them to take care of everything in one stop. Get gas, use the facilities, buy some food, and then get back on the road and eat along the way.

Evelyn understood the logic of all that, it was just that her body didn't always cooperate. "Can we stop, Russell?"

He shot her a look. "Can't you wait? We're almost there."

"Please. I would like to freshen up before meeting your mother."

Russell sighed. "Alright. I'll stop at the next gas station."

Evelyn was sure another short break would be good for Russell too. They had been driving for nearly ten hours. The first five, mostly in the dark, hadn't been too bad, and Evelyn had even dozed a bit when sleepiness engulfed her. They'd been able to go faster through the flatter land of Ohio, but as they got into Pennsylvania, the terrain had changed to low hills and winding roads. Then the low hills had turned into mountains, and the last few hours had been trying. She could tell that Russell was tired, and that made him irritable. Did she dare suggest that he wash up and comb his hair?

Glancing at how tightly he was gripping the steering wheel, she decided against it.

After the hasty stop, they drove for another hour and a half in the twisting mountain roads. The scenery was stunning, but the sheer drop to the right made Evelyn's nerves jangle when she dared to look down. Finally, after going halfway up a very steep hill—the car engine groaning and almost stopping at one point—Russell turned onto a dirt street, then stopped in front of the fourth house from the corner. Evelyn looked out to see a pretty brick house, not unlike some of the houses in Detroit. A tiny, spry woman came down the steps from a porch that was nearly hidden behind a tall, dark green hedge. Small pink and white flowers bordered both sides of the walk up to the house. The woman stopped halfway down.

Evelyn smoothed the skirt of her cotton dress and waited for Russell to come around and open her door. For once, Juanita did not waken when the car stopped, so Evelyn let her sleep in the space they had made for her in the back and stepped out to meet her mother-in-law. Russell took her elbow and led her up the sidewalk, then he let go to give his mother a brief hug before presenting Evelyn. That he knew how to do it very properly surprised her, as did Emma's curt nod, before she said, "Come in and eat. Beans are ready."

During the drive, Russell had told Evelyn a little about what to expect, especially the fact that food was a major part of life with his family. No matter where they would go, the coffee would always be hot and the beans were always simmering on the stove. And there was plenty of cornbread and biscuits to sop up the juice. The affection he felt for his family was apparent in the stories he told, yet there had been so little displayed in the greeting she was left wondering. And the cool reception from her mother-in-law was disconcerting.

Emma went inside, and Russell helped Evelyn get the baby and a few bags out of the car. "I'll get the rest later," he said, leading her into the house.

The interior was surprisingly cool, considering the temperature outside was scorching, and they stepped directly into a living room that had a fireplace adjacent to the front door. The fireplace faced two large windows on the opposite wall, where Evelyn could see that the house butted up to the side of the hill, letting in very little light.

Emma came into the living room and walked over to Evelyn, who was still holding Juanita. "This your girl?"

"Yes. Her name's Juanita."

"Odd name for a baby," Emma said. "Never heard none like it before."

Russell dropped the suitcase he was holding and stepped closer. "I heard it in a song."

"Did you now?"

"Yup."

"Well, okay then." Emma stepped closer to look at the baby. "She's a purty little thing. Looks like you, Russell."

"She does have his hair," Evelyn said. "And her eyes are the same clear blue. You'll see when she wakes up."

"Let her sleep for now. You can take this here room." Emma led them into a bedroom that opened right next to the fireplace.

Stepping in, Evelyn saw a double four-poster bed with a lovely heirloom quilt. At the sight of a cradle next to the bed, Evelyn warmed a bit to her mother-in-law, who had obviously taken some pains to prepare for the visit. So maybe the odd greeting was just the older woman's way, as Russell had told her. Smiling in relief, Evelyn gently put Juanita down, careful not to jostle her awake.

"Come into the kitchen when you're ready," Emma said. "You can wash up in there." She pointed out a second doorway in the bedroom to a hall that had an open door to the bathroom. Evelyn could see a washbasin against the wall.

"You go first," Russell said after his mother walked out. "I'll get the rest of our things."

Evelyn stepped into the large bathroom, noting the claw-foot tub along one wall, the commode on the back wall, and the washbasin in front. A little window to the left of the basin offered a view of the house next door, which was only a sliver of yellow siding above a sidewalk that separated the houses. The close proximity was a bit unnerving, but Evelyn figured since she could see no windows, nobody could peek in unless they took great pains to lean way down as they passed by.

Evelyn quickly took care of business, then stepped into the hall, glancing to her left where she saw a doorway to the kitchen. She went in and found Russell there at the table that was set for two. She hardly had time to wonder about that before Emma said, "Sit right there by Russell. I'll bring the food."

Which she did, never once sitting down herself. She kept an attentive eye on her guests and was quick to bring more cornbread or another helping of beans. Evelyn noticed that Emma had a small bowl on a little counter next to the stove. When she wasn't serving them, Emma would spoon a few bites.

"Wouldn't you like to sit down?" Evelyn looked over at Emma.

Russell laughed. "I don't ever recall my mother sitting at the table."

Over the course of the week-long visit, Evelyn discovered that was the way with most of the women in the family, except Anna, who was the youngest and not married. At every home, they visited the men, children, and guests gathered at the table and were served by the woman of the house. Being the only adult female to be seated most of the time made Evelyn a bit uncomfortable, but her offers to help were brushed aside.

Everybody was very polite, and Evelyn never had a moment to be hungry, but there was a certain coolness that seemed led by Emma. Sometimes conversations stopped abruptly when Evelyn walked into a room, and she was never sure if it was because they were discussing private family business or perhaps talking about her. In an effort to win them over, Evelyn tried her best to be a good guest, tending to the baby quickly when she cried, offering to help clean up after a meal, and smiling politely at everyone, but the sheer number of people was often overwhelming. She thought perhaps Loren's wife, Erma, would be the friendliest, both of them being in-laws, but she never had much time with Erma to see if that would be true.

Russell's father, Sheridan, came to some of the dinners, but not all. Evelyn found it a bit strange that he came and went like that, and nobody said anything about it. She was eager to know more about the estrangement and the odd way everyone had of handling it, but she wouldn't dare to ask. A couple of times, she tried to find out more about how Russell might feel about it, but he deflected her questions when they were alone. Sheridan was a pleasant man, and Evelyn could see the strong family resemblance of father and sons. During the meals, the men talked about farms or the coal mines, and the women talked about quilting and the next session of making apple butter. Since Evelyn did neither, she felt very much the outsider, struggling just to keep a polite smile on her face.

Late the third evening of the visit, Evelyn took advantage of the privacy of their little bedroom and asked Russell what she needed to do to make his mother and sisters warm up to her.

"Is that why you've been so quiet?" he asked, taking off his trousers and laying them across the trunk at the foot of the bed.

"I don't know what to say." Evelyn lifted a sleeping baby out of the crib and laid her on the bed for a diaper change. Juanita often slept through the night with a fresh diaper late in the evening.

"They're women." Russell put on his pajamas. "What do women talk about?"

Evelyn glanced at him to make sure he wasn't joking. "Don't you listen at the table?"

He shrugged and Evelyn shook her head. "I'm excluded when your mother and sisters talk about sewing and canning."

"You could join in."

"And say what? I have nothing to contribute." Evelyn put Juanita back in the cradle, thankful that the baby had barely stirred during the change. "They never invite me to talk about things I like. I did ask what books they read, and they all just stared at me."

Russell laughed. "We're not much on books here."

"I gathered."

At the petulant tone in her voice, Russell walked over and put his arm around her. "Just relax and give it some time."

"I don't think your mother likes me."

"Don't be silly. It's just her way. If she didn't like you, she wouldn't offer a second helping of beans."

"Don't make jokes. I'd just like some indication that I'm truly welcome into the family."

Russell huffed. "You're making too much of this. I told you that we aren't a family that shows much affection. Or talks about feelings. Things just are. And you are in the family."

Evelyn sat on the edge of the bed and kicked off her shoes. She didn't want to fuss at Russell anymore. He'd been looking forward to this visit with his family, so she could hardly whine and ask him to pay more attention to her. But that's what she wanted him to do. She wanted him to be so proud to be married to her that he made her the centerpiece of his life, especially here among strangers. She sighed. That was the way it happened in novels. Could real life ever be the same?

Standing, she took off her dress then went over and hung it in the closet. Then she put on her light cotton nightgown, turned off the light, and slipped into the bed where Russell was already stretched out, uncovered. It was warm, so she didn't pull the sheet over them. He rolled over and nuzzled her neck. When he spooned her, she could feel his hardness pressing into her hip; her body responded as it always did.

"Russell, we can't," she said as his advances became more insistent. "The bed squeaks. She'll know."

He chuckled. "She knows where babies come from."

"It's not funny. I don't want her to hear us."

"Okay. I'll be quiet." He trailed his fingers down her tummy and then...

Then there was no turning back.

Afterward, when they were sated, Evelyn rested her head on his shoulder and let the contentment wash over her, along with the slight breeze from the fan that dried the sweat. These were the moments when her doubts were stilled and she believed in his love. The moments right after they had been so wonderfully joined.

Listening to his gentle snore as he fell asleep, Evelyn resolved to hang on to these perfect feelings, keep her concerns at bay, and just enjoy the rest of the vacation.

———

Most evenings Russell, his brother, Loren, and his sister, Anna, played guitar and sang, their voices blending in lovely harmony. The nights Sheridan was there, he joined in as well. He had a beautiful baritone voice, and it was obvious where the musical talent originated. It was also obvious that the music bonded them as a family. It may have even been a substitute for open affection. Watching them sing and play their instruments gave Evelyn another glimpse of what the music really meant to her husband. It was a family legacy that went much deeper than what it appeared to be on the surface. As they sang, they looked at each other, exchanging glances that seemed to be sending silent messages.

There was one last get-together the evening before Russell and Evelyn planned to head back to Michigan. The entire family was invited, including Sheridan, Loren, and Erma. Russell's two other sisters, Opal and Maesel, came as well, bringing their husbands and children, which made quite a houseful for supper and for singing afterward. It was a warm, humid evening, but windows were opened to let in the breeze and fans were turned on.

Once the fried chicken, beans, and cornbread were thoroughly disposed of, the kids spilled out onto the front porch and the grownups gathered in the front room, where it was a bit cooler than in the kitchen. Evelyn sat in the rocking chair in the corner next to Erma, who was in a ladder-back chair. Evelyn held Juanita, who was smiling and cooing. Erma leaned over. "She likes the music."

"Yes. She's always happy when Russell plays his guitar and sings."

"Does he do that often?"

"As much as he can. But he's busy. He works a lot."

Erma gave a slight shake of her head. "It's too bad he couldn't keep playing professionally. He's good enough."

At first, Evelyn wasn't sure how to respond to that. Was there an undertone of judgment in the comment? "Well, yes. It is too bad. But it was a decision he made freely."

"I see."

Again, a tone that didn't set well, but Evelyn pulled on her earlier resolve and tamped down her paranoia. She smiled and said, "Russell is a good man. A good husband. And a good father."

Erma nodded. "So is Loren. They take after their father."

Again, Evelyn was uncertain about a response. She'd promised Russell not to bring up the subject of his parents' odd arrangement, but she couldn't just let Erma's last comment stand. Evelyn took a breath, then said, "But he left."

Erma waved off the comment. "Just because he and Emma have some problems doesn't mean he isn't a good man."

Evelyn couldn't argue with that, but she was still curious as to what had happened and how Emma and Sheridan had come to the point of living in two separate places. There seemed to be no rancor between them, which made it even more puzzling.

Despite the loud singing and the noise of the kids running in and out, Juanita fell asleep in Evelyn's arms a little after eight, so Evelyn took her into the bedroom, closed the door to the front room, and put Juanita in the crib. Then Evelyn went out the other door to the hall and crossed to the bathroom. After taking care of her business, she stepped out and heard voices in the kitchen. She started toward the doorway when she saw Emma and Opal but stopped abruptly when she could make out some of the conversation. "He says not. But I know she trapped him."

Evelyn pulled back into the shadows, her heart thumping. Even though she didn't know who had said it, there was no mistaking the meaning.

"She seems nice enough."

"I told him to be careful of those big city girls."

It was hard to be sure, but Evelyn suspected that it was Emma who said the hurtful things. Had the women been talking about her and Russell and the marriage like that all along? All those quickly ended conversations she'd stumbled into the past few days. Was this... this belief that Russell was trapped what caused the undertone in Erma's voice earlier? And if they were so free in discussing her situation, why were they so circumspect when it came to talking about Sheridan? A flare of anger propelled her into the kitchen, just to see if the women would be embarrassed to be caught in this uncharitable conversation, but they turned to her without reaction. "Do you need something?" Opal asked.

"I did not force Russell to do anything he didn't want to. You need to know that."

Evelyn quickly turned and went back into the bathroom. She did not want those women to see the tears pouring out of her eyes. She stayed there for a full five minutes, then she splashed her face with cold water before crossing to the bedroom and slipping through that door to the front room. Emma and Opal were there, but they kept silent about the confrontation. Luckily, Russell was so engrossed in the music that he didn't notice the chill in the room.

The magic was gone from the evening, but Evelyn put on her bravest smile and got through it until company left. She was so hurt and so humiliated she didn't even want to talk about it later when they retired to the bedroom. She was thankful that Russell was so exhausted that he went right to sleep.

Early the next morning, they packed up the car for the trip back home. As they transported the luggage, Evelyn said nothing about what had transpired between her and Emma and Opal. She was surprised that Emma had loaded them down with food. There were a dozen jars of green beans and as many of apple butter, along with fried chicken, sliced fresh vegetables, and biscuits to eat on the road. Evelyn accepted the gifts and the cool embrace from her mother-in-law, but she knew the generosity was more for Emma's beloved son than for the woman who had ruined his life.

She could hardly hold back the tears as they drove away, and Russell picked up on her mood. He shot her a quick glance and said, "I'm always a little sad to leave too."

If only he knew.

———

They drove well into the night, and the sky was black as ink when they finally drove up to the front of the apartment house. As quickly as they could, they got everything unloaded, had a bite to eat, and settled the baby down for what was left of the night. Russell was helping Evelyn put the canned goods his mother had sent with them into a cabinet when she suddenly threw a jar across the room, splattering the wall with apple butter.

"What the hell?!" Russell took three quick steps and grabbed her arm, turning her to face him. "Why'd you do that?"

"I'll clean it up." Evelyn couldn't look him in the eye and fought to keep her lip from trembling and hot, wet tears from falling.

"Tell me what's wrong." He accompanied the demand with a not-so-gentle shake.

"Okay." Evelyn pulled back, her anger providing the courage to let the words tumble out. "Your mother told Opal that I tricked you into marriage."

"That's ridiculous. She would never say a thing like that."

"No?" Evelyn let that question hang there for a moment, then asked, "And where might she have gotten the idea you were tricked?"

Russell didn't respond, the telltale signs of his anger brewing in the red spots on his cheeks, but Evelyn didn't back down. "Is that what you told her? That I got pregnant on purpose to trap you? So she can hold a grudge against me the rest of her life?"

Russell pushed past her, shoving her roughly out of the way. "Don't you ever talk about my mother that way again."

"Or what? You want to hit me? Go ahead. Hit me. I don't care."

Russell paused and balled his fists, and for a moment, Evelyn thought he would follow through. She braced herself for the blow that never came as he stormed out of the room. "I'm going to bed. I have to go to work in the morning."

Evelyn went over to clean up the mess, careful not to cut herself as she picked out the shards of glass, then scooped the globs of apple butter up with a spatula, dumping that in the trash on top of the glass. Then she mopped the floor and washed the residue of apple butter from the wall. The work gave her time to regret her childish display of temper. She shouldn't have confronted Russell about this tonight. Not when he was so tired from the long drive. Of course, he would be short tempered. But wasn't a husband supposed to put his wife above his mother?

Evelyn leaned on the handle of the mop, thinking about the

interplay between Russell and Emma. It was love. Real love. The way a mother loves a child and wants the best for him.

A pang of longing hit her so hard Evelyn stood stock still for a moment, while the tears ran warm down her cheeks. Again, she was that little girl wanting—

Evelyn shook the tears and the thoughts away. It did her no good to cry and even less to wish. She busied herself with the last of the cleanup and then put the cleaning supplies away, turning out the light as she left the kitchen.

When she went into the bedroom, Russell was already fast asleep. Juanita was whimpering, so Evelyn quietly changed the wet diaper, then slipped into bed, careful not to disturb Russell. This was the first big fight they'd had since they married. Actually, it was the first big fight ever, and Evelyn couldn't believe how she had challenged him. Part of her wanted to reach across the invisible barrier between them. Wake him up and tell him she was sorry for creating a scene. Then he might hold her. Comfort her. Make her feel loved. But she was afraid to touch the sleeping bear.

19

EVELYN – JUNE–DECEMBER 1941

E velyn stood and stared at the house in dismay. It really wasn't a house, just a framed structure with a roof and tar paper on the outside walls. How could Russell have been so excited about this?

He'd come home from work last week happier than she had seen him since their vacation and told her about the man who wanted to sell the house. Harold Murphy was a friend of Hoffman and had started to build the place for his wife. They had only been married a few years and this was going to be the home where they would raise their family. Last month, the wife had been killed in a car accident, and Harold couldn't face the job of finishing the house and living there alone. He wanted to get rid of the place as quickly as he could, so he was practically giving it away.

As much as Evelyn wanted to move out of the small apartment that had gotten considerably more cramped when the baby was born in March, it didn't feel right that their good fortune should come at the expense of someone's ill fortune.

And the house wasn't even ready to move in. She had no idea how long it would take to make it livable.

"What do you think?" Russell asked.

"It's barely even started." Evelyn wiped the sweat from her forehead then put her handkerchief back into the pocket of her light cotton dress. It was already summer-hot even though it was only mid-June.

"I know it looks rough," Russell said. "But the hardest part is done. Look. It has a basement. That and framing are the hardest parts of building. We can finish it. We can work together when I get home from the shop."

"I don't know anything about that kind of work. And I've got the baby to take care of." Evelyn shifted a restless Juanita from her hip to her shoulder, patting her to quiet her down.

Russell stepped closer to the house and ran his hand down one of the corner beams. "We shouldn't pass this up, Evelyn."

There was a tone in his voice that Evelyn recognized. He was normally easygoing and not demanding, but now and then, he had to let her know that he was the man. The head of the house. The boss. She never fought him when he took a stand, figuring she could bow to his wishes when she had to in order to keep him happy. The doubts raised by the experience with his family earlier in the summer had never quite gone away, and even though she and Russell had since eased back into a somewhat comfortable routine, she knew the marriage would only work if she made him happy instead of angry. This was one of those times that she could make the choice to keep peace, so she swallowed her protests and nodded. "Whatever you think."

"Okay." Russell smiled. "I'll let Mr. Murphy know."

———

Every weekday evening for the next three months, Russell went to work on the house, only stopping at the apartment first for a quick supper after his shift at the shop. It was hard on Evelyn to be alone with the baby all day long and then well into the evening, but it was good to see Russell so happy to be able to provide a better home for them. Since weekends were the only times they could spend much time together, Evelyn went with Russell on Saturdays to help however she could. Now and then, she would hand him a tool, or a piece of wood, but often, she just sat with the baby and watched. Most Saturdays it was fun. She'd pack a picnic lunch, and at noon, they'd sit in the shade of the big elm tree in the back and eat sandwiches and drink iced tea out of Mason jars.

Today, the August sun beat down without mercy, and Evelyn was reluctant to leave the comfort of the shade. Juanita was sleeping on a blanket on the other side of the picnic basket. Katydids buzzed in the tree, and Evelyn felt her eyelids start to droop as she sat there.

Russell moved closer and pulled her over. "Maybe we should take a nap... or something."

He ran his hand along her thigh, and there was no doubt what the "something" might be. "Russell! We can't. Not here in broad daylight. What if somebody saw us?"

"We're hidden by the house. And the tree. Nobody can see us."

Even though she was tempted—her body always seemed to respond to him no matter what her mind was saying—she was relieved when Juanita started to cry, and she didn't have to admit that she was too embarrassed to do it out in the open like this. "I have to see to the baby."

"Damn!" Russell got up abruptly and stomped back to the construction, hefting a piece of sheetrock.

Evelyn knew he was disappointed. And maybe even a little

mad. She could tell by the way he moved. The first few months they'd been married, they had sex every night. Sometimes twice a night. Evelyn had worried that there was something wrong with how much she wanted him. It just didn't feel right. But Viola told her that being horny was part of being pregnant. Evelyn appreciated the explanation, but did wish Viola wasn't always so vulgar in her language.

Whatever was making Evelyn so wanton—it seemed more ladylike to use that term rather than horny—Russell took full advantage, and he seemed to think it was all perfectly normal. Then, after the baby was born the opportunities to take advantage were less and less. Too many times, like today, a crying baby interfered.

After settling Juanita back down, Evelyn went to where Russell was nailing up a piece of sheetrock. The way he was wielding the hammer, Evelyn could tell he was still angry. "I'm sorry," she said. "I had to—"

"Forget it."

The words matched the rhythm of the hammer, and Evelyn winced. "The baby cried. What was I supposed to do?"

"I said forget it."

His tone was sharp and she fired back. "It wasn't my fault."

He stopped hammering for a moment and faced her, red splotches forming on his cheeks. "Let it be," he said.

Normally, she would let it be, but her own anger trampled any sense of reason. "You don't have to get so mad just because you couldn't have your way."

"I'm not mad. Just frustrated."

"You sure look angry to me."

He turned back to his work. "You don't know how I'm feeling. Just leave me alone."

Evelyn retreated to the blanket where Juanita was still sleeping.

When the shadows of dusk approached, Russell loaded his tools in the trunk of the car, and Evelyn packed up the picnic basket, slipping it into the back seat along with a bag with diapers and bottles for the baby. "Ready?" Russell asked. The first thing he'd said to her since the argument and the second to the last thing he said to her that day.

After they got home, he washed up and changed clothes, then walked to the front door. Evelyn turned from the stove where she'd started heating some leftover stew for supper. "Where are you going?"

"Out."

She motioned to the pot on the stove. "Don't you want to eat?"

The sound of the door slamming was the only response.

Evelyn ate her meal in solitude. She took care of the baby when she woke up for her supper, then went to bed as soon as Juanita was asleep again. Sometime in the night, Russell came home and slipped into bed beside her. He brought the strong stench of beer and cigarette smoke with him, so she turned her back.

———

Summer turned into fall and then into winter, and still the house was not finished. All the extra work put a strain on them both. If Russell wasn't gone in the evenings, he was dozing on the couch after supper. Evelyn tried to be patient. She tried to be a better wife, but little things upset him. Like his response to her burning the roast. "We don't have enough money to waste it burning food."

When he snapped at her, she tried to hold her temper back, but there were times it flared, and they would be at each other like two angry cats.

This wasn't the life she wanted. The life she'd dreamed about, but it was what she had, and sometimes, when they weren't fighting, it was almost good. The good happened on the rare days Russell would stay home and not fall asleep after supper. He'd get out his guitar and sing, much to the delight of Juanita, who would clap her hands and grin. During those peaceful evenings, Evelyn felt the tension between them ease, and afterward, in the dark of night, he might turn to her to make love.

Sundays were the most pleasant. Despite his feelings about church, Russell always agreed to watch Juanita in the morning so Evelyn could go to church, which is what she was doing this cold December day.

Wrapped in a heavy coat and scarf, Evelyn walked to the church a few blocks from their apartment. The first snow of the winter feathered the ground, but thankfully, the sidewalks were still clear. Snow clung to the branches of trees that lined the sidewalk, and the wind blew chunks off that stung her face, so she hurried. Once inside, she brushed the moisture off her coat, removed her scarf, and settled in a pew toward the back. When the Mass started, she listened to the priest drone on while her mind wandered. She'd long ago given up on any attempt to follow what the priest was saying at the altar. It was all in Latin, and even though she could use the Missal that had English on one side, she didn't want to bother as she never could read fast enough to keep up. The only Latin she remembered from all those chapel days at the orphanage was what the priest would say as some kind of greeting, "Dominus vobiscum." To which the congregation was to respond, "Et cum spiritu tuo."

There were other places in the service where the people were allowed to speak, but Evelyn could never remember when, so she was content to be quiet and let the priest's unintelligible words wash over her. Here, now, in this church in

Detroit, it didn't matter if Evelyn said the responses or not. There were no nuns to scowl their disapproval.

The drone of the priest's voice was rhythmic, almost like music, and a soothing backdrop to whatever issue Evelyn wanted to fret about.

Today, she was fretting about the state of Russell's soul. She wished he would come to church with her and had even asked him a number of times, but he'd recently told her to stop asking. He'd reminded her of what he'd said about church the first time the subject had come up, and that feeling had not changed. He was not joining a church even if that meant going to hell when he died. Which he said he did not believe would happen. Of course, Evelyn had been told that anyone who didn't go to church would definitely go to hell. It wasn't something she wanted for Russell, or their daughter, who was still not baptized.

Evelyn sighed. This was just one of the things they fussed about. The tension that had been slowly building between them since last summer would ebb and flow, depending on Russell's mood, and she didn't know what to do. She made herself available to him for sex, even though her body had lost most of its heat. Caring for the baby took so much of her energy, and she didn't feel pretty, what with the extra pooch to her belly that hadn't gone away since Juanita was born. And he stayed away so much, either working on the house or going out after work with the guys; it was almost like living with a stranger. She sometimes thought that if they could share one thing, church, it might make a difference. And she wouldn't have to worry about him going to hell.

Still, Russell was good with the baby when he was home. And maybe, when Juanita was older and Evelyn was not so tired, they could get back to the excitement of those early months of marriage. The memory was pleasant, and she momentarily gave herself over to it then stopped. Was it sacrilegious to think about sex at church? That thought made her chuckle, much to the dismay of the woman next to her. Now there was a scowl of disproval.

When the last "amen" was said, Evelyn left the warmth of the church and turned down the street that would eventually take her to the apartment. She didn't mind the walk, not even in the cold, but on this blustery day, she was glad she only had to walk a few blocks. She glanced at the sky and saw dark clouds hanging heavy overhead. More snow was coming, so she hurried her steps. This would be a good afternoon to stay in and listen to the radio. The Philco console was a gift from Hoffman when he and his wife got a new radio, and Evelyn was thankful for the generosity. The radio provided hours of entertainment when Russell was away. She especially liked *The Inner Sanctum Mysteries* and *The Great Gildersleeve*. When she'd first heard the show, she laughed at the name, and even Russell laughed when she told him about it.

Evelyn stepped into the apartment and slipped out of her coat, hanging it on the hall tree by the door. The living area of the apartment was one large room with the kitchen to the left. Russell sat on the sofa with his guitar. "The baby's asleep," he said.

"Good. I'll set the roast to cook for our dinner."

"Won't burn it this time, will you?"

Alarmed, Evelyn turned quickly and relaxed when she saw his smile. She smiled back. When he teased her like that, it seemed nothing would go wrong, at least for a day. "I'll set the timer."

Russell grinned then continued strumming his guitar.

"Do you want anything in the meantime?"

He shook his head. "I had toast and jam a little while ago. I'll wait."

Evelyn peeled carrots, potatoes, and onions and arranged them in a big pot with the roast, thinking about how many Sundays she'd done this. Pot roast had been a staple at Sarah's house, and there was always something so comforting in the peaceful Sunday afternoons with the family gathered around the table.

When Juanita cried, Evelyn started to wipe her hands on her apron to tend to her, but Russell held up a hand. "I'll get her." He put his guitar away, wiping the strings with a soft cloth before closing the case, and then ambled into the bedroom. A few minutes later, he came back, Juanita giggling in his arms. He walked over and turned on the radio before sitting down on the couch.

Evelyn had to smile. Her husband and baby laughing in the living room. Evelyn happy to be cooking dinner. This reality could almost match her fantasy.

Later, sitting at the table with Russell, Juanita in a high-chair between them, Evelyn played some more with the fantasy, creating a mental picture of what her family might look like ten years from now. Juanita would be a young lady, and maybe there would be other children. They would live in a red brick—

"Listen." The outburst shattered the peacefulness of that daydream.

There was an unmistakable urgency in Russell's voice, but Evelyn had no idea why. "What?" she asked.

"On the radio."

She had been only half aware of the radio playing in the living room, and the fact that the music had stopped had not penetrated her musings. "What's happening?"

"A news bulletin. I think a man said there was an attack. On an American naval base."

"What? Where?"

Russell held up his hand to quiet her, and they both heard, "The naval base at Pearl Harbor was attacked by Japanese planes early this morning."

"Oh my God," Evelyn said. "That can't be true."

"Wait." Russell got up from the table and went into the living room to turn up the volume on the radio.

"Details are sketchy," the reporter said. "Stay tuned to World News Today for updates. I repeat this news bulletin just in. The Japanese attacked Pearl Harbor today, sinking several ships and killing hundreds of people."

Evelyn walked over to stand beside Russell. "Do you suppose this could be a hoax? Like that one a few years ago? When that actor tricked us about an invasion from Mars?"

Russell shrugged. "Nobody should joke about something like this."

Evelyn thought nobody should have joked about an alien invasion, either, but she didn't voice that opinion.

After a few moments of static and garbled transmission, the reporter came back on air. "Ladies and gentlemen, I have the first eyewitness account of the horror that is happening in Hawaii. This comes from an NBC Blue Network reporter who climbed to the roof of a building in downtown Honolulu, microphone in hand. He said, 'This battle has been going on for nearly three hours... It's no joke, it's a real war.'"

"Oh no." Evelyn sank into a nearby chair. "That's terrible."

They listened to the report for a few more minutes as the announcer said that their country needed all able-bodied men to join up to fight the Japanese.

Russell stood. It was as if he needed to do that for this declaration. "First thing tomorrow, I'm going to enlist."

"Enlist?" She looked at him, aghast. "You could get killed."

"Don't think that way."

"How should I think?"

"That I will do my duty and make it out alive."

"But what about me? The baby? The house?"

"That can wait."

"You would just leave me and maybe never come back?"

Russell grabbed her gently by the shoulders. "Evelyn. Don't you understand what has just happened? Our country has been attacked. We have to defend ourselves."

"Why can't single men with no families do the defending?"

Russell dropped his hands and shook his head. "This is not open for discussion."

The peaceful afternoon Evelyn had anticipated was shattered by the news on the radio and Russell's declaration. She was so stunned she couldn't let her mind even consider the possibility that he would go off to fight in this war and perhaps never come back.

———

At the shop on Monday, all the guys were talking about those dirty rotten Japs and how they wanted to go kill all the fuckers. While Russell wanted to join up, he wasn't so sure about the killing. He remembered how he always had to look away when his mother killed the chicken for Sunday dinner. When he was a young teen, his sister, Anna, laughed and teased him about it, saying he shouldn't make their poor mama do that nasty job. Truth was, Russell hated the idea of killing of any kind. He accompanied friends on hunting trips because that's what boys and men were supposed to do, but he only enjoyed the comradery and the whiskey they put in the coffee at the end of the day. He left the killing to the others.

Despite his misgivings about actual combat, when the shift ended at five, Russell went with one of the guys, Gary, to the army recruiting office. Lots of men were eager to sign up, and they joined the group, first filling out forms, then moving into another area for an initial physical screening. That entailed an eye test, and Russell was surprised when he was turned down because he was colorblind. He hadn't even thought about that for years, having grown accustomed to his black and white and gray world, and he really didn't see what difference it made. But the doctor was adamant as he stamped Russell's paperwork "ineligible." The army wanted men with perfect vision.

Russell drove slowly, trying to get rid of his anger and frustration before he got home. Evelyn hated his flares of anger, so he tried to keep them out of the house as much as he could. It wasn't her fault that there had been so many disappointments that made him feel inadequate. First it was the music. The dream of being a performer blown away by responsibility. Not that he didn't love his daughter. He did. He just wished she'd waited a few more years before arriving.

By the time he got home, he'd calmed down some, but he still walked into the apartment and threw his coat in the general direction of the hall tree. It fell to the floor in a heap. He saw Evelyn on the sofa feeding Juanita a bottle. Evelyn had seen him toss the coat. It was so unlike him that she asked, "What's wrong?"

He shrugged.

Evelyn put the baby on her shoulder to burp and said, "I can tell something's the matter."

Russell walked back and picked up his coat. "I was rejected."

"Rejected? From what?"

"From doing my duty?"

"What?"

"I went to the recruiting station with a buddy from work. Went through all the paperwork. Then found out I can't serve because I'm colorblind."

Evelyn lowered Juanita to her arms and put the bottle back into the eager mouth. "I don't understand."

Russell turned to face her after putting his coat on the rack. "I don't see colors."

"None?"

He nodded.

"I never heard of that."

"It's not common."

"Oh. Why didn't you ever tell me?"

Russell went to the kitchen and lit the fire up under the coffee pot. "It never came up. And I hardly think about it anymore." He turned and faced her. "Until today."

Evelyn brought the baby to her shoulder for another burp."What are you going to do?"

"Keep working. A lot of the tool and die shops will change manufacturing to support the war effort." He tried to keep his tone confident, but he couldn't hold back a surge of frustration.

"I'm sorry. I know you're disappointed."

He shrugged, then got a mug out of the cabinet. He poured the steaming coffee before turning back to watch Evelyn finish with Juanita. There were times his heart swelled with love for his family. Which was good, because there were plenty of times that Evelyn made loving hard. And despite how much he wanted to join the other men in fighting against that evil monster that had attacked his country, this family was his responsibility, and maybe it was better that he stay here.

20

EVELYN – DECEMBER 1942

Evelyn had started to wonder if the war would ever end. It had gone on for a whole year, and she was dismayed when the news broadcasts included the numbers of men who had been killed. Whenever she went out, to the store or to walk to church, her stomach would clench when she saw the gold stars in neighbors' windows, black wreaths on the doors. She told herself not to look. She didn't have to look. She could just walk on by. But something always nudged her to take a quick glance. And always there would be one more.

At first, she didn't know what those stars meant, but Russell told her it was a sign that the family had lost a son in combat. At the time, Evelyn thought it odd that the family would get a gold star, but as the weeks and months of the war dragged on, and she saw more and more of the stars, it had gone from odd to incredibly sad.

She never told Russell how relieved she was that he had been rejected, but she knew he wasn't. The first time he hit her was because she had voiced that. It wasn't really much of a hit. More like a push, but it had been strong enough that her head banged into the sheetrock. Luckily, she was not hurt physically, but the fact that he could do that made her stomach clench. He was acting out of frustration. She knew that. But the knowing didn't make his anger any easier to take.

Today, he was hanging curtain rods in the living room. The walls were still bare sheetrock, but she had told him she wanted curtains before Christmas. He had two weeks. She walked into the room after putting Juanita down for the night and saw that the brackets were not even. She pointed to one, "That one is too low."

"I measured. They're even."

"No, they're not. From here, I can see the one on the left is a little lower."

"What does it matter?"

"I don't want crooked curtains."

"It's only temporary." He stepped down from the ladder.

"Everything in this house is only temporary. I'm so tired of it."

"What do you want me to do about it?"

"Fix it." Evelyn poked him in the chest, and he reached out to push her away. The push was hard. Full of anger. And she hit the wall so hard it left a large dent.

She stepped away, rubbing the back of her head.

"Oh, Evelyn. I'm so sorry." He started to step toward her, but she held up a hand to keep him away. "Believe me. I didn't mean—"

Hand still raised to wave him off, Evelyn went into the kitchen, got a glass of water, and sat down at the table. A few minutes later, Russell came in, looking every inch the repentant child. "Do you need anything?"

The question was so ludicrous she shook her head in disbelief. "Do not hit me again."

"I didn't—"

A raised hand stilled his words. "My head hurts too much to argue."

"Can I get you an aspirin?"

"Just let me be."

He did.

That night, he slept on the couch, and the night after that. It took several days for the ice between them to thaw enough that they could be more than civil to each other.

On the fourth day, Evelyn looked at him across the supper table and said, "We need to do what we can to make Christmas good for Juanita."

Russell put down his fork, nodding.

"So can we be more than polite to each other? For her?"

Russell nodded again.

———

This Christmas was going to be a meager one. Right after America joined the war effort following the Pearl Harbor attack, the government had started rationing rubber and gasoline. Food products were also rationed, and Evelyn often felt pressured by the folks waiting in line behind her at the checkout. Evelyn would try to hurry and then get flustered when the clerk told her she had too many cans of vegetables. She could feel the heat of the other customers glaring at her as the clerk helped her straighten everything out.

It was at times like that that she would again become that child standing before the wrath of Sister Honora, feeling stupid, useless, and totally humiliated.

Hanging another piece of tinsel on the tree, Evelyn shook those thoughts away. Even though there would be few presents to put under the tree, and she would probably only manage to get half a chicken to cook for a Christmas dinner, there was much to be happy about. They were living in the house with a lot more room than they'd had at the apartment. Juanita was over a year old, walking and jabbering a mile a minute.

The small shop where Russell worked had changed from producing parts for General Motors to government contracts. The shop owner had told the men that the government considered the parts they made for military vehicles as vital to the war effort as what the men on the front were doing, and that seemed to help Russell get over the frustration of not being able to enlist. He had also been promoted to shop foreman. That carried a lot more responsibility, and he was often called in at night if a problem arose on the line, but he'd received a raise that had allowed him to buy the rest of the materials to finish the house.

Well, almost finish.

The living room where Evelyn was decorating the tree still had bare sheetrock for walls, and she tried to avoid looking at the slight dent about head high in the corner. Things had almost gotten back to normal in the past two weeks since the fight that had ended in that dent, and she didn't want to spoil that with negative thoughts. She didn't know what it was that made them both so quick to anger. Viola had told her that it was normal for couples to fight, but Evelyn didn't think other couples fought like she and Russell did. She couldn't remember Sarah and her husband ever raising voices or fists. When she'd said that to Viola, her sister had laughed and said that maybe Sarah and her husband weren't normal. Or maybe they did their fighting in private.

Evelyn shook her head and pulled her thoughts back to the task at hand, putting bulbs on the Christmas tree. She was determined to live up to her end of the bargain to make this Christmas special for Juanita. While Russell had grudgingly agreed, it seemed like he was really trying the past few days. He was home every evening, going down to the basement to work on something he said would be a surprise. And he helped her with dishes after supper without her having to ask him about ten times.

Then there was last night. The lovemaking had been wild and exciting. Evelyn was still surprised, and slightly embarrassed, about how much she enjoyed sex. The *Wife's Handbook* had stated that what went on in the bedroom was merely to be tolerated by a refined young lady, and Evelyn so desperately wanted to be seen as such.

A blush warmed her cheek as details of last night played through her mind. Then another thought interrupted the reverie.

"Oh my," she murmured, halting the hand that was reaching for a strand of tinsel. It was much like that day she'd had the realization about Juanita, and she hurried to the kitchen where a calendar hung above the lowboy that held her dishes until Russell made the cabinets. Quickly, she flipped pages back to November, then October. She had her last monthly on October 15. There it was, clearly marked, and nothing for November. It was now a week past her normal start date for December too. She slid her hand below her waist. The little pooch she had not lost since the birth of Juanita was still there. Was it bigger? Was she pregnant again?

She barely had time to let the possibility sink in before she heard a cry from the other room. Juanita was awake. Evelyn went to the crib and lifted the child out, carrying her to the changing platform Russell had made on top of the dresser.

Juanita stopped crying the minute Evelyn laid her down, the tears replaced with a smile and a gurgle. Evelyn smiled back, finished changing the wet diaper, then took Juanita out to the kitchen for a snack. While the child sat in her highchair eating some slices of banana, Evelyn sat at the table and thought about how another child would disrupt the comfortable pattern she'd established to keep up with the housework and the demands of a child. And how would Russell react? She wasn't sure if he would welcome another child. She wasn't even sure if she could. But then, she had no choice. Neither of them did.

That evening, Russell came home late for supper and told her that he would probably have to go back to the shop for a few hours.

"Do you have to?" Evelyn set the bowl of potatoes on the table then went to get the meatloaf out of the oven. "We have hardly had time to talk all week."

"One of the machines broke down." Russell spooned a helping of mashed potatoes to his plate and fed some to Juanita who was in her highchair next to the table. "I have to go. So talk quick."

Evelyn slid the platter of meat on the table and sat down with a sigh. "Okay. I'm pregnant."

He shot her a quick glance, but she couldn't read his expression.

"At least I think I am."

"Why don't you not scare me until you know for sure?"

"I'm as sure as I was about Juanita at first. I just need the doctor's confirmation."

Russell didn't respond. He looked away, feeding Juanita a small piece of the meatloaf with a spoon.

"What's the matter? Do you not want another baby?"

"It's not that." Russell put down the spoon. "The timing could be better, that's all."

"I thought so, too, but..." she let the rest of the words fade into a shrug.

He sighed. "We'll just have to manage."

"I suppose." Evelyn filled her plate, then took over feeding

Juanita so Russell could eat. "Will you be able to spend more time at home? Finish the other bedroom so there's a place for Juanita and the new baby?"

"I don't know." Russell took a bite of meatloaf.

"They'll need a place to sleep."

Russell swallowed. "Just put the cradle in our room. That worked before."

"There wasn't already a crib in the bedroom." Evelyn paused a moment to tamp down her irritation. She didn't want to argue.

Russell took a couple more bites of potatoes, then said, "Could we talk about this later?"

"When, later? You're never home to talk. You're never home to help."

"What do you want me to do?" He dropped his fork to his plate, the clatter sounding like a backfire. "I can't make the war go away. I can't make the work stop."

"I'm not saying you can. But you don't have to do Civil Service patrols almost every evening you're not working. You could stay home more often."

"What I'm doing is important."

"We're important too."

Russell took so long to respond Evelyn held her breath, not knowing what to expect. Finally, he said, "Don't even suggest that I shirk my responsibility to you. I've done nothing short of my duty since..." he didn't finish with words but nodded to Juanita who was watching the exchange with wide eyes.

"Your?... Your duty?"

Juanita started to cry, and Evelyn knew that the last thing they needed was to fight in front of her. But how could he have said those horrible, crushing words? Is that how he really felt or was it just the anger talking?

Swallowing hard to keep her own tears at bay, Evelyn

pulled Juanita from the highchair and bounced her until she quieted. The rest of the dinner was eaten in silence, tension simmering underneath it, then Russell stood and got his jacket. "I have to go to the shop."

Clipped, cold, emotionless words.

"When will you be back?"

"Late."

When the door closed and she was alone with Juanita, Evelyn let the tears run in a warm river down her cheeks.

———

A trip to the doctor's office confirmed the pregnancy. Evelyn made up her mind to be positive about having another child. She would forget about the last argument and the harsh words and just try to be happy. Russell seemed to pick up on her mood, and life was almost back to normal as they worked on getting the room ready for the new baby. Russell stayed home a couple of evenings to cover the bare two-by-fours in the second bedroom with sheetrock. Evelyn found some curtains with Teddy bears on them at a thrift store, and her neighbor, Mary, helped her paint the room a pretty yellow. It turned out to be the loveliest room in the house.

The excitement as Christmas Day approached also brought a merriment to the house that seemed to be contagious. Evelyn enjoyed keeping the secret of the scarf she was knitting for Russell, for once actually glad when he was gone so she had time to pull it out of hiding and work on it. The day she'd shopped for the curtains, she'd found two skeins of Pearl Wool. She didn't recognize the type of yarn, but Mary did and told Evelyn the wool would make a lovely scarf. It was a deep burgundy and tan two-toned yarn, and the finished scarf would match well with Russell's brown overcoat.

Christmas day dawned with a bright blue sky and heavy snow weighing down the branches of the elm tree in the yard. The scene was magical. Evelyn turned away from the window, fingering the pearls at her neck. A present from Russell. They were not real. She knew that, but the fact that he'd thought enough to give her something pretty made her smile. He'd made wooden blocks for Juanita and the child seemed delighted with them. She sat on the floor stacking the blocks into crooked towers and then knocking them down amidst peals of laughter.

Russell sat beside their daughter, his scarf wrapped around his neck, the ends trailing on the floor. He looked so happy Evelyn thought her heart would burst. If only she could capture this moment and preserve it in one of her canning jars.

———

Then the holidays were over and the cold dreary winter dragged on. Evelyn was so tired of being alone that she decided to take the bus to visit her sister, who lived in Dearborn. She sincerely hoped that Lester would not be there. He was still working as a long-haul truck driver, so he could be gone for weeks at a time, but she never knew when. The few times he was there when Evelyn visited, he had little to say to her and often left the table right after dinner. She didn't care for Lester, but she kept that to herself. She didn't want to upset Viola by telling her that there was something almost sinister about the man's cold, lifeless hazel eyes. His unblinking scrutiny was always most disconcerting.

After the long, uncomfortable bus ride, Evelyn hurried with Juanita to Viola's door. When Evelyn knocked, Viola opened it and her eyes widened in surprise. "Evelyn. I wasn't expecting you."

"Oh. I'm sorry. I thought... well, didn't we talk about it the other day when I called?"

"Yes. But I thought you would call again before you left. You usually do."

"I'm sorry. I didn't think. Can I come in? I really need a bathroom."

Viola stepped aside. "Of course. I'll take Juanita."

"Thank you." Evelyn quickly slipped out of her coat and laid it across the back of the sofa as she passed through the living room to the bathroom.

When she came back out, Viola said, "You'll have to leave soon."

"Why?"

"Lester's coming home. He doesn't like it when someone is here."

"He didn't seem to mind last time."

"He didn't say anything until after you left." Viola nodded toward Juanita who was toddling over to play with Viola's daughter, Regina. "Lester says we don't need another kid around. One's enough."

"What about..." Evelyn gestured toward the slight bulge in Viola's abdomen.

"He was furious when I told him. Wants me to get rid of it."

"Why didn't you tell me?"

Viola shrugged. "What was I going to say? My husband wants me to kill our baby? I remember how you acted the first time I considered an abortion."

Evelyn didn't know what to say in response to that, so she just stood there. Finally, Viola turned and headed to the kitchen. "You must be hungry. I'll make sandwiches you can take with you."

Evelyn followed her sister. "I was hoping to stay at least for the day."

"You can sit and rest for a bit while I make you a lunch, but then you must go. Lester will be mad."

Evelyn started to go to the living room to get her coat. Then she stopped and turned to her sister. "Is he mean to you?"

The other woman glanced away quickly, and Evelyn stepped to her, laying a hand on her arm. "Vi?"

"He's strict. That's all."

Evelyn froze for a moment. It had been a long time since she'd seen her sister like this. A bit cowed. All of her normal fire and bravado vanished. "Does he... hurt you?"

Viola shook her head then took a deep breath. "Is peanut butter okay?"

"Do you want to talk?"

"No." Viola went to the sink and poured a glass of water, then handed it to Evelyn. "Here, sit for a moment while I make the sandwiches."

Evelyn took a sip of the water and swallowed before putting the glass on the table. She considered telling her sister about the fights she'd had with Russell. Maybe it would help them both to talk about the problems in their marriages. Then she decided not to. If Vi didn't want to talk, she wouldn't, and Evelyn wasn't sure she wanted to, either. Some things were better left unsaid. "I should go see to Juanita. She might need a change before we leave."

Viola merely nodded.

The sandwiches were ready when Evelyn returned to the kitchen, so she took the brown paper bag and hugged her sister. "Thank you."

"I'm sorry you can't stay, but..." Viola shrugged the rest away.

"That's okay. I don't want to make trouble for you."

A shadow crossed Viola's face, which was quickly replaced with a forced smile. Evelyn didn't know what else to say or do, so she hugged her sister again and walked out the door.

On the bus ride home, Evelyn thought about the change in Viola since she'd married Lester. It hadn't been obvious at first, but reviewing the last year, Evelyn remembered other instances when she'd been a little afraid of Lester. Too often he had that look in his eyes that was almost predatory.

She unwrapped a sandwich from the waxed paper and ate half, slipping small bites to Juanita. It didn't look like Evelyn or her sister were going to have the fantasy life they had talked about in the darkness of night at the orphanage. Sure, she was better off than Vi. Russell was a much better husband than Lester. But neither she nor her sister had married the men of their dreams.

The part of the fantasy Evelyn never shared with Viola was the prince she would marry who would whisk her off to a great mansion. There would be room enough for her and Viola and all the children in the orphanage.

In the fantasy, her mother would never set foot in that mansion.

21

REGINA – FEBRUARY 1943

Regina liked her job at the Cadillac hotel. Cleaning rooms was a lot easier than cooking at Coney Island and then scrubbing the stoves and mopping the floors. No matter how hard she scrubbed, she never could get all the grease off the floors or off herself when she got home. At the hotel, she just had to change beds, vacuum, dust, and clean bathrooms. Some guests left their rooms so neat, it was almost like nobody had been there. Others? Well, that was another story. Regina didn't know how some people could be so disrespectful as to leave garbage overflowing the wastebaskets, tubs that looked like someone did their business there, and bathroom sinks coated with something she didn't recognize. At times like that, she was thankful for rubber gloves.

Today, she was at the hotel as a guest. Henry had booked them a room for Valentine's Day. "Put me down," she said, as Henry swept her up and carried her into the room. "This isn't our wedding day."

Henry eased her to her feet and gave her a kiss. When he stepped back, Regina caressed his cheek, and then took a look around at the luxurious furnishings and décor. Heavy dark furniture rested on cream carpeting, and light tan satin graced the windows. Since this suite was on the top floor of the hotel and not one of the rooms she routinely cleaned, she had not seen it before. "Henry. You shouldn't have. This is too expensive."

"I got a special rate because I know someone who works here." Henry winked at her. "Now, get ready. The girls will be here soon. We have reservations downstairs at seven."

Regina went into the bathroom that was done in black and white marble with gold faucets and fixtures. She paused a moment to take in the glamorous atmosphere, feeling like a queen, and took her time refreshing her makeup. When she finished applying lipstick, she took one of the tissues out of the box on the counter to blot the excess. These were not the same kind of tissues normally put in the lower-priced rooms. This one was unbelievably soft and had just a hint of lavender perfume.

She was about to step out when an errant thought crossed her mind. Was this the room where Lester had entertained his hussy? She'd seen him last week when he was supposed to be on the road. At first, she hadn't been sure it was him. There was a tall man standing there at the elevator with his hand on a woman's back, but when he turned for a just a moment, there was no mistaking him. They stepped into the elevator, and Regina watched the floor indicator until it stopped at this floor. Was it really him?

That was the question she'd kept coming back to every time she thought about what she had seen, and every time the question arose, so did her doubts. Maybe she'd been mistaken. Lester certainly couldn't afford a room on this floor.

Regina stepped out of the bathroom, wishing that the

memory had not come back so vividly. Henry walked over and touched her arm. "Are you okay? You look a little upset."

"I'm fine." Regina forced a smile. It wasn't fair to Henry to be dismal.

"Okay. Let's go."

After the elevator took them to the ground floor, Regina and Henry walked into the dining room to see Evelyn and Russell already seated at the table. They walked over, and when Evelyn stood to greet them, Regina noticed how her daughter's hand rested on her tummy. Was Evelyn gaining weight, or was she...? Surely, she would have told them if she was pregnant.

Regina glanced at Evelyn's hand then brought her eyes back to meet her daughter's. "Are you expecting again?"

Evelyn hesitated just a beat before answering. "Yes."

"And you didn't tell us?"

"Well, I—"

"That's terrific," Henry said, pumping Russell's hand. "Hoping for a boy this time?"

"Of course."

After they were seated, Regina turned to Evelyn. "How far along are you?"

"A few months."

Regina put her napkin in her lap. "I'm surprised you kept it a secret all this time."

Evelyn fiddled with her napkin, and Russell spoke up. "It wasn't a secret. But we didn't want to tell anyone until we were sure."

"Well, it is good news," Henry said, then turned to Evelyn. "Are you feeling okay?"

"I'm fine. Not as much morning sickness as last time."

Nothing more was said for a moment, then Regina looked up and waved to a couple who had just stepped into the entrance. "There's Lester and Viola. She's expecting too. Did you know that, Evelyn?"

"Uh... yes. Yes, I did." Evelyn turned to watch Viola and Lester approach the table.

"Nice to see you. Mother. Henry." Viola gave them each a quick hug and sat down, Lester holding the chair for her.

Evelyn had made no move to offer such a warm greeting, and face to face with the difference between her daughters, Regina felt a pang of sadness. She had hoped in time that Evelyn's cool exterior would melt and they could be friends, but even though they were always polite, there was nothing like the bond she felt forming between her and Viola. Was that wrong of her? Was that like choosing one over the other? No. Regina wasn't choosing. This time, it was Evelyn who was making the choice to be distant.

"Thanks so much for inviting us to dinner," Viola said with a smile that didn't look quite right to Regina, and she glanced at Lester, searching his confident demeanor for cracks. She'd never cared for him when Viola first brought him around. And she cared even less now. Something ugly lurked in the shadows of his eyes that seldom stayed at rest, and his glance flitted from place to place like a fly evading a folded newspaper. Henry had told her that people who couldn't maintain eye contact were hiding some lie or guilt. What was Lester hiding? The hussy? Or something else?

A uniformed waiter brought menus and a wine list to the table. "We have a special for Valentine's Day," he said. "Chateaubriand for two, accompanied by a bottle of our finest claret, and followed with chocolate mousse."

"Very well," Henry said. "We would like three orders."

Russell sucked in a breath as if to protest and Regina quickly spoke, touching Henry's arm. "Perhaps they would like to order for themselves."

"Yes," Lester said. "I would appreciate the courtesy of a choice."

"By all means," Henry said. "I just thought I would eliminate the awkwardness of what moderately priced item to choose since this is my treat. There is no need to be concerned about prices."

Well, that was a surprise to Regina. "Honey?" she said, touching his arm to get his attention.

Henry seemed to know what she had not put into words. He smiled. "It's okay. I won big at the poker game last week."

"Well, it's not okay with me," Lester said. "I am a man who prefers to pay his own way."

The waiter looked from one man to the other then settled his gaze on Henry. "Uh, sir? Shall I come back?"

"No. No," Henry said. "We'll have one order of the special dinner. The other couples can choose for themselves."

Regina squirmed in embarrassment. Why did Lester have to create such a scene? The waiter was being so diplomatic about it, but she was sure he wished he was serving a different table where tensions were not as thick as January molasses.

"Henry, I appreciate your offer," Russell said, relieving the tension. Then he turned to the waiter. "We'll have the same."

"Very good, sir." The waiter stepped over to Lester. "For you and the lady?"

"Do you serve tongue?"

Regina choked on the sip of water she'd taken, and the waiter seemed to be having trouble finding his voice. He gave a slight cough then said, "No, sir. We do not."

"Then we will have a plate of vegetables and some bread."

Viola touched her husband's arm. "Could I please have a steak? I've been craving meat."

"We have a very fine—"

"No, you may not," Lester said, cutting off the waiter. "You will eat what I say you can eat."

The waiter nodded, doing his best to pretend that there was nothing wrong at the table. Regina bit her lip, glad when Henry struck up a conversation with Russell about how work was going on the house. When the food came, they ate for several minutes in an awkward silence, then Viola stood. "I need to visit the restroom."

Regina dropped her napkin beside her plate. "I'll go with you."

"Me too." Evelyn stood and followed.

When Viola came out of the stall to wash her hands at the sink, Regina caught her daughter's eye in the mirror. "What's the problem with Lester?"

Viola turned away, walking toward the drying towel. "I don't know what you mean."

"Viola. Look at me." Regina waited until her daughter complied. "When did he turn into a tyrant?"

Viola shrugged and tears slowly slipped out of her eyes. Regina took her daughter into an embrace, holding her tight while sobs shook her shoulders.

After a few moments, Viola pulled away and swiped at her wet cheeks with the back of her hands. "We should return to the table. Lester will..."

Evelyn came to the sink. "Will what? Hit you in front of all of us?"

"Of course not. He isn't like that."

"Really?" Evelyn waited for a response, and when it didn't come, she continued, "Lester has far too much control over you."

"She's right," Regina said. "This marriage isn't good for you."

"Of course it is." Viola gave a weak smile. "Lester loves me."

The absurdity of that statement was so strong Regina couldn't help herself. "Lester loves Lester. And maybe that woman he brought to the hotel a few weeks ago."

The devastation on her daughter's face made Regina regret the words. If only she could pluck them out of the air and put them back.

"What woman?" Viola's voice rose to a shrill pitch.

"What woman?" Evelyn repeated, almost in a whisper.

"I don't know who she was. Just some woman." Regina reached out a placating hand. "And maybe I was mistaken."

Viola stood rigid for a few seconds then nodded. "That's right. Lester wouldn't..."

The sentence dropped off as if Viola couldn't bring herself to finish it, and Regina waited the moment out. Maybe Viola would convince herself that it wasn't true, and they could go back to the table and have dessert and everything would be okay.

Viola squared her shoulders and started to walk out. "That bastard!"

Regina grabbed Viola's arm. "Wait. What are you going to do?"

"Kill the son of a bitch." She struggled to pull free.

"Stop." Regina pushed Viola away from the door. "Think about what you need to do. For you and for the baby."

Viola didn't respond. She just stood there, her free hand on her tummy, her other arm trembling in Regina's grasp.

"What if you confront him and he walks out?" Regina asked. "What will you do?"

"I don't know. I'll figure it out."

"Just wait," Evelyn said. "You don't want to be on your own. Not now." She gestured toward Viola's swollen stomach. "And Mother said she might have been mistaken."

"You're not even sure?!" Viola jerked free, glaring at Regina. "Why the hell didn't you just shut up about it?"

Regina didn't know what to say, and Viola stormed out. She turned to Evelyn, hoping for some understanding, but got an icy glare instead. "How could you?" Evelyn said. "How could you ruin her life again?"

22

EVELYN – JULY 1943

The strongest contraction hit Evelyn when they were standing on the corner watching the parade. She'd had mild ones for the past two hours, but the baby wasn't due until next week, so she'd ignored them. This one couldn't be ignored. She turned to Russell. "We need to go home."

"But the parade isn't over." He shifted Juanita from one shoulder to the other. He'd put her up there so she could see over the heads of the adults gathered along the street to watch the Fourth of July parade.

"I need to go to the hospital."

That got his full attention. "Now?"

Another contraction squeezed her abdomen, almost making her go to her knees, and that was enough answer for Russell. He eased Juanita to the ground. "You're going to have to walk. Daddy has to help Mommy."

"Mommy hurt?"

"No. Don't worry. Just keep walking."

Juanita trotted ahead, and Russell put his arm around Evelyn, supporting her as they walked the half a block to the house. It was a good thing that the house wasn't any farther away. The contractions had started coming every few minutes. Once they were inside, she sat on the sofa while Russell hurried to take Juanita to the backdoor neighbor, Mary. A few weeks ago, she had agreed to watch Juanita when it was time for Evelyn to go to the hospital, and a bag was already packed. All Evelyn had to do was sit and wait until Russell came back. Thank goodness for helpful neighbors.

Another contraction tightened like a metal band around her belly, and Evelyn moaned with the pain. She wished Russell would hurry back. The pains were coming hard and fast.

Moments later, Russell ran into the living room. "Are you ready?"

"Thank God you're here. I don't think this is going to take as long as it did for Juanita."

Evelyn stood and made it to the car as fast as her pains would let her move. It wasn't far to the hospital, which was another stroke of luck. She could feel the urge to push and remembered from when Juanita was born that the urge meant the baby was ready. Russell drove the few blocks as if he were in a race car, then pulled to a screeching halt in front of the hospital. He turned off the engine and ran around to open the passenger door for Evelyn. "Can you walk?"

"I don't know."

"Never mind." He swept her up in his arms and ran to the door. Once inside, a nurse spotted them and hurried over, pushing a wheelchair.

"Put her down, sir." Russell did and the nurse told Evelyn to breathe in short pants and "don't push" as she was whisked down the hall. Another nurse helped get Evelyn onto an exam table.

"The baby's coming," Evelyn said, panting through another contraction. "Oh my God."

The nurse pushed Evelyn's dress up and pulled her panties off just seconds before Evelyn's water broke in a warm rush and flooded the area. The other nurse grabbed towels to catch the flow of water as the doctor walked in. "She's crowning," the nurse said. "We'll have to deliver her here."

The doctor grunted a response and lifted the sheet the nurse had draped over Evelyn's knees. The nurse standing beside Evelyn said, "Okay. Now you can push."

Four excruciating pushes later, another baby girl was born. Hair matted with sweat and breathing heavily, Evelyn collapsed against the bed. Another girl. Russell wanted a boy. Would he be horribly disappointed? She tried not to worry about that as the nurses cleaned her up, then wheeled her down to the maternity ward. After the nurses got her settled in bed, with strict instructions that she was not to get up, Russell was allowed to come in.

"We had a girl," Evelyn said.

"Yes. The nurse told me." He sat on the hard wooden chair that had been put there for visitors.

Nothing had changed in the hospital routine since she'd been here before, but she wished that he would be allowed to sit on the bed. And maybe they could hold hands. Anything to make her feel more connected to him. Evelyn sighed. "They said she was healthy."

"That's good."

"Are you happy?"

"Sure." He gave her a smile, but it wasn't like the smile when Juanita was born.

Evelyn had hoped that once the baby was here, Russell would be more excited about another child. She didn't doubt that he loved children. That was clear in the way he treated

MARYANN MILLER

Juanita. He often sang to her, and always picked her up and swung her around when he came home from work.

"Are you horribly disappointed that it is another girl?"

"Not horribly." He gave her another small smile. "But a man does look forward to having a son."

Warm tears escaped Evelyn's eyes. "I'm sorry."

He patted her hand. "It's not your fault."

Before they could finish the conversation, a nurse bustled in to tell Russell he had to leave. Another rule that hadn't changed. Visitors, even husbands, could only stay a few minutes after the birth. The new mother needed her rest.

Russell leaned over and gave Evelyn a brief kiss before following the woman out. Then moments later, the nurse came in with the baby. Evelyn looked at this girl-child as she nursed, and thought about how her entrance into the world would change their lives. Russell had already said he would have to work more, now that there would be another mouth to feed, and he wasn't going to give up his responsibilities for the Civil Defense Corp. When the war first started, he'd spent weeks training to help victims should the United States be bombed, and even though that threat had declined, he still had bi-weekly meetings to attend, and he patrolled one night a week. Evelyn was proud of what Russell was doing, but couldn't help the occasional surge of resentment at the hours he was away.

Once Russell had finished the interior of the second bedroom, he'd made it clear that he was not to be nagged about finishing the rest of the house or buying things. He didn't have time to work on it, and they had to save money somehow. Evelyn had tried to respect that, but it had been hard because she was the one staring at bare plasterboard walls most of the time and trying to figure out how she would take care of two kids with little money. The worse part of it all was there was no time to talk to him about how she felt. And she didn't know

220

what he was thinking or feeling. Sometimes she had a sense that their relationship was as fragile as an eggshell and the wrong move could crush it.

———

Russell slid onto the stool and motioned to the bartender to pour him a draft. He'd been here enough times that Ed knew to pour a Stroh's. Evelyn didn't know how often Russell stopped at the bar between work and home, and it was better that way. The wife didn't have to know everything a man did.

"Bad day?" Ed asked, setting the mug in front of Russell.

"Yeah. But I should be happy." Russell took a swallow of his beer, then licked the froth off his lip. "Got a new baby."

"Congratulations. Boy?"

Russell shook his head. "I was hoping. But it's another girl."

"Maybe next time."

"Yeah. Maybe." Russell sighed as Ed moved on to wait on a woman who had just come in.

Russell wasn't sure about a next time. While he was disappointed about not getting his boy, he knew that wasn't the only source of his discontent. He kept trying to talk himself out of resenting the whole fact of the marriage and the responsibilities, but when he was alone with his beer, he couldn't deny the feeling. Or the questions. Did he make a big mistake getting married? Could he have made a career in music? Hell, he hardly had time for music anymore.

He shook the thoughts away. No sense in dwelling on what could have been. He needed to be happy with what he had. And sometimes he was. His mother had been right about family being the most important thing in life. Russell just wished Evelyn was easier to live with. Her moods and flares of anger were like nothing he had ever experienced before.

Certainly nothing like his mother or sisters. They seemed always content with life.

After finishing his beer, Russell swiveled around on the stool, thinking he'd go home. He needed to pick Juanita up from Mary's house. Mary didn't mind keeping the girl while Russell worked and for the little while he could visit Evelyn in the hospital, but she'd rather not have Juanita all night. She had her own kids to see to.

The woman who had come in a few minutes earlier looked up and smiled as Russell passed, and he stepped back, now recognizing her. "You're the new hire at the shop, aren't you?"

"Yes. Eileen." She smiled.

"Russell." He leaned against the stool next to her.

"Join me in a drink?"

"Can't. Got to pick up my kid."

"Oh. You married?

"Yeah. Wife's in the hospital. Just had our second baby last week."

She raised her glass in a salute. "Congratulations."

"Thanks." He knew he should leave, but he hesitated. There was something about the pretty smile. "You like the job?"

She nodded. "Keeps food on the table."

"You married?"

"My husband's overseas." Eileen cocked her head and gave him a long look. "Surprised you're not. You look to be draft age."

"I was rejected."

"You're better off. War does horrible things to people."

Russell sensed there was more to her statement, but he didn't ask. It wasn't his place, and he had to agree. There wasn't anything nice about killing, even when it was sanctioned.

"I'd better go." Russell pushed away from the stool. "See you at work."

Driving home, Russell thought about the woman's smile and how it had made him want to smile in return.

Eileen had started working at the shop a week ago. She had the night shift, so Russell had only seen her once when she'd stayed past seven. Greg, the night supervisor had been with her, and Russell figured she was getting the tour.

Russell realized that he wouldn't mind seeing her again, and quickly pushed that thought away. Too much beer and too little sex lately. He needed to be careful.

———

Evelyn pulled the baby away from her sore breast. These first days of nursing were torture. Her nipples hurt until they got tougher, and when the milk came in in a great rush, her breasts ached deep inside. The discomfort only lasted a few days, and she knew it was better for the baby to have mother's milk. She'd learned that when Juanita was born,

She was on day three.

Evelyn ran a finger down the soft cheek of her baby, who still did not have a name. In the nursery, she was listed as Baby Girl Van Gilder, and the nurses kept reminding her that she needed to give the child a name. They couldn't fill out the birth certificate without one, and that needed to be done before Evelyn left the hospital.

During his short visit this evening, Russell had finally told Evelyn to just pick a name. He really didn't care, although he didn't want the baby named after his mother. He wasn't fond of the name, Emma. The name didn't appeal to Evelyn, either, especially considering how her mother-in-law seemed to feel about her, but she'd suggested it, thinking he might be pleased. It might even please his mother, who still barely acknowledged her existence. Emma sent brief letters addressed to Russell, giving him news of the family that she said he could share with his wife. As if Evelyn was simply an appendage.

No. She would not call the child Emma.

Watching her baby's eyes twitch in sleep, Evelyn considered a few other names. Maybe Viola after her sister? No. The child looked nothing like a Viola. Sarah? Evelyn thought that would be perfect until she realized that the choice could cause hard feelings. Despite all the disappointments she'd experienced at the hands of her mother, Evelyn did not want to deliberately hurt her, and she remembered how thrilled their mother had been when Viola named her first child Regina.

A nurse pulled back the curtain that separated Evelyn's bed from her neighbor's and stepped up to the bed, her stiff uniform rustling against the bedclothes. "It's time for the baby to go back." The nurse took the child from Evelyn. "It would be nice if she had a name."

Evelyn heard a tone of reproach, but she had to agree. "I... we decided when my husband was in earlier. I forgot to tell you when you brought her in."

The nurse had already started toward the door. She stopped and looked back, "Well?"

"Marion," Evelyn said, not even knowing where that came from.

"Middle name?"

"None. Just Marion."

Later, when another nurse brought the paperwork in for Evelyn to sign, she saw that the nurse had put Maryann instead of Marion. She must have misunderstood. Evelyn hesitated for a moment, wondering if she should correct the mistake, but the nurse's impatient body language flustered her. She hated the pressure she always felt when someone waited for her to read any kind of papers. It was like they knew she was slow to read and understand and judged her as stupid.

"Is there a problem?" The nurse finally asked.

"No." Evelyn quickly signed the form and handed it back. Maryann was a nice name, and it honored the Blessed Virgin. Maybe that would make up for the fact that Evelyn was living in sin.

23

EVELYN – SEPTEMBER 1943

I t didn't take long for Evelyn to realize that she was ill-equipped to care for two children. She thought about all her experience working for Sarah, and then the Gardners, would have given her all she needed to know about raising children, but it was so different with children of her own. No set hours for work. No time when the children were in the care of someone else. Russell had new responsibilities at the job that kept him there for long hours. At least he said it was the job keeping him away, and Evelyn didn't have the emotional energy to question him.

Come to think of it, she didn't have much energy for anything. Once the mandatory six weeks of no intercourse had been over following the birth, Russell made sure he was home several evenings in a row, but Evelyn fell into bed exhausted once the girls were settled. And she didn't even feel the urges. Not like she had after Juanita was born when Evelyn was eager to satisfy that tingle that persisted long after nursing the baby.

There wasn't even any energy for talking, and when they did, it always escalated into a fight. Evelyn's nerves were on edge all the time, and often she felt like she would explode if she didn't get away from the girls.

The first time she left, it was only for an hour. Both of the girls were down for a nap, so she slipped out of the house and went to the library on the corner. Once inside, she sat down on a wooden chair with a book in hand, but instead of reading, she just sat there, letting the quiet envelope her.

"Would you like me to bring another?" The Librarian asked, motioning to the closed book on Evelyn's lap.

"No. But thank you." Evelyn opened the book and did her best to read a bit, glancing at the clock now and then to make sure she didn't stay too long. An hour at most, but she got caught up in the story, and the next time she looked at the clock, an hour and a half had passed.

She jumped up, put the book on the shelf and raced out the door. Please God, let the girls be okay.

Hurrying into the house, she stopped short when she saw that Russell was there. "Oh. You're home early." Evelyn managed to push the words out through the constriction in her throat.

"Light load today. Where were you?"

"Just... uh... went for a quick walk."

"Not that quick. I've been home a half hour."

There was a hint of a challenge in his voice and Evelyn scrambled for a way to avoid it. "Are the girls still asleep?"

Russell nodded. "But you should have taken them with you."

"They were napping."

"Then you should have stayed here with them."

On one level, Evelyn knew that was true. On another, it seemed imperative that she just get out of this house, if only for a little while. "I didn't think it would hurt to take a short walk while they napped."

"It could have."

"Nothing happened. They're fine." She pushed past him. "I'll start supper."

"Evelyn."

When he didn't say anything else, she turned to face him. "What?"

"Don't ever leave my girls alone again."

"Oh. So now they're your girls? Then why don't you take care of them for a change." Evelyn grabbed her purse and stormed out.

She didn't know where to go and didn't have much money, so she walked to Main Street and went into the drug store. She sat at the counter of the soda fountain and bought a Coke. Then she bought another so she could sit there a little longer. Finally, the boy who worked the soda fountain told her that she had to leave. They were closing soon, and he needed to clean up. She nodded and left, walking aimlessly for a little while as dusk settled and the heat of the summer cooled off. She thought about just walking forever. Walking away from her past, her present, and her pain. But she knew she could not do that. She would never walk away from her children.

———

Evelyn's resolve to stay home only lasted a couple of months. Then she started slipping out for some peace and quiet. Just once in a while before she exploded in frustration. Each time, she went to the drug store or the library and was careful to only stay an hour. And when she returned, she was always relieved that the girls were still asleep and Russell was not there.

Until today.

She walked into the kitchen to see him holding Maryann,

who was crying while he bounced her, trying to settle her down. He whirled on Evelyn. "Where the hell have you been?"

His voice cut her like a knife, and the red spots on his cheeks almost glowed. Evelyn couldn't push her voice past her fright.

"How long were you gone this time?"

He had softened his tone, so she managed, "I don't know. I was at the library, reading—"

"You left them alone to read a goddam book? They let you bring them home you know."

Evelyn swallowed hard. "It's so quiet there."

Russell just stared at her, still bouncing the baby.

"I didn't mean to—"

"You didn't mean to? You said you would not do this again. What's wrong with you?"

Evelyn tried to hold back the tears, but they ran hot down her cheeks. "I don't know."

Russell handed the crying baby over. "This has got to stop. You can't just go off and leave the children."

"I know." Evelyn held Maryann on one hip and dug a bottle out of the refrigerator. "I'll try to do better."

"Woman. You have got to do more than try."

"It's just..."

"What?"

Evelyn hesitated. Would he understand? She didn't understand herself. She had no clue as to what caused her feelings of sadness and despair and frustration. "I just don't feel right."

"Are you sick?"

The concern in his question gave her courage. "No. Not sick. I just have all these strange feelings since the baby was born."

"Oh, my God." The concern was gone now. "Feelings?

Every woman has feelings, but they don't make stupid decisions."

Evelyn turned away, putting the bottle on the stove to heat. Stupid, stupid, stupid. Now even Russell thought she was stupid. Would she ever get smart? "I'm sorry."

"Yeah. Well. Don't be sorry. Just take care of your responsibilities."

He walked out, and his parting comment hit Evelyn like a physical blow. She leaned against the counter to keep from falling. When the bottle was warm enough, she took it and Maryann to the table and sat down to feed her.

Juanita toddled into the room. "Hungry, Mama."

With her free hand, Evelyn opened the tin of crackers on the table and passed a few to Juanita. "I'll fix supper in a bit."

Juanita took the crackers and chewed on one, then touched a wet spot on Evelyn's cheek. "Baby cry. Mama cry."

Evelyn choked back the sob that rose in her throat. All this crying had to stop.

———

Russell slid onto the barstool and motioned to Ed to bring him a beer.

"How's it going?" Ed asked, setting the glass in front of Russell. A bit of foam slid over the lip of the glass, and Ed expertly wiped it before it reached the surface of the bar.

Russell picked up the glass and downed half the beer before answering. "Why does life have to be so damn hard?"

"I'm a bartender. Not a philosopher."

Russell laughed. The little joke was what he needed; just enough of a deflection from the original question. No way was Russell ever going to tell the bartender just how bad of a day it had been, or how those bad days were piling up like a stack of old newspapers that nobody bothered to toss out. What the hell was going on? This irresponsible shrewish Evelyn was not the woman he'd fallen in love with. Or at least he thought he'd fallen in love. Actually, it was probably more lust than love. If only she hadn't gotten pregnant. He hadn't planned for that. His plans were for music. Always music. He just knew that if he'd had the chance he could have done more. Made something of himself in the music world but that dream took a dive down the toilet.

To be fair, it wasn't all Evelyn's fault. Not the current situation or the pregnancy that had gotten them to this current situation. It took two to make a baby, as his mother was fond of saying, so maybe he could have been more careful that early summer day three years ago.

He was on his second beer when Eileen came in and slid onto the stool next to him. "How's it going?" she asked.

"It's going. You?"

She shrugged, and there was something in the gesture that made him wonder. "You got a problem at the job, you know you can talk to me," he said.

Eileen signaled Ed for a beer, then smiled at Russell. "Things are great at work."

They drank their beers in silence for a few minutes, then Eileen put her glass down. "My husband came home."

"Really? Good news, right?"

"Of course."

She didn't sound convincing. "He okay?"

"Yeah. Just... different."

Russell didn't have to wonder about what she wasn't saying. Some guys coming back from the war were damaged in ways that couldn't be seen. He saw some men coming to work at the plant that had dead, lifeless eyes, and he'd heard about one who went a little crazy and killed his wife. He hoped Eileen's husband wasn't one of those. He looked at her intently. "You okay?"

She shrugged again.

"Has he done anything... bad?"

"No. It's just..." she let the sentence fade and took a swallow of her beer. Then she continued. "He came back a stranger, and I don't know if I like this stranger."

Russell ran a hand across his face. What the hell should he say? What the hell should he do? He couldn't even solve his own problems.

"It's going to be okay," she said. "I can handle it."

He nodded, hoping his relief wasn't too obvious.

She laughed. "Sorry," she said through the laughter. "You look like a kid who just dodged a whupping."

"I didn't know what to say. You deserve better." He glanced away and took a swallow of beer.

They sat there in silence for a few more minutes, then Eileen fished some nuts out of the bowl on the bar and turned to him. "What has you here instead of home?"

He shrugged.

"Come on. Fess up."

"Needed to get out for a while."

Eileen eyed him over the rim of her glass. "I suspect there's a bit more to it than that."

Russell slowly finished his beer and motioned to Ed for another. He was tempted. Sorely tempted to unload, but he hesitated. She had enough troubles of her own. All the while, Eileen kept watching him. He tried not to notice the warmth he saw in her eyes or the rush he felt when she leaned closer, and their legs touched. He pulled back. Jesus. He needed to watch it.

After Ed brought the fresh beer, Eileen said, "If you don't want to talk, that's fine. But I am a good listener."

"It's just…"

"What?"

"Oh, hell." Russell drank half of the new beer, then he told her. A condensed version of how rough it had been the past few months, stopping short of telling her that he was beginning to regret ever meeting Evelyn.

"Christ," Eileen said when he finished. "How can she just leave the kids like that?"

Russell shrugged.

"Listen. I don't mean to butt into your business. But if you ever need me to check on the kids, just let me know."

"Couldn't do that."

"Sure you can. I have a phone."

That made Russell smile.

———

He didn't think it would happen so soon, but just a few weeks later he had to take Eileen up on her offer. He was at work when his boss, Roger, called out to him, "Phone call for you, Russell."

He shut off his machine, wiped his greasy hands on a rag and followed his boss into the little office in the corner of the machine shop. Roger motioned to the phone on his desk. "I'll leave you alone."

After Roger stepped out, Russell picked up the receiver. "Hello?"

"Russell, this is Mary. Your neighbor."

There was a tone in her voice that caused prickles of alarm to run down his spine. "Is something wrong?"

"Yes. I'm so sorry to bother you at work, but I didn't know what to do."

"What is it?"

"I was out in my backyard hanging laundry, and I heard your girls crying."

He didn't have to ask. He knew he didn't have to ask, but he did anyway. "Evelyn is gone?"

"Yes."

Oh my God. "Are you with them now?"

The minute the question came out, Russell realized the answer. Of course she wasn't at his house. No phone there. "Sorry. Can you go back? Stay with my girls until I can get home?"

"How long would that be? My little one is sick, and I have to take her to the doctor."

Russell ran his hand across his stubble of beard, thinking. He couldn't leave for at least another half hour. He had to get that machine working for the night shift. And then it was 45 minutes to home. What to do?

"Russell? Are you there?"

"Yes, Mary. Listen, can you go back and stay just a little while. Maybe ten minutes? I think I can get someone to come sooner than I can make it home."

"Okay," Mary said. "I can leave Margie to watch Judy. But just for ten minutes. That's all."

"Thank you." Russell hung up the phone and called Eileen. Her number was on the work schedule.

———

As soon as Evelyn had settled on the bus that morning, she realized it was a stupid move to leave and go so far away without the children. As the bus wheezed away from the curb, she'd almost pulled the cord to stop it, but let her hand drop into her lap. She needed this. She needed the time away, even if it was just for part of the day. The girls would be okay. She had fed them both. Made sure they had clean diapers and clothes. They would be okay for a couple of hours. Russell would be home by four, and Evelyn could make it home soon after. Russell wouldn't have to know that she had been gone more than a few minutes.

Forty-five minutes later, she got off on the corner of the street that led to Viola's and walked the two blocks to her sister's house. She didn't know what to expect when she got there. She hadn't gone to the corner phone booth to call this time. She just hoped that Lester wasn't at home.

When she arrived, she knocked on the wood of the screen door and waited. It seemed to take forever for Viola to come to the door, and when she did, she only opened it a crack, peeking out. "Yes?" Then she seemed to recognize her sister. "Evelyn?"

"I know I should have called but—"

"What are you doing here?" Viola still held the door to a narrow crack and Evelyn couldn't see her face in the dim interior.

"Is Lester home?"

"No."

"Can I come in?"

Viola seemed to take forever to come to a decision, then she opened the door wider. Evelyn gasped when she stepped inside and her eyes adjusted. Ugly yellow bruises marred her sister's face, and her lip was swollen. "Viola! What happened?"

"Should I lie and say I ran into a door?"

"Did... did Lester do this?" Evelyn reached out and let one finger gently touch her sister's face.

Viola winced and pulled away. "I threw the bastard out."

Evelyn walked into the living room and saw Viola's oldest holding baby Jimmy on the couch. "Are the kids okay?" she asked, turning to her sister.

"Yes. That's why I made him leave. I figured he'd start on the kids next."

"Oh my God." Evelyn put her purse down on the coffee table. "What are you going to do?"

"I don't know. Maybe move away. One of the girls I used to work with at the hotel got a job up north. She called a while back and said there were openings."

"What kind of job? Where?"

"In a town called Grayling. Lots of men go there hunting, and she works at a lodge."

The baby started to cry, so Viola went over and took him from her daughter. "You go play, Reggie. Mama and Aunt Evelyn need to talk."

After the child left and Viola settled on the couch to nurse Jimmy, Evelyn said, "Are you really going to do it?"

"Maybe. I have to see how it would all work with the kids and all. But, yeah, I'm tempted."

Evelyn tried to adjust to the idea of losing touch with her sister once again. "How far away is this Grayling?"

"My friend said it's about a five-hour drive. I don't know how many miles."

"That's a long way."

Viola shrugged, and then shifted the baby from one breast to the other. "There's fresh coffee in the kitchen if you'd like some. And I wouldn't mind a cup."

"How can we just casually drink coffee while you're planning on moving away?"

"What are we supposed to do? Just sit here and cry?"

"That's not fair."

Viola sighed. "I know. I'm sorry." She smiled. "But I would really like a cup of coffee."

Evelyn couldn't help but smile back, the rancor dissolving. Viola always had the ability to either escalate an argument or cut it short with a funny comment. Evelyn preferred the humor. The little smiles always connected them in a way nothing else could. She went into the kitchen and got them each a mug of coffee.

After Viola finished nursing the baby, he fell asleep, so she put him in the nearby playpen. Then she settled back on the sofa and picked up her mug. "So? Are you going to tell me what prompted this unexpected visit? And where are your girls?"

Evelyn burst into tears.

"What's wrong?"

"I don't know. I just keep doing this."

"Doing what?"

"Needing to leave. Crying for no good reason."

Viola took a swallow of coffee, then set the mug down. "Well, there has to be a reason. People don't cry for nothing. Although you used to be good at that when you were a kid."

Evelyn knew that last bit was meant to be funny, but this time she didn't smile. She wiped the wetness from her cheeks with the palms of her hands and tried to stem the stream of tears.

"I'd ask if you were unhappy," Viola said. "But it appears that would be a silly question. So what is making you so unhappy?"

"It's just... rough since Maryann."

"What do you mean 'rough'?"

"I'm so tired all the time, and Russell's no help. He doesn't stay home long enough to be much help. And sometimes I just don't know what to do with Juanita. She gets into trouble, and I spank her, so then she's crying and the baby's crying. I can't stand all the crying and all the work."

"Is Russell stepping out on you?"

That wasn't a possibility Evelyn was comfortable responding to out loud. Sure she had wondered in the dark recesses of her mind. Wondered about the nights that he was gone. But there had never been anything to turn that wondering into suspicion.

"I'm thinking your silence means that's a 'no,'" Viola said. "So what on earth is so goddamned rough in your life besides what mothers deal with all the time?"

Evelyn looked at her sister, stunned, then glanced away. She'd expected understanding and sympathy from Viola. Not anger. Viola's baby started to cry, so she went over and picked him up, then faced her sister. "Look at me, Evelyn." Viola waited, then said again, "Look at me! I'm covered in bruises for God's sake. And you're complaining about how tough your life is."

"I'm sorry, I didn't mean..." Evelyn let the sentence fade. She was always saying sorry. Why couldn't she stop before she had to say I'm sorry.

"I can't believe it." Viola shook her head. "You don't even know how good you have it. You got the good guy."

Viola stood and walked toward the kitchen with her mug. "I should have stayed with him when I had the chance."

"What?"

"Nothing." Viola kept walking.

Evelyn hurried after her. "It's not nothing. What the hell do you mean?"

Viola put her mug in the sink and turned. "We dated a few times. That's all. After we first met and things weren't serious between the two of you."

"Dates? That's all?"

Viola glanced away and didn't say anything.

Evelyn sank into a kitchen chair. "Oh my God."

"Don't get all dramatic about it. It was only a few times."

Evelyn flew out of the chair and stopped just short of slapping her sister. The woman had enough bruises. "You knew," she said, the words coming out in a strident hiss. "You knew that I loved him long before he met you. But you couldn't resist taking one more thing from me."

Before Viola could respond, Evelyn stormed out of the kitchen, grabbed her things, and walked out. She wasn't sure if she could ever forgive her sister.

24

EVELYN – SEPTEMBER 1943

E velyn came in through the back door and took the few steps from the landing to the kitchen. She paused a moment when she heard voices in the back bedroom. She quickly put her purse down on the kitchen table and hurried into the bedroom. A woman was holding Maryann, and Russell sat with Juanita on the rocking chair. What on earth? She looked at her husband. "Russell. Who is this woman?"

"Where have you been?"

Maryann started to cry, and the woman jostled her just a bit, crooning to quiet her.

"Give me my baby." Evelyn marched over and pulled Maryann away. "Who the hell are you?"

Instead of answering, the woman turned to Russell. "I should leave. I'll see you at work."

Evelyn hoisted the baby to her shoulder, patting her back, and watched the woman walk out.

"What the hell were you thinking?"

Evelyn turned back to her husband. She couldn't remember

the last time she'd seen Russell so angry. The fire in his eyes rendered her speechless.

"You left the kids. Again. After you promised not to."

"It was just for a few hours. They were sleeping."

Russell didn't say anything for the longest time, then he stood and put Juanita in the rocking chair, giving her a teddy bear to hold. He walked out of the bedroom, through the short hall and into the kitchen. Evelyn quickly put Maryann into the crib and followed. Stepping into the kitchen, she saw a bucket near the sink filled with dirty water. A rag floated on top. "What's this?"

"There was shit all over the crib. Eileen had to clean it up when she got here."

"Eileen? That's her name? Is she a friend of yours?" Evelyn didn't keep the sarcastic tone out of her voice.

Russell lifted the bucket and poured out the water. The rag plopped into the sink. "She works with me, Evelyn. That's all."

Evelyn shrugged her jacket off and hung it on a peg by the doorway leading to the back-door landing and the basement. "Why did she come here?"

"To see about the kids. You weren't here." His anger flared again, and Evelyn watched the red spots on his cheeks get bigger. "You knew I was working a double shift today."

Her own anger matched his. "And that's the problem. You're always working, and I'm always stuck here with two kids."

They glared at each other for a few moments, then Russell slumped into a kitchen chair. "I can't believe you just left them."

There was a long minute of strained silence then Evelyn asked, "How did you even know I was gone?"

"Mary called me."

"Mary? Our neighbor?"

"Yes. She heard the girls crying and came over. When she

discovered that you weren't home, she called me. I couldn't come home right away, so I asked Eileen to come over to see what was going on."

"You asked a perfect stranger to take care of our children?"

Russell sighed. "She's not a stranger."

"Oh? Just how well do you know this woman?" Evelyn was well aware of how catty she sounded, but she couldn't stop herself. Jealousy triggered all kinds of unreasonableness.

"From work. She's on the night shift, so sometimes I see her when I work double. She lives a few blocks over."

"That's convenient."

"Oh for heaven's sake, Evelyn. Will you just stop?"

When she started to speak, he held up one hand. "Not now. I'm exhausted. I'm going to sleep."

"But what about supper? Aren't you hungry?"

"No. Don't leave again."

With that, Russell stomped to the front bedroom and slammed the door. The noise triggered cries from the other bedroom, and Evelyn hurried in. She had to quiet the girls so he could sleep, but part of her was still fuming. She didn't like the way that woman had looked at Russell before she left. He could tell her all day that there was nothing going on, but there was just something about that look. Or was it just her imagination?

That thought caught her up short as she picked up Maryann and shushed her. There was no basis for the jealousy, was there? Then she thought about her sister. For so long, Evelyn had fought back her suspicions about Viola and Russell. What a fool she'd been.

If not for the need to keep the children quiet, Evelyn would have screamed in frustration.

———

Evelyn had just settled Juanita and Maryann down for a nap when there was a knock at the door. She was surprised to see her mother and Henry standing on the front porch. They rarely made the drive from downtown Detroit to Van Dyke Township. Regina always said it was too far to come, but never seemed to think it was too far for Evelyn to travel the other direction to visit them.

"Henry. Regina. How nice to see you." Evelyn opened the door wide enough for them to step inside. "I just put the girls down. I could get them if—"

"No. Let them be," Regina said. "We just came to see if everything is all right."

"All right?" Evelyn took her mother's wrap and Henry's hat and headed to the hall tree. "What do you mean?"

"We talked to Viola."

"Oh."

"She told us about your fight last week."

Evelyn turned toward them. "Perhaps she should have been more discreet."

Henry chuckled. "When has your sister ever been discreet?"

Evelyn had to smile in agreement. Full steam ahead is the way Viola handled everything. "Would you like some coffee?"

"That would be nice," Regina said.

Evelyn went into the kitchen and turned the fire up under the coffee pot. Regina and Henry sat down at the table. After the coffee was served, Regina said, "Viola was quite upset that you just left the way you did."

"Did she tell you why I left?"

Regina took a sip of her coffee before answering, as if the pause could keep this from escalating from a mere conversation to a confrontation. "She said you accused her of improprieties."

Evelyn had to laugh. "I didn't accuse her of anything," she

said when she'd sufficiently tamped down the laugh. "She told me about her relationship with Russell."

Regina held up a hand. "She did not have a relationship."

"What about having sex with him?"

Those words hung in the air for a few awkward moments. Henry stood and took his coffee into the living room, obviously uncomfortable with this turn in the conversation. Evelyn waited for her mother to respond. Finally, Regina said, "Viola made it clear that the sex happened before you and Russell were seriously dating. Viola didn't think it mattered."

Oh, it mattered. It gave credence to the suspicions that Evelyn had lived with for so long. The doubts came in waves that were sometimes high and strong and overwhelming. Other times they pushed softly at the edges of her mind, and she could ignore them. Since her fight with Viola, the waves had beat at her relentlessly, and she was tired. So very tired.

Still, there was a certain amount of anger. It had followed her home last week and refused to go away, no matter how hard she tried to ignore it. Today she tamped the anger down and swallowed the retort that her anger wanted to make. What good would it do to fight with her mother?

Evelyn got up, arranged some oatmeal cookies on a plate, and brought it to the table. Her mother obviously took that as a sign that the subject of Viola and Russell was closed. She picked up a cookie and took a bite. "These are very good," she said after she had swallowed. "Did you make them?"

"Yes. From a recipe on the oatmeal box."

Regina finished her cookie, then said, "Viola's leaving."

"I know. She told me about the job up north."

"You should patch things up with her before she goes. She's been through a lot you know."

Once more Evelyn swallowed words that were fighting to

get out. She took a deep breath and sighed. "I'm not sure I can do that yet," she said.

Henry wandered back in with his coffee. "Did I hear there are cookies?"

Evelyn gestured to the plate. "Help yourself."

Henry settled back at the table, and the silence that settled over the room was a bit strained, then Regina asked, "Are things okay with you and Russell?"

Evelyn looked up in surprise. "Why do you ask?"

Henry reached over and patted her hand. "Now, don't get upset again. But he called us last week. To see if you were with us."

"He shouldn't have bothered you."

"He was worried."

Evelyn took a sip of her coffee. "I never thought he'd call you."

Regina said, "This wasn't the first time. Did you know that?"

"First time for what?"

"We know. Every time you leave, Russell calls."

Evelyn stood and walked to the counter, turning her back on them. "I'm sorry he bothers you."

"It's no bother," Henry said. "Only we never know where you are. So we can't help."

Nothing was said for a moment, so Evelyn rinsed her hands and went back to the table. "Sometimes I go to the library. Just for a bit. And sometimes I go to Viola's."

"Why do you have the need to leave?" Henry asked.

Evelyn shrugged.

"Russell said you don't take the girls," Regina said.

It was a flat statement, not an accusation, but it felt like one, and Evelyn shot out of the chair. "You're a fine one to judge me."

Regina's eyes widened, and her cheeks flushed as she rose from her chair.

"At least I didn't abandon my girls in some goddam orphanage," Evelyn finished.

The slap caught Evelyn by surprise, and by the expression on her mother's face, it hurt her, too. "I'm so sorry." Regina took a step closer, but Evelyn backed away.

"No. Don't touch me."

Henry reached out a hand to Evelyn, but she stepped away from him, too. She locked eyes with her mother. "You need to leave."

"Evelyn please," Henry said.

"No. Both of you. Just go."

Regina stood rooted to the floor while Henry got their things. He wrapped the cape around Regina and eased her to the door. Then he looked back at Evelyn. "Your mother is trying."

"She should have tried harder a long time ago."

"That tone is not called for," Henry said.

Evelyn stood in rigid silence as Henry, and her mother walked out. Then she went to the heavy wooden door and leaned against it. She was sorry. Sorry for the whole mess of things. But she wasn't sorry for what she said. Maybe she should have told her mother how she felt a long time ago and had this great weight lifted from her chest.

How long had that boulder been there?

————

When Russell came home from work, Evelyn waited until he was finished with supper, but then she told him about the unexpected visit from Regina and Henry. "I don't like you telling them things about me," she finished.

"I'm not telling them things about you." He pushed his empty plate aside and sighed. "I just ask if you are there."

"Well, don't." She rose and took the empty plates to the sink.

"Then stay home, goddamit."

"Russell, please. I don't want to fight."

"I don't either." He tipped his cup. "Is there any more coffee?"

"Sure." She brought the pot over and filled his cup. After replacing the pot on the stove, she came back to the table and sat down. "Maybe I'd be better if we had our marriage blessed."

"What?" Brown liquid sloshed over the edge of his cup and spread in a circle on the white tablecloth.

"You know how important the church is to me." Evelyn sopped at the spilled coffee with her napkin. "And I can't take communion because we're not married in the church."

"Why now? Why after almost three years?"

Evelyn hesitated then said, "The last time I asked the priest about it. He said I was forever banned. And he said our children were..." she stumbled over the last word. "Bastards."

"What?" Russell glared at her. "How could a priest say such a horrible thing about a child?"

"I don't know." Evelyn shrugged. "The priest said that if we got our marriage blessed, it would make everything legal in the church."

"I don't care what your church thinks."

"I was hoping—"

"Hoping what?" He stood and threw up his hands. "I'm so tired of your hopes and your dreams."

His angry interruption had reduced her to a stammer. "I... I..."

They faced each other in strained silence for a moment, then he said. "I told you before we married what I think about

247

any church. And I keep telling you. Yammering away at me is not going to change my mind."

"I wasn't yammering."

"Woman. All you do is yammer. If it isn't about the damn church, it's about the house. 'Russell, when are you going to finish the cabinets in the kitchen? Russell, could we have a real front porch? Russell, it wouldn't kill you to go to church once in a while.'"

He turned and started toward the door.

"Well, it wouldn't," she called to his retreating back. "And if you spent more time here, maybe you could get the damn house finished."

He whirled. "I'd spend more time here if the atmosphere was a lot more pleasant."

"Oh. That's right. Blame everything on—"

The last of her sentence had been cut off by the slamming of the door.

———

Evelyn didn't mention the church again. Or the unfinished house. And she managed to stay home for the next few months. Lester had come back, so Viola had left her children with him and gone up north. That news had stunned Evelyn when Regina told her, breaking the cold war of silence that had existed since that last disastrous visit. How could Viola have left her children? After all they had gone through without a mother. And to leave them with Lester?

Despite all her unhappiness at times, Evelyn never thought of leaving her girls for more than a few hours, and she simply could not comprehend how Viola had just walked away from her children.

The rancor between her and Russell had finally eased once

again, and Evelyn made every effort to avoid giving in to the need to get away from the pressure of caring for the girls. Sometimes she went into the bathroom for long periods of times, but at least she didn't go out of the house and leave them. And she didn't tell Russell about the times she lost control and hit them to make them stop crying. She was thankful that Juanita never said anything, either.

Still, Evelyn could sense his discontent and wished there was something more she could do to make him happy. Something she could do to make herself happy. Something she could do to keep her life from disintegrating.

25

EVELYN – MARCH 1945

E velyn was simmering a pot of chicken and dumplings on the stove when Russell came in from work. Something about his heavy tread on the linoleum made her turn to look at him. He wasn't smiling. Not even the forced smile he sometimes wore when things were particularly bad between them and he tried to act like everything was okay. The Woman's Handbook said that a wife should always greet her husband cheerfully, but this didn't seem to be the time for cheer. Had something terrible happened at work? "What's wrong?" she asked.

He leaned against the doorway to the kitchen and looked at her for the longest moment before answering. "I'm tired."

"Then sit down. Supper is almost ready." She turned back to the stove.

"I don't want to sit. And I don't want to eat."

His tone, cold and lifeless, drew her attention. "Russell? Are you okay?"

"No. I'm not okay. And neither is this?" He waved a hand to generally encompass the room.

"What are you saying?"

"We're not happy together, Evelyn."

She looked at him, disbelief keeping her mute.

"I'm moving out. I want a divorce."

Evelyn braced herself on the little cabinet next to the stove as the words assaulted her. Why now? She thought things were getting better. "I don't understand, Russell."

Even as she said that, she did understand. Even though she had tried to believe that everything was okay with them, she knew it was not. Ever since that last time Evelyn had left, Russell had pulled slowly away from her. All of the pretending in the world would not make the reality any different.

Russell didn't say anything, so Evelyn asked. "Where will you go?"

"I'll take a room at the boardinghouse."

The way he said it struck a chord. Not any old boarding-house. The Boardinghouse. "Eileen's?"

He nodded.

"Is she...? Is that the reason?"

"No," he said quickly. "She's married. Her husband just came back from the war. How could I?"

"The same way you fucked my sister."

He rushed her then. Slapping her hard across the face. "Don't you dare accuse me."

They locked eyes, and the glares could have cut concrete. Then Evelyn pushed him hard in the chest and stepped away. "Go. Get out of here."

Russell stormed out, and Evelyn collapsed in a chair. Even though she had been secretly dreading something like this, she couldn't believe it was actually happening. Couples didn't get divorced. They worked things out. But even as those thoughts ran through her mind, she knew that the problems between her and Russell were beyond working out. Still, her mind reeled with the realization that it was over, and she didn't know what she was going to do. Who could she turn to? Viola was too far away, and Evelyn was not sure this was something she wanted to talk to her mother about. Would Regina take some delight in Evelyn's failure?

No. That was an awful thing to consider. Regina had disappointed her in so many ways, but she was not that cold-hearted. Evelyn felt the heat of shame for even entertaining the thought.

Russell came back late that evening after the girls were down for the night. He nodded at Evelyn, who was sitting on the sofa in the living room, then went into the front bedroom and came out a bit later with a suitcase in one hand, guitar case in the other. "Can I see the girls before I leave?"

Evelyn almost said no, just to spite him, but she softened and nodded. He put the suitcase and guitar down and walked quietly into the second bedroom. When he came out a few minutes later, he said, "There's money on the dresser in our room. It'll have to do for groceries until we... uh, settle everything."

Evelyn stood. "I don't want to settle anything. Why can't you just stay?"

He stepped closer and took her by the shoulders. For a moment, she thought he was going to pull her into an embrace. She wished he was going to pull her into an embrace, but he just stood there, locking eyes. "Evelyn, I'm sorry for all the angry words. And I'm sorry for all the fights. But don't you see? We can't keep living like that. The fights will never end with us both so... so..." He couldn't seem to find the right words, so he just dropped his hands and stepped away.

"I have to go," he said, picking up his suitcase and guitar again. "I'll be in touch."

I'll be in touch? Like she was some casual acquaintance he was leaving.

The reality and the pain hit her all at once, and she muffled a loud cry as she raced into her bedroom. She knocked all the glass figurines off her dresser with a sweep of her hands, feeling a sense of release as they crashed to the floor in a jumble of broken shards. Then she opened drawers and threw some of the clothes Russell had left behind in a heap on top of the mess.

The next morning, Evelyn woke with a start when she heard Maryann crying. Evelyn wasn't sure when she had fallen asleep, but she was sprawled on the bed, still wearing her housedress. She quickly got up, took care of necessities in the bathroom, and then went to tend to her children.

Maryann had wet the bed, again, and Evelyn fought down a surge of frustration. When was the girl ever going to get trained? That thought brought a manic laugh. Toilet training was the least of her problems now.

A solemn-faced Juanita carefully watched her mother strip the bed, and Evelyn knew it was because the child didn't know what the response would be to the accident. Evelyn was aware of how much uncertainty was in the girls' lives because of the times that she would erupt in anger, and there were too many times that she couldn't control it. "It's okay," she said to Juanita. "Take your sister to the kitchen and give her some cereal."

Juanita quickly took Maryann's hand and led her out of the room. Evelyn set the blanket aside. Thankfully, it wasn't wet, and she balled up the sheet. She would have to wash the rubber sheet protecting the mattress later, but right now she'd get the bed clothing into the washing machine.

It took another day before Juanita asked about their father. It broke Evelyn's heart that the girls were so accustomed to him being gone all day and many evenings, that his absence just now registered. Evelyn didn't know how much to say to them, or how, but took a deep breath and started. "Daddy is moving out."

"Where is he going?" Juanita asked.

"To a boardinghouse."

"Will he come back?"

That was the hardest question to answer, so Evelyn decided to deflect it for now. "I don't know."

That seemed to satisfy the girls, so Evelyn said no more.

For two weeks, Evelyn mindlessly took care of her children, barely taking any care of herself, until one day the rank smell of her body drove her to the bathtub. She dressed in clean clothes. Not because she wanted to, but because the ones she had been wearing smelled like day's old garbage. She threw them out. She knew she couldn't go on this way. Her emotions were in a turmoil, and she felt like she would erupt if she didn't have anyone to talk to. So, she dressed the girls in warm coats as protection against the cold March day and rode the bus to her mother's apartment. It was a Wednesday, one of her mother's usual days off. She would probably be home.

The bus let them off three blocks from the apartment house, and Evelyn carried Maryann while Juanita walked beside them, carrying a bag that Evelyn had packed with bottles and diapers. By the time they got to Regina's door, Evelyn's arms ached, and she pushed the button with one hand while balancing the toddler on her hip. Thankfully the door was opened quickly, and Henry looked out. "Evelyn how nice to see you. Come in."

Henry reached out and took Maryann, so Evelyn helped Juanita in with the bag. Then she took off her coat and hung it on a peg by the door, along with Juanita's. Henry started toward the living room, calling out, "Regina. Evelyn's here."

A few seconds later, Regina came from the hall leading to the bedrooms. She walked over and hugged Evelyn. It was a warm, welcoming embrace, and so long wanted that Evelyn's defenses broke. She burst into tears.

"Evelyn. What's wrong?" Regina eased Evelyn onto the sofa.

Evelyn slumped into the soft cushions and struggled to get her voice past her sobs. "Russell... wants... a divorce."

Henry was still holding Maryann, and he took Juanita by the hand. "Let's go to the kitchen and find some cookies."

After he was gone, Regina said, "That's quite a shock."

Evelyn pulled a tissue out of her purse and mopped her cheeks. "I don't know what to do."

"Wait a minute. Let me get something to drink."

Regina got up and went to the kitchen, coming back a few moments later with two tumblers of an amber liquid. Evelyn took a big swallow and choked. "What is this?"

"Whiskey. I thought you needed it."

"I don't drink."

"I know. But you were pale as a ghost when you walked in. Now you have a little color."

Evelyn couldn't help it. She laughed. Then the tears started again. First, just a slow trickle that ran in warm rivulets down her cheeks, then a torrent that scalded her skin. Regina put her arms around her, and they rocked.

It took a few minutes for the tears to stop and Evelyn to speak, "Oh, Mother, what am I going to do? I'll be lost without Russell. And the girls? How will I take care of the girls?"

"You'll do whatever it takes. You'll manage."

Evelyn pulled out of the embrace. "Manage? How? I barely manage now with Russell's paycheck."

"You'll do it. You're a strong woman. Stronger than you think."

Evelyn tried to believe that. She took the words home with her later and tried to hold on to them.

The next evening, Evelyn had just put the girls down when there was a knock on the front door. She opened it to see Russell. "Well, uh... you didn't have to knock. This is your house."

"I thought it best."

He didn't say any more, so she stood aside so he could enter. He walked over to the little chair facing the sofa, draped his coat over the back of it and sat down.

"Do you want coffee?"

He shook his head. "I won't stay. I just want to talk about the terms."

"Terms?"

"Of the divorce."

"Oh." She sank slowly to the sofa.

"You can have the house. You need a home for the children."

She didn't say anything, so he went on. "I will stay at the rooming house. It's close. It's convenient. And I can come to see the girls."

"You've worked it all out?" She spoke softly.

"I talked to an attorney. He suggested the settlement."

"Settlement?"

"Yes. What we can agree on."

"But I don't agree. I don't want a divorce."

Russell sighed and rubbed a hand across his face. "It'll be better if you don't contest it."

"Better?... Better for who? For you and your floozy?"

"I'm not leaving you for another woman. I'm just leaving." Again he swiped a hand across his face. "God, Evelyn, don't you see. All we do is fight. I can't stand it. And I can't stand not knowing when you will leave again. And maybe not come back. I can't work and raise two kids. Hell, we never should have gotten married in the first place."

That comment had hit her like a whip with barbs. What was she supposed to say to that? Had the whole four years been one big lie? Was everything in her life just one big lie?

"Okay." The word was a whisper.

"What?"

"I said, okay. You want a divorce. I won't fight you."

But Evelyn did want to fight him. Despite the hardships of the past few years, she loved him. She would always love him. How could she live without him?

26

EVELYN – APRIL 1946

Evelyn sat in the ladder-backed chair facing the desk and the attorney, George J. Amos. Russell was in a similar chair to her right. The attorney had been recommended by Hoffman, and Russell had told her that if she didn't contest the divorce, the one attorney could handle the legalities of filing the petition. They had already met with the man several times to map out the agreement, and Evelyn had struggled to maintain her composure at each one. How could she nod and smile and say she agreed, when she didn't agree? Damn it! She didn't want this, but she was powerless to stop it. Russell would not bend to her pleas to try to work things out, so this was it.

Today was the final review of the terms. Henry was here, too, making sure that everything was fair for Evelyn.

"Okay," Amos said. "As previously outlined and agreed to, one Evelyn Van Gilder will have ownership of the house at 804 Timpken. Custody of the two minor children, Juanita Van Gilder and Maryann Van Gilder, will be awarded to the mother, Evelyn Van Gilder. Russell Van Gilder will have possession of the car, one Model T coupe, and will be allowed weekly visits with the minor children. He will also be given permission to take the children on vacations to West Virginia."

He paused and looked up at Evelyn and Russell. "Is that correct?"

Evelyn nodded.

"You must verbalize your response."

"Yes," she said, the word catching in her throat and sounding like a croak. Russell had no difficulty in saying yes.

"The terms of the child support are as follows." Amos flipped to a second page of the document. "Russell Van Gilder will provide $17 a month for each minor child until such child reaches the age of 18." In an earlier meeting, Henry had tried to champion for a little more. Something for Evelyn, but Russell had been firm. He only made $130 a month. Out of which he had to pay room and board, Union dues and other expenses.

"If this is all in order, I will file the petition in the county courts tomorrow. I will contact you when it is time for you to appear before the judge for the final declaration. Any questions?"

Evelyn was out of questions, so she just shook her head. Russell did, too.

Two weeks later they were at the same courthouse where they had gotten married, getting unmarried. Mary was watching the girls, and Evelyn had taken the early morning bus downtown. Henry had offered to drive her, but she had declined. The only person she wanted with her this day was several hundred miles away, and she hadn't heard from her sister in several months.

She stood rigid as the judge read the papers; the attorney standing between her and Russell. Thank goodness, they weren't in front of the same judge who had legalized the marriage, and thank goodness, this one didn't look at them and smile. That would have killed Evelyn.

The judge questioned her and Russell in turn, and at the appropriate times each said, "I agree."

Then the judge made it official. "Based on the pleadings before this court and the evidence reviewed today, the Agreed Decree of Divorce is granted this 19th day of April in the year of our Lord, 1946. The proposed division of property and parenting plan are accepted and therefore ordered by this court. Your attorney will take the final decree to the clerk to have it filed, and you will each get certified copies. Good luck to you both."

Evelyn stood for a moment, her feet like lead. She didn't know what to do. She was afraid she would not be able to move. She was afraid she would burst into tears.

She was simply afraid.

The attorney touched her lightly on the arm. "Come out to the hall."

She followed him, wondering why her shoes did not sound like cement hitting the hardwood floor with each step. It was so hard to move.

Russell came out behind them but stood several feet away from where the attorney eased Evelyn down on a bench. "Will you be okay?" Amos asked.

"Yes. I just need a minute."

"I have to file these." He held up the sheaf of papers the judge had turned over to him.

"Of course."

"Your copy of the decree will be mailed to you."

Evelyn nodded, not looking at the attorney as he walked away. Her eyes were on Russell, who was pacing the narrow confines at the end of the hall. Was he as lost as she was? She wanted to wave him over. Talk to him. Ask if they could take it all back. But before she could move a hand, he gave her one last look, then strode out of the building, taking the last of her strength with him.

She slumped against the hard wood like a rag doll. She was alone. So utterly alone.

Who would love her now?

27

EVELYN – OCTOBER 1946

Pulled suddenly awake by a noise she couldn't quite place at first, Evelyn groggily got off the couch and hurried to the kitchen to look at the clock. "Oh, no," she murmured. "The house is a wreck, and the caseworker will be here any minute."

She could hear Maryann crying and Juanita telling her to hush. "Mama's asleep. We can't wake her."

Not knowing if she should tend to the crying child, or try to clear the mess of papers and toys and a few dirty dishes from the living room, Evelyn stood rooted to the floor in the kitchen. It had been six months since the divorce. At first, Evelyn had been able to hold fast to the vow that she made after Russell walked out of her life. The vow that she would do everything she could to hold herself together and make a home for the girls. She would not leave them. She would stay home and take good care of them.

Determination had only lasted a few months before Evelyn had been overcome by the weight of the responsibilities. The lack of money. The constant whining from the girls that they were hungry. The end of every month was the hardest when she didn't even have a quarter to buy a box of crackers or a loaf of bread.

There were times she thought about how easy her life would be without the girls. The possibilities danced around in her mind, teasing, tempting. She could just walk away like her sister had. Leave the kids and find a new life somewhere else. And maybe a new somebody to love her.

Could she?

Would she?

As tempting as the thought was, the answer was always, no.

She would not abandon her girls. Not the way she had been abandoned.

Maryann had stopped crying, so Evelyn ran back to the living room and cleared old magazines off the coffee table and folded the afghan across the back of the sofa. Taking a few more precious moments, she went to tend to the toddler, changing her wet pants and telling Juanita to keep her sister quiet. In the bathroom, she quickly washed her face and combed her hair. It might be good to look clean and tidy.

A few minutes later, a knock sounded on the front door. Evelyn hurried to open it and admit the caseworker from Aid to Dependent Children. Henry had told her she might qualify for assistance and had helped her fill out the necessary paperwork to apply three months ago. Last week, she had received a letter saying that she had been approved, pending a home visit. So now, a middle-aged woman with bushy red hair sticking out from a black hat stood in the doorway.

Evelyn stepped aside so the woman could come into the living room and motioned toward the sofa. "Come in and sit down."

They spent some time going over the details of the application and what Evelyn could expect in assistance, then the woman gave Evelyn a quick smile, then stood. "May I see the children?"

Evelyn rose and led the woman to the bedroom where the girls were playing, hoping the woman would not catch the faint odor of urine from the wet clothes Evelyn had hastily shoved into a hamper. "This is Juanita," Evelyn said, gesturing to the eldest girl. "The younger one is Maryann."

"Hello," the woman said to the girls, then turned to Evelyn. "They look healthy."

"I do my best."

The woman glanced around the bedroom, then nodded. "This is fine. We can finish in the other room."

"Of course." Evelyn looked to Juanita. "Take care of your sister for a little while longer."

"Yes, mama."

Once again, the woman opened her briefcase and pulled out a paper. "This is the official document that authorizes $20 a month in Aid to Dependent Children. You will also qualify for Welfare assistance with food items." She pointed to a line on the paper. "You sign here."

While Evelyn carefully wrote her name on the line indicated, the woman slid a small pamphlet across the coffee table. "This tells you how surplus USDA foods are distributed. You can use this card to pick up the food."

The woman gave Evelyn a small card, no more than three inches square.

"Are you sure this is what you want to do?" The woman asked, starting to close her briefcase. "Some mothers in your situation consider an option."

Evelyn didn't even have to ask what that option was. She knew.

She fingered the card that would get food for her girls. "I won't change my mind," she said. "I will never give my children away."

EPILOGUE

While my mother never stopped loving my father, the day he married his second wife was the day she stopped believing in a hopeful future. That was three years after the divorce, and his remarriage made it final. Russell was never going to be hers again, and she was left with two kids, no education, and no job. Even with the government assistance, times were hard and each day was a struggle.

When I was very young, I didn't always like my mother. In fact, there were times I hated her. Not the "I hate you" reaction to not getting my way that is so typical of a child, but a hatred that came out of a deep-seated fear and uncertainty. I didn't understand why anger ruled our house so much of the time. I didn't understand why she would fly into a rage and beat me and my sister. I didn't understand why she hoarded snacks and ate them late at night when my sister and I were supposed to be asleep, but the hunger in our bellies kept us awake.

There were so many things I didn't understand until I got older and realized my mother didn't know any other way. She was a product of her upbringing, which was hard and often cruel.

Yet, she survived, and survival made her strong, even though she never saw herself that way. This novel, based on the true events of her life, is my way of reconciling the mother that I feared as a child, and the woman I grew to love, but never completely got to know. She hoarded secrets the same way she hoarded potato chips.

The End

ABOUT THE AUTHOR

Maryann Miller is an award-winning author of numerous books, screenplays, and stage plays. She started her professional career as a journalist, writing columns, feature stories, and short fiction for regional and national publications. In addition to women's novels and short stories, she has written a number of mysteries, including the critically-acclaimed Seasons Mystery Series that features two women homicide detectives. Think "Lethal Weapon" set in Dallas with female leads. The first two books in the series, *Open Season* and *Stalking Season* have received starred reviews from Publisher's Weekly, Kirkus, and Library Journal. *Stalking Season* was chosen for the John E. Weaver Excellence in Reading award for Police Procedural Mysteries. Her mystery, *Doubletake,* was honored as the Best Mystery for 2015 by the Texas Association of Authors.

Other awards Miller has received for her writing are the Page Edwards Short Story Award, the New York Library Best Books for Teens Award, first place in the screenwriting competition at the Houston Writer's Conference, placing as a semi-finalist at Sundance, and placing as a semi-finalist in the Chesterfield Screenwriting Competition. She was named The Trails Country Treasure in 2011 by the Winnsboro Center for the Arts, and Woman of the Year in 2014 by the Winnsboro Area Chamber of Commerce.

Miller can be found at her Amazon Author Page her

Website on Twitter and Facebook and Goodreads. She is a contributor to The Blood-Red Pencil blog on writing and editing.